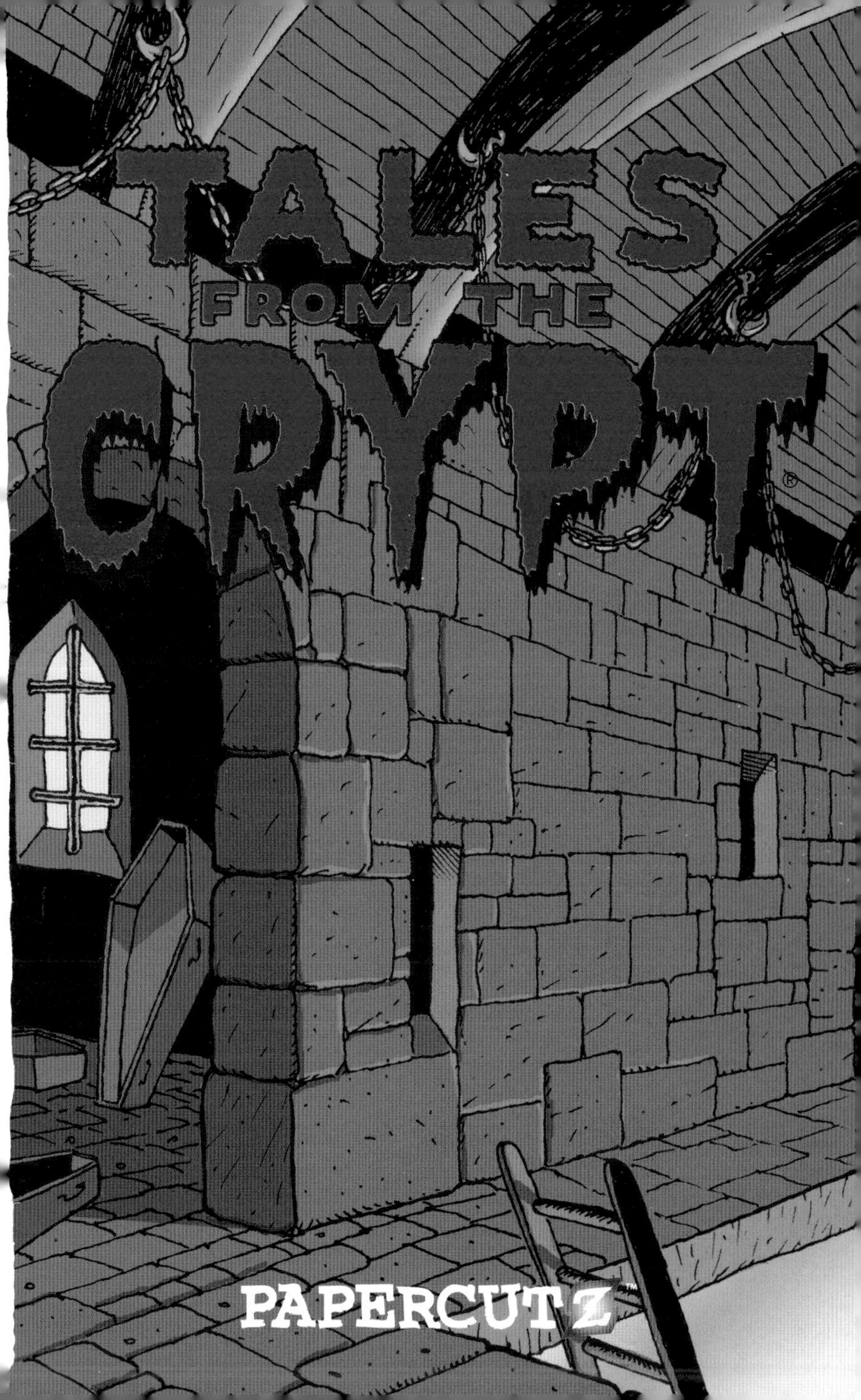

TALES FROM THE CRYPT®
PAPERCUTZ™

TALES FROM THE CRYPT®

Graphic Novels Available from Papercutz

$7.95 each in paperback, $12.95 each in hardcover
Please add $4.00 for postage and handling for the first book, add $1.00 for each additional book.
Make checks payable to NBM Publishing.

Send to:
Papercutz
40 Exchange Place, Suite 1308
New York, NY 10005
1-800-886-1223 • www.papercutz.com

ALL-NEW STORIES! FULL-COLOR GRAPHIC NOVEL!
TERROR
TALES FROM THE CRYPT
FEATURING...

Graphic Novel #1
"Ghouls Gone Wild!"

ALL-NEW STORIES! FULL-COLOR GRAPHIC NOVEL!
TERROR
TALES FROM THE CRYPT
FEATURING...

Graphic Novel #2
"Can You Fear Me Now?"

ALL-NEW STORIES! FULL-COLOR GRAPHIC NOVEL!
TERROR
TALES FROM THE CRYPT
FEATURING...

Graphic Novel #3
"Zombielicious"

ALL-NEW STORIES! FULL-COLOR GRAPHIC NOVEL!
TERROR
TALES FROM THE CRYPT
FEATURING...

Graphic Novel #4
"Crypt-Keeping It Real"

ALL-NEW STORIES! FULL-COLOR GRAPHIC NOVEL!
TERROR
TALES FROM THE CRYPT
PLUS AN ALL-NEW STORY BY JOE R. LANSDALE & JOHN L. LANSDALE CHAMPION MOJO STORYTELLERS!
FEATURING...

Graphic Novel #5
"Yabba Dabba Voodoo"

ALL-NEW STORIES! FULL-COLOR GRAPHIC NOVEL!
TERROR
TALES FROM THE CRYPT
FEATURING...

Coming March 2009:
Graphic Novel #6
"You Toomb"

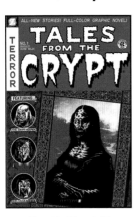

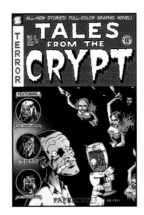

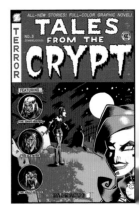

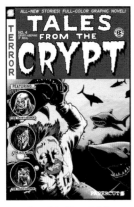

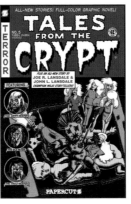

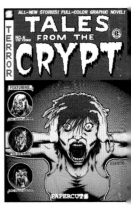

TALES FROM THE CRYPT

NO. 5 – *Yabba Dabba Voodoo*

FRED VAN LENTE	MORT TODD
JOE R. LANSDALE	JAMES ROMBERGER
JOHN L. LANSDALE	CHRISTIAN ZANIER
CHRISTIAN ZANIER	RYAN DUNLAVEY
JIM SALICRUP	RICK PARKER
Writers	Artists

MR. EXES
Cover Artist

Based on the classic EC Comics series created by WILLIAM M. GAINES.

New York

"IGNOBLE ROT"
FRED VAN LENTE — Writer
MORT TODD — Artist, Letterer, Colorist

"VIRTUAL HOODOO"
JOE R. LANSDALE & JOHN L. LANSDALE — Writers
JAMES ROMBERGER — Artist
MARK LERER — Letterer
MARGUERITE VAN COOK — Colorist

"SHE WHO WOULD RULE THE WORLD"
CHRISTIAN ZANIER — Writer, Artist, Letterer, Colorist
MARVIN MARIANO — Colorist

"GLASS HEADS"
FRED VAN LENTE — Writer
RYAN DUNLAVEY — Artist, Letterer, Colorist

GHOULUNATIC SEQUENCES
JIM SALICRUP — Writer
RICK PARKER — Artist, Title Letterer, Colorist
MARK LERER – Letterer

CHRIS NELSON & CAITLIN HINRICHS
Production

MICHAEL PETRANEK
Editorial Assistant

JIM SALICRUP
Editor-in-Chief

ISBN 10: 1-59707-116-1 paperback edition
ISBN 13: 978-1-59707-116-1 paperback edition
ISBN 10: 1-59707-117-X hardcover edition
ISBN 13: 978-1-59707-117-8 hardcover edition
Copyright © 2008 William M. Gaines, Agent, Inc. All rights reserved.
The EC logo is a registered trademark of William M. Gaines, Agent, Inc. used with permission.
Printed in China.

10 9 8 7 6 5 4 3 2 1

THE CRYPT OF TERROR

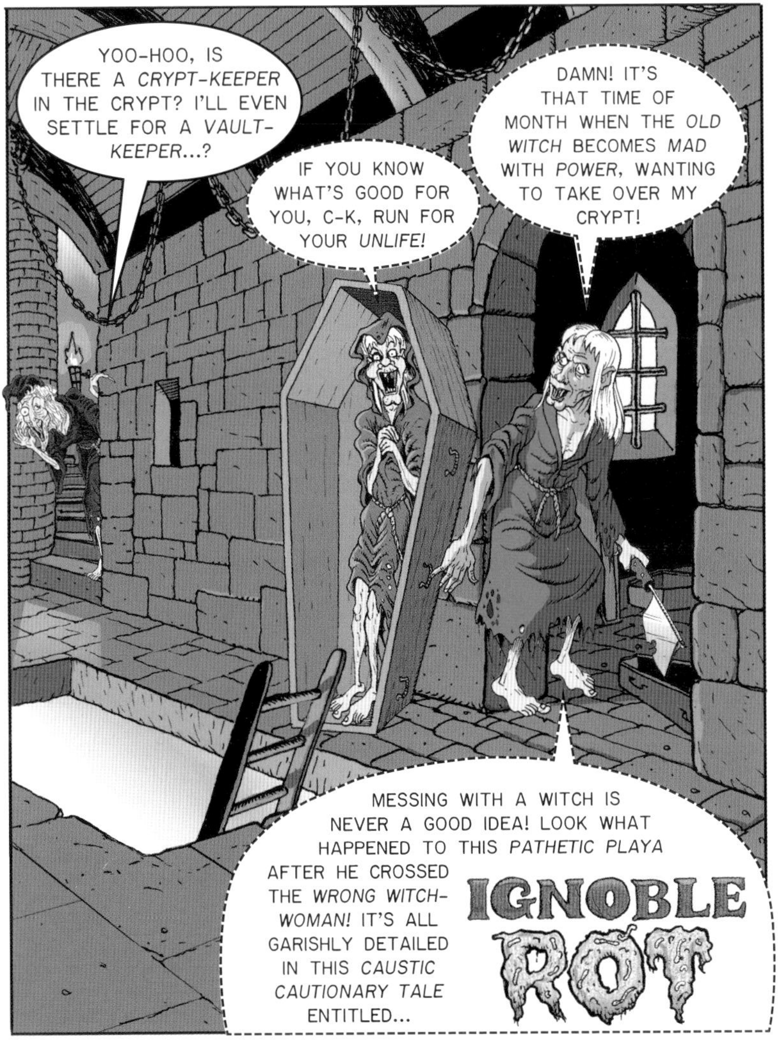

YOO-HOO, IS THERE A *CRYPT-KEEPER* IN THE CRYPT? I'LL EVEN SETTLE FOR A *VAULT-KEEPER*...?
IF YOU KNOW WHAT'S GOOD FOR YOU, C-K, RUN FOR YOUR *UNLIFE!*
DAMN! IT'S THAT TIME OF MONTH WHEN THE *OLD WITCH* BECOMES *MAD* WITH *POWER*, WANTING TO TAKE OVER MY CRYPT!
MESSING WITH A WITCH IS NEVER A GOOD IDEA! LOOK WHAT HAPPENED TO THIS *PATHETIC PLAYA* AFTER HE CROSSED THE *WRONG WITCH-WOMAN!* IT'S ALL GARISHLY DETAILED IN THIS *CAUSTIC CAUTIONARY TALE* ENTITLED...
IGNOBLE ROT

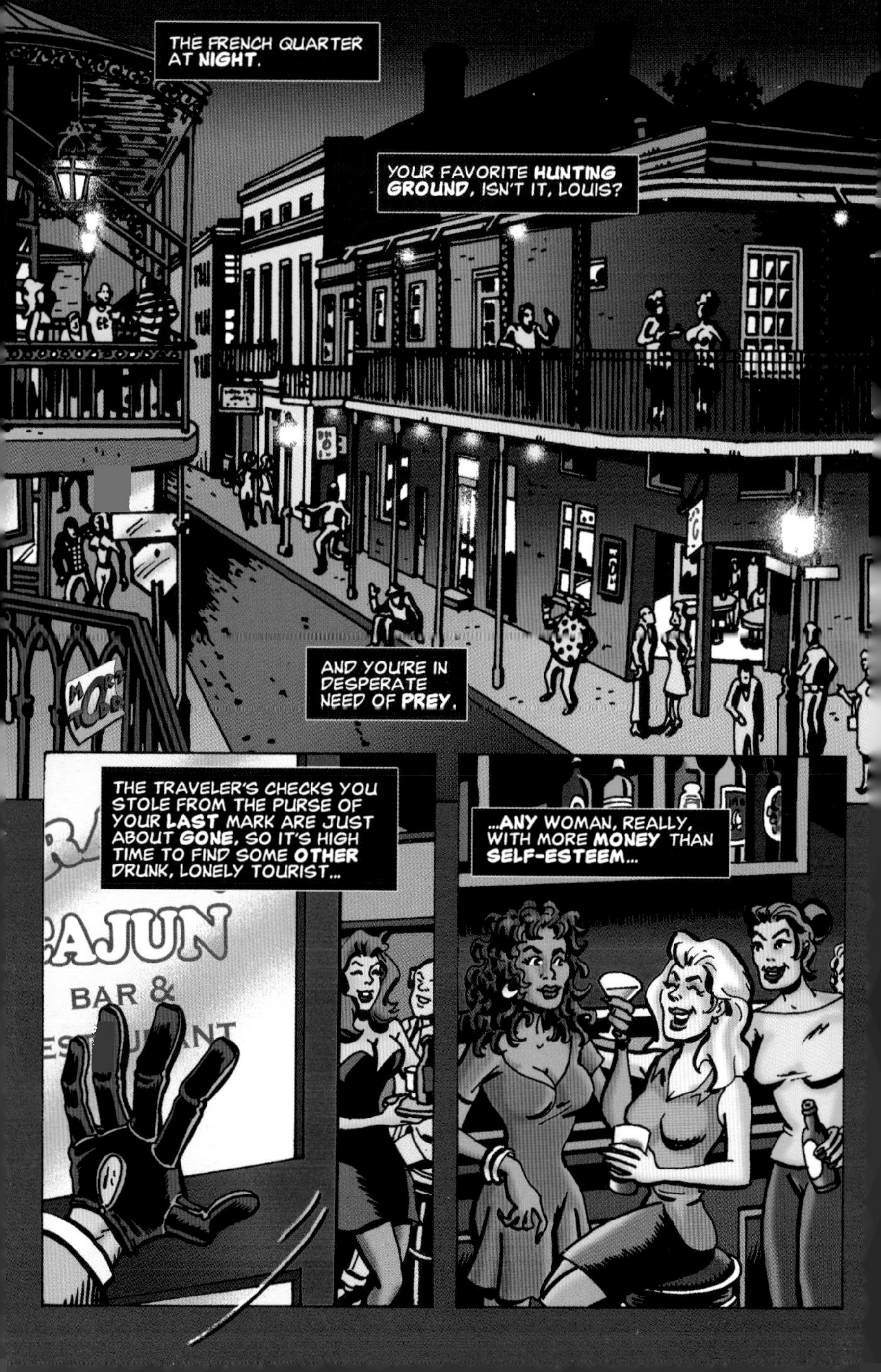
THE FRENCH QUARTER AT NIGHT.
YOUR FAVORITE HUNTING GROUND, ISN'T IT, LOUIS?
AND YOU'RE IN DESPERATE NEED OF PREY.
THE TRAVELER'S CHECKS YOU STOLE FROM THE PURSE OF YOUR LAST MARK ARE JUST ABOUT GONE, SO IT'S HIGH TIME TO FIND SOME OTHER DRUNK, LONELY TOURIST...
BAR &
...ANY WOMAN, REALLY, WITH MORE MONEY THAN SELF-ESTEEM...

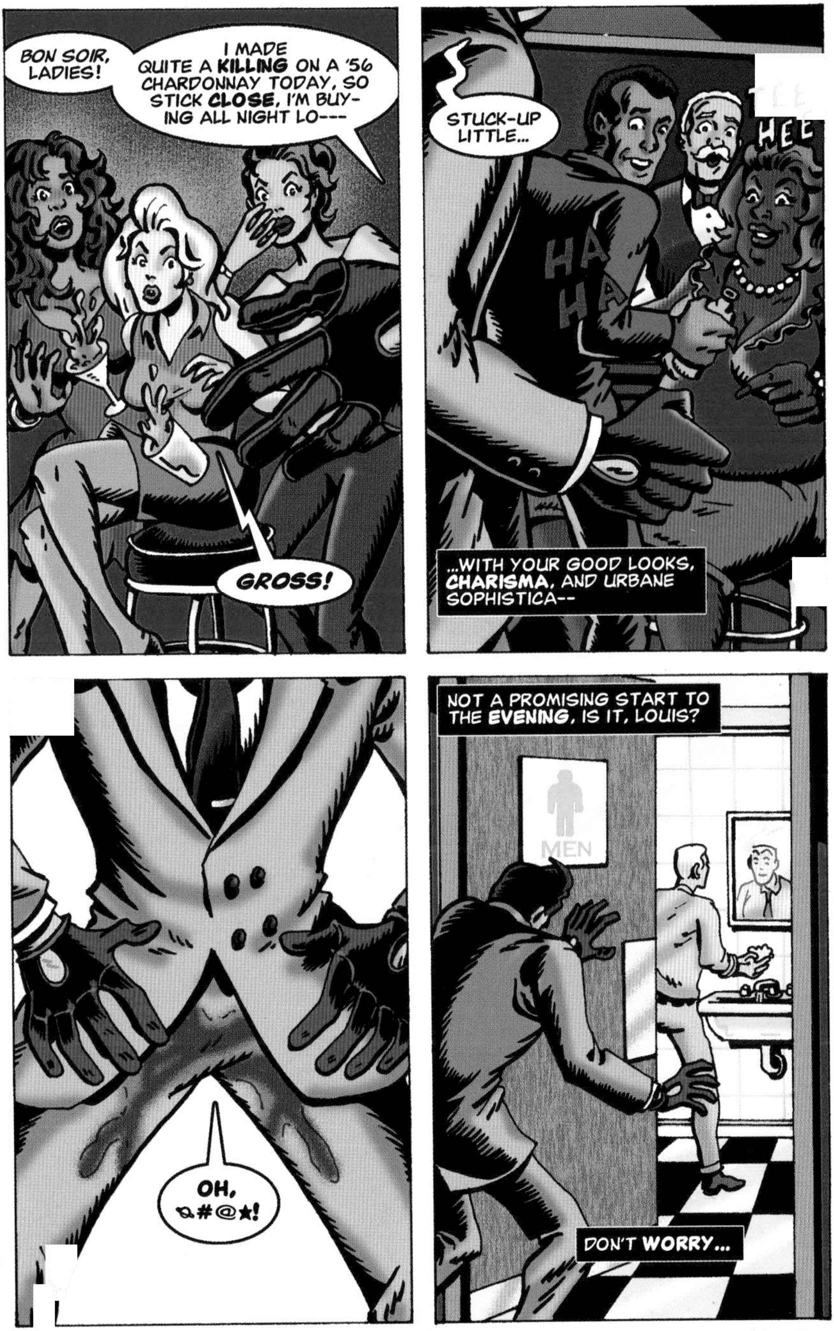

BON SOIR, LADIES!
I MADE QUITE A **KILLING** ON A '56 CHARDONNAY TODAY, SO STICK **CLOSE**, I'M BUY-ING ALL NIGHT LO---
GROSS!
STUCK-UP LITTLE...
...WITH YOUR GOOD LOOKS, **CHARISMA**, AND URBANE SOPHISTICA--
OH, ⊘#@★!
NOT A PROMISING START TO THE **EVENING**, IS IT, LOUIS?
MEN
DON'T **WORRY**...

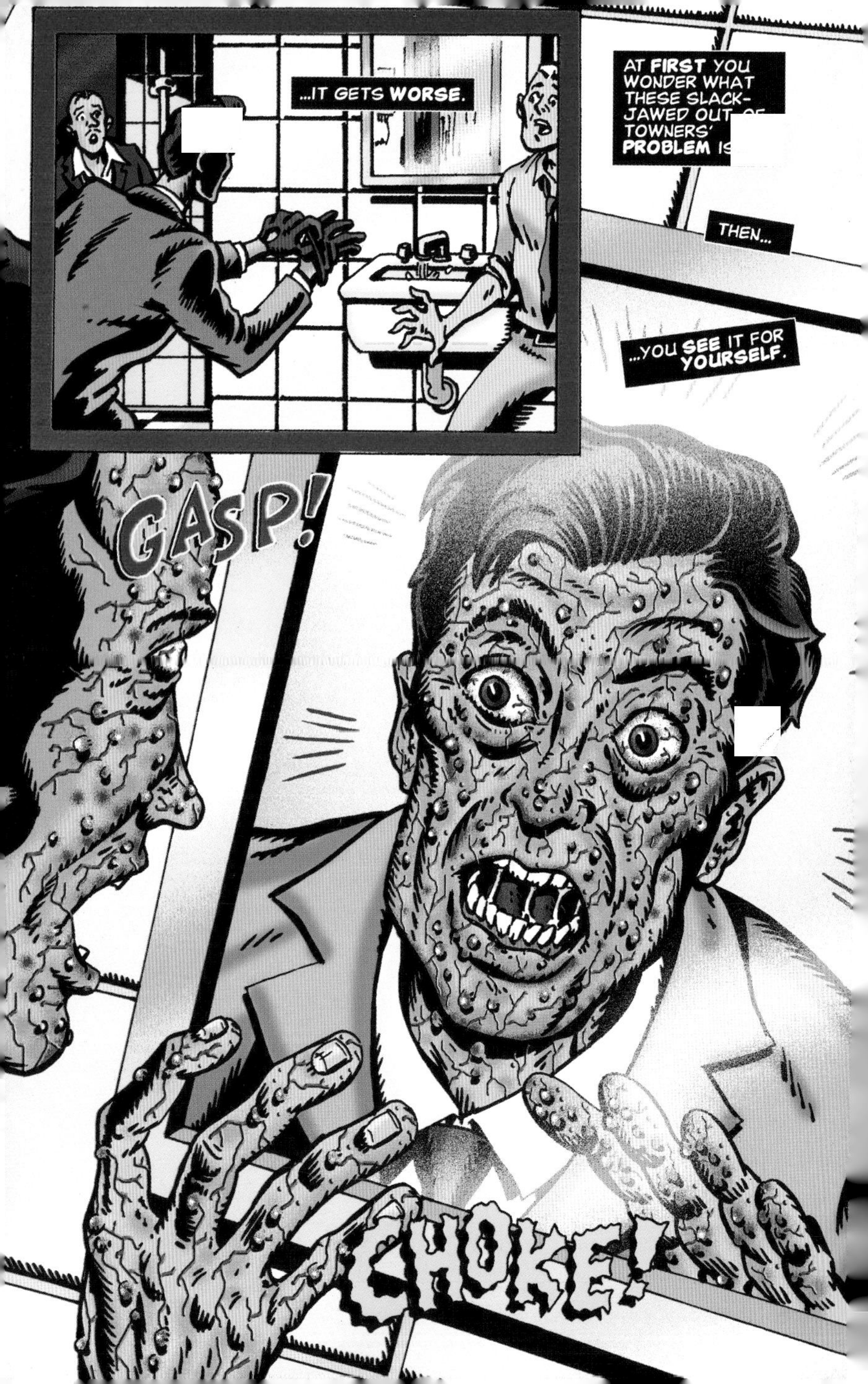
...IT GETS WORSE.
AT FIRST YOU WONDER WHAT THESE SLACK-JAWED OUT- TOWNERS' PROBLEM IS
THEN...
...YOU SEE IT FOR YOURSELF.
GASP!
CHOKE!

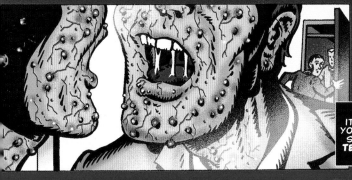

WHAT YOU **SEE** IS BAD ENOUGH...

...BUT IT'S WHAT YOU **DON'T** SEE THAT **TERRIFIES** YOU!

YOU DON'T SEE **FOG** ON THE MIRROR FROM YOUR **BREATH!** FOR NO MATTER HOW HARD YOU STRAIN YOUR LUNGS...

...YOU CANNOT **BREATHE!**

NOR IS THERE A **PULSE** BENEATH YOUR WRIST---

---AND THE SKIN IS **COLD** AND **CLAMMY** TO THE TOUCH--- LIKE **RUBBER** LEFT OUTSIDE OVERNIGHT!

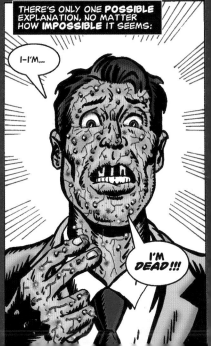

THERE'S ONLY ONE **POSSIBLE** EXPLANATION, NO MATTER HOW **IMPOSSIBLE** IT SEEMS:

I-I'M...

I'M **DEAD!!!**

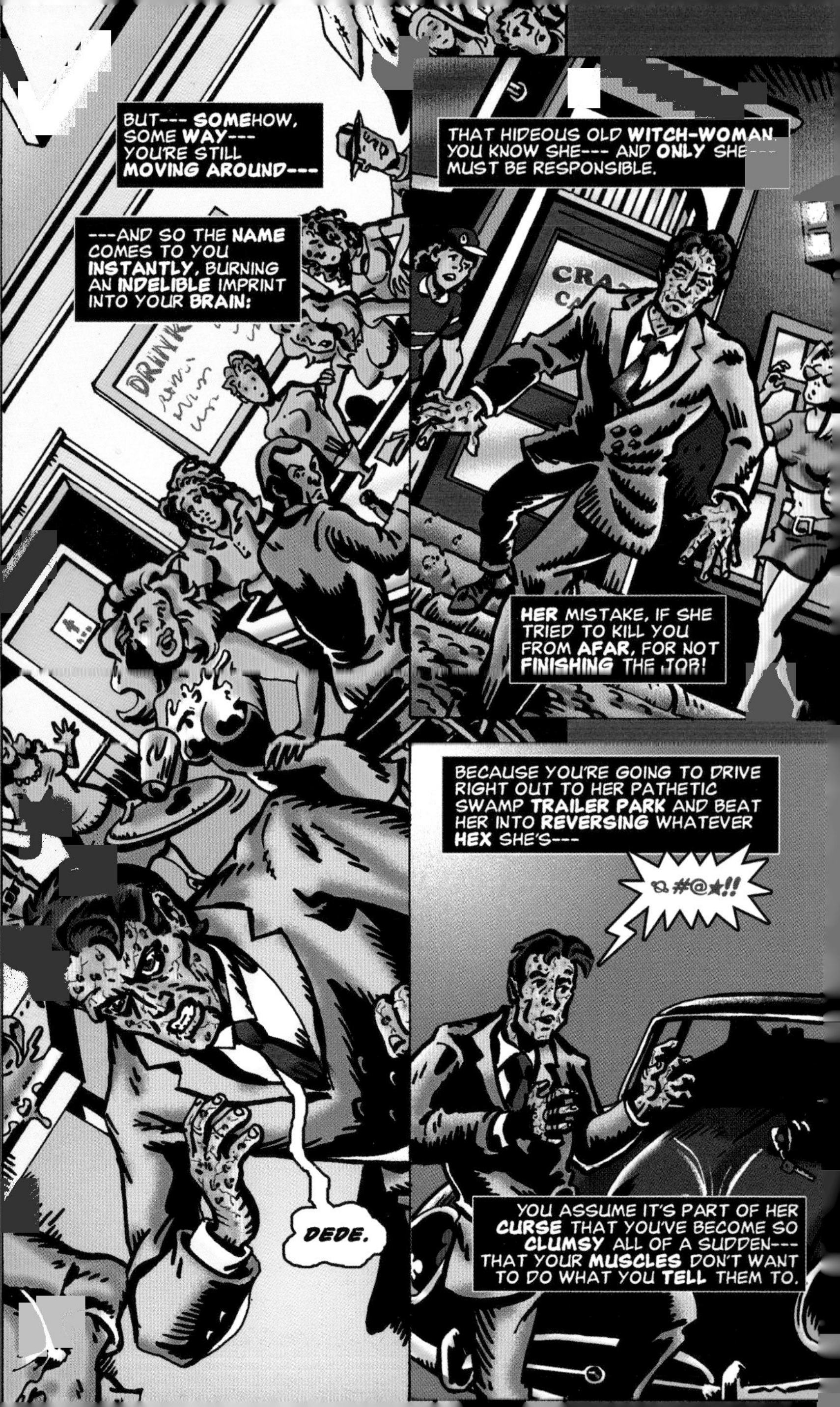
BUT--- SOMEHOW, SOME WAY--- YOU'RE STILL MOVING AROUND---
---AND SO THE NAME COMES TO YOU INSTANTLY, BURNING AN INDELIBLE IMPRINT INTO YOUR BRAIN:
DEDE.
THAT HIDEOUS OLD WITCH-WOMAN. YOU KNOW SHE--- AND ONLY SHE--- MUST BE RESPONSIBLE.
HER MISTAKE, IF SHE TRIED TO KILL YOU FROM AFAR, FOR NOT FINISHING THE JOB!
BECAUSE YOU'RE GOING TO DRIVE RIGHT OUT TO HER PATHETIC SWAMP TRAILER PARK AND BEAT HER INTO REVERSING WHATEVER HEX SHE'S---
#@★!!
YOU ASSUME IT'S PART OF HER CURSE THAT YOU'VE BECOME SO CLUMSY ALL OF A SUDDEN--- THAT YOUR MUSCLES DON'T WANT TO DO WHAT YOU TELL THEM TO.

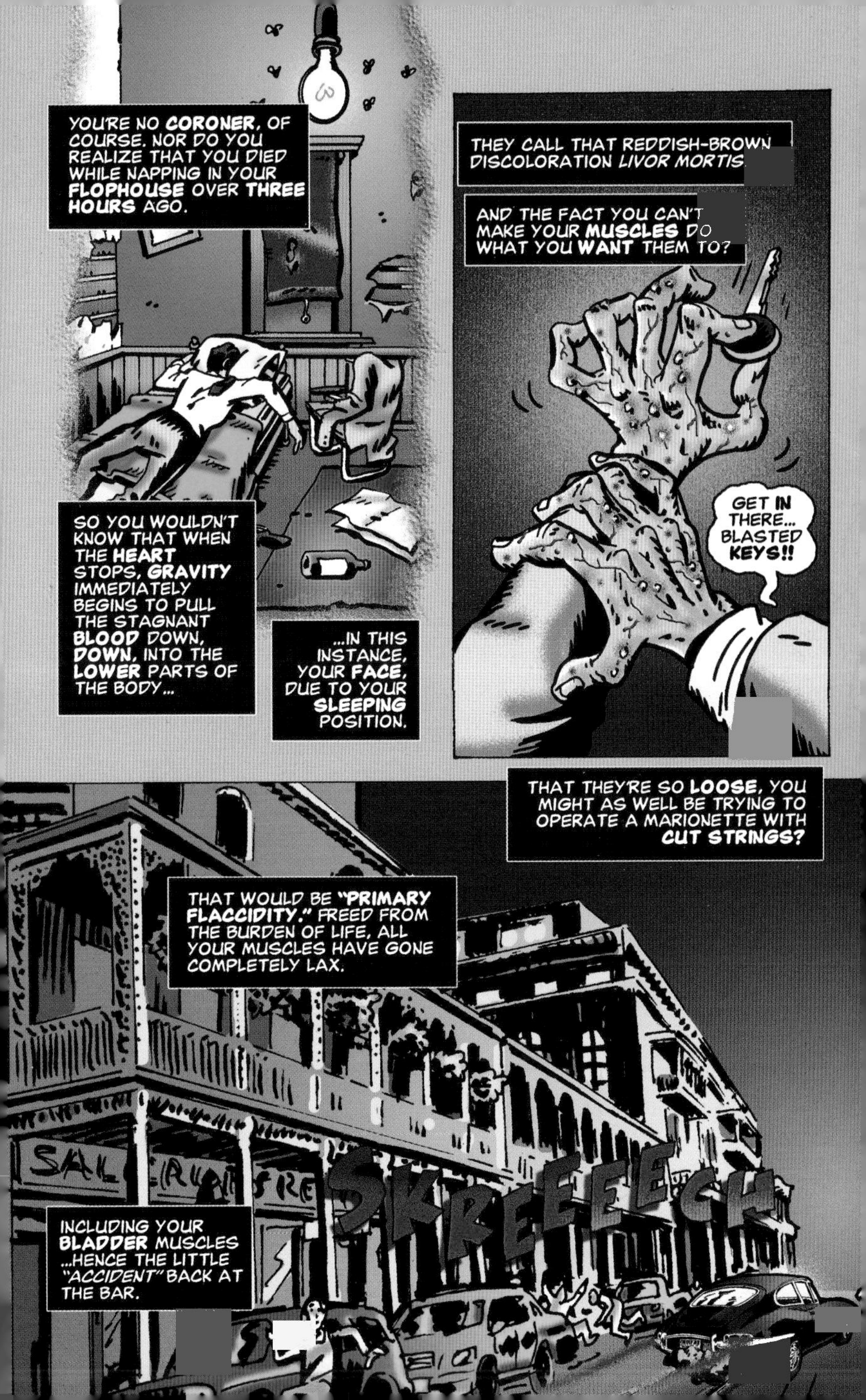
YOU'RE NO **CORONER**, OF COURSE. NOR DO YOU REALIZE THAT YOU DIED WHILE NAPPING IN YOUR **FLOPHOUSE** OVER **THREE HOURS** AGO.
SO YOU WOULDN'T KNOW THAT WHEN THE **HEART** STOPS, **GRAVITY** IMMEDIATELY BEGINS TO PULL THE STAGNANT **BLOOD** DOWN, **DOWN**, INTO THE **LOWER** PARTS OF THE BODY...
...IN THIS INSTANCE, YOUR **FACE**, DUE TO YOUR **SLEEPING** POSITION.
THEY CALL THAT REDDISH-BROWN DISCOLORATION *LIVOR MORTIS*
AND THE FACT YOU CAN'T MAKE YOUR **MUSCLES** DO WHAT YOU **WANT** THEM TO?
GET **IN** THERE... BLASTED **KEYS!!**
THAT THEY'RE SO **LOOSE**, YOU MIGHT AS WELL BE TRYING TO OPERATE A MARIONETTE WITH **CUT STRINGS?**
THAT WOULD BE **"PRIMARY FLACCIDITY."** FREED FROM THE BURDEN OF LIFE, ALL YOUR MUSCLES HAVE GONE COMPLETELY LAX.
SKREEEECH
INCLUDING YOUR **BLADDER** MUSCLES ...HENCE THE LITTLE *"ACCIDENT"* BACK AT THE BAR.

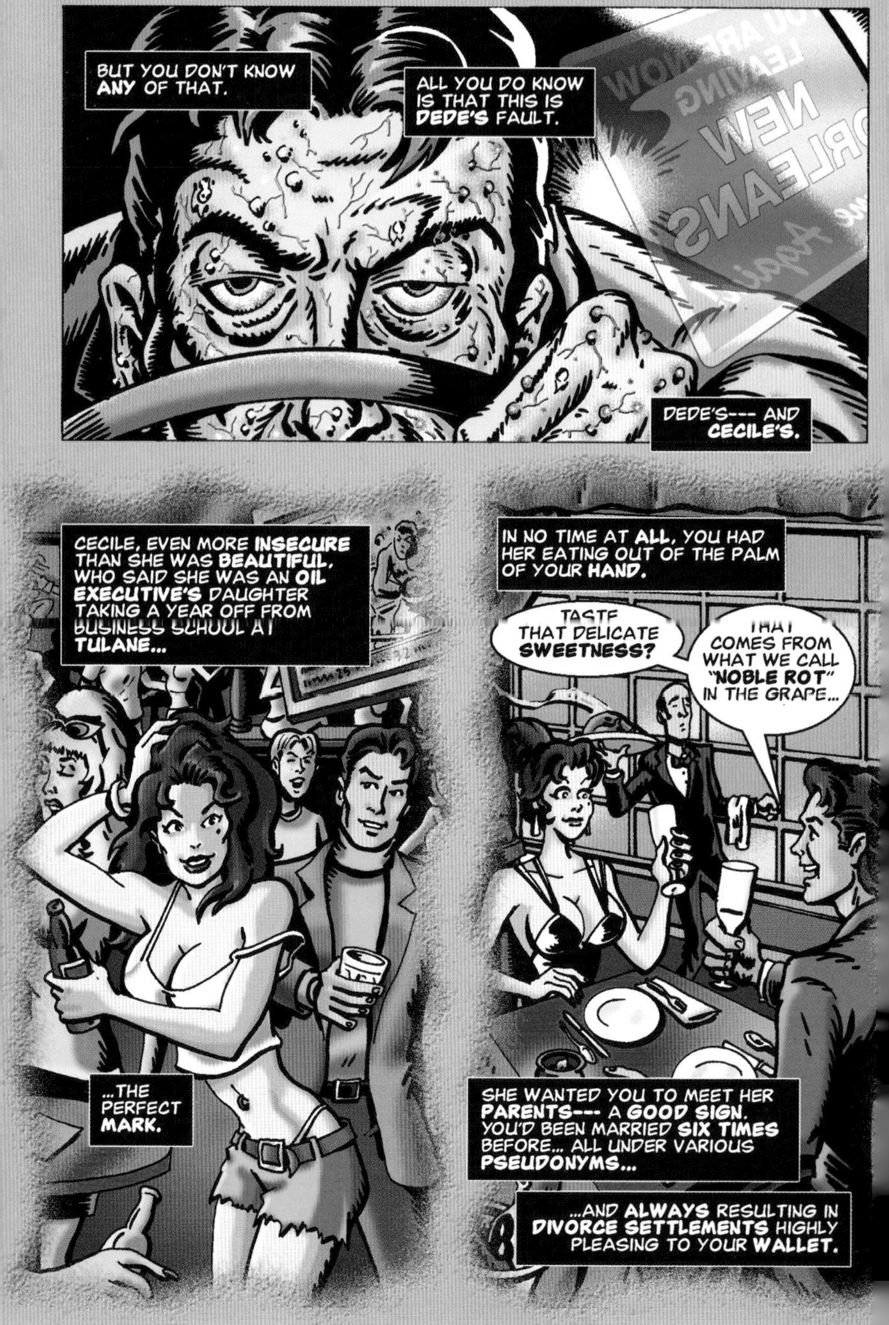
BUT YOU DON'T KNOW ANY OF THAT.
ALL YOU DO KNOW IS THAT THIS IS DEDE'S FAULT.
DEDE'S--- AND CECILE'S.
CECILE, EVEN MORE INSECURE THAN SHE WAS BEAUTIFUL, WHO SAID SHE WAS AN OIL EXECUTIVE'S DAUGHTER TAKING A YEAR OFF FROM BUSINESS SCHOOL AT TULANE...
...THE PERFECT MARK.
IN NO TIME AT ALL, YOU HAD HER EATING OUT OF THE PALM OF YOUR HAND.
TASTE THAT DELICATE SWEETNESS?
THAT COMES FROM WHAT WE CALL "NOBLE ROT" IN THE GRAPE...
SHE WANTED YOU TO MEET HER PARENTS--- A GOOD SIGN. YOU'D BEEN MARRIED SIX TIMES BEFORE... ALL UNDER VARIOUS PSEUDONYMS...
...AND ALWAYS RESULTING IN DIVORCE SETTLEMENTS HIGHLY PLEASING TO YOUR WALLET.

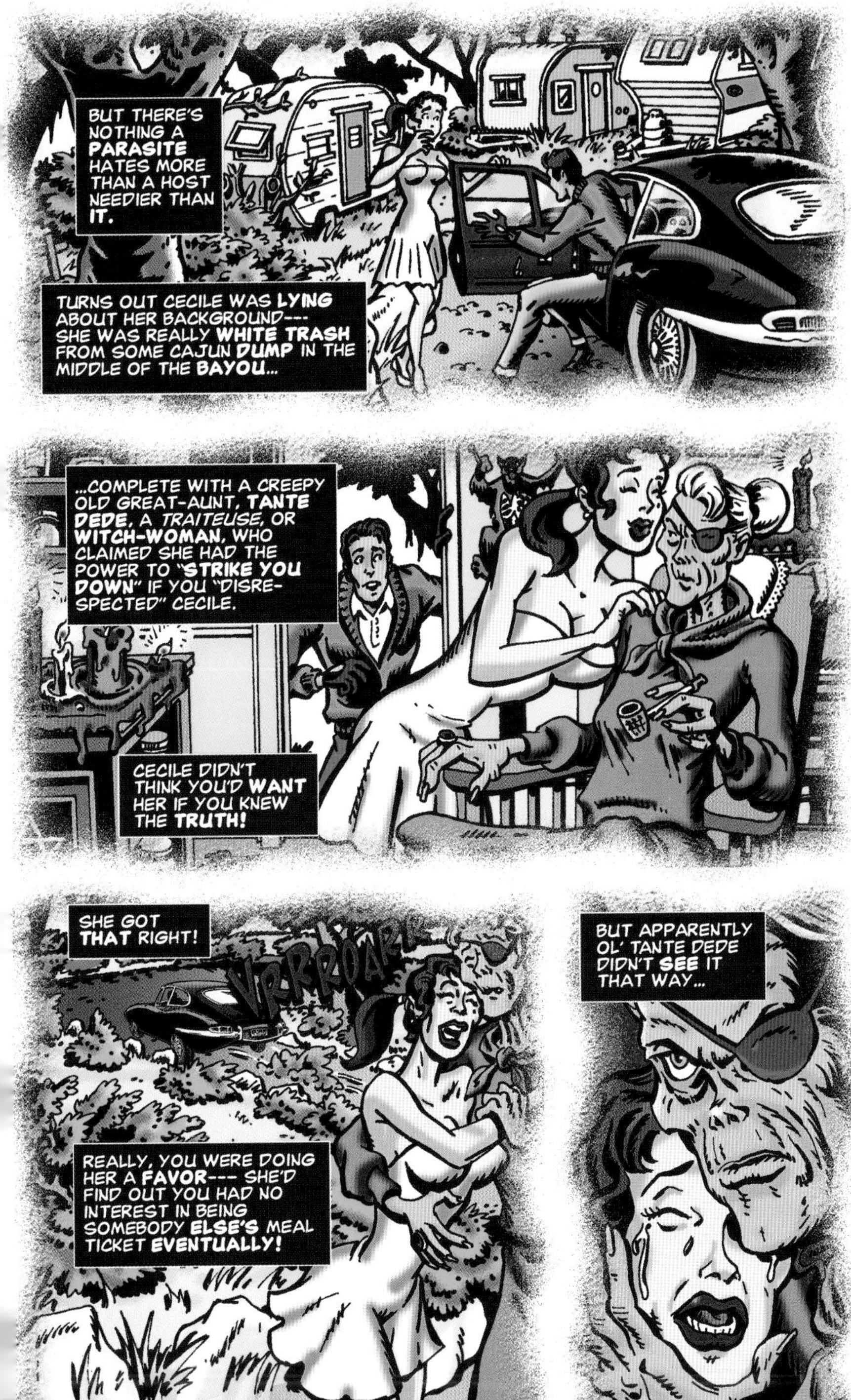
BUT THERE'S NOTHING A PARASITE HATES MORE THAN A HOST NEEDIER THAN IT.
TURNS OUT CECILE WAS LYING ABOUT HER BACKGROUND--- SHE WAS REALLY WHITE TRASH FROM SOME CAJUN DUMP IN THE MIDDLE OF THE BAYOU...
...COMPLETE WITH A CREEPY OLD GREAT-AUNT, TANTE DEDE, A TRAITEUSE, OR WITCH-WOMAN, WHO CLAIMED SHE HAD THE POWER TO "STRIKE YOU DOWN" IF YOU "DISRESPECTED" CECILE.
CECILE DIDN'T THINK YOU'D WANT HER IF YOU KNEW THE TRUTH!
SHE GOT THAT RIGHT!
VRRROAR!
REALLY, YOU WERE DOING HER A FAVOR--- SHE'D FIND OUT YOU HAD NO INTEREST IN BEING SOMEBODY ELSE'S MEAL TICKET EVENTUALLY!
BUT APPARENTLY OL' TANTE DEDE DIDN'T SEE IT THAT WAY...

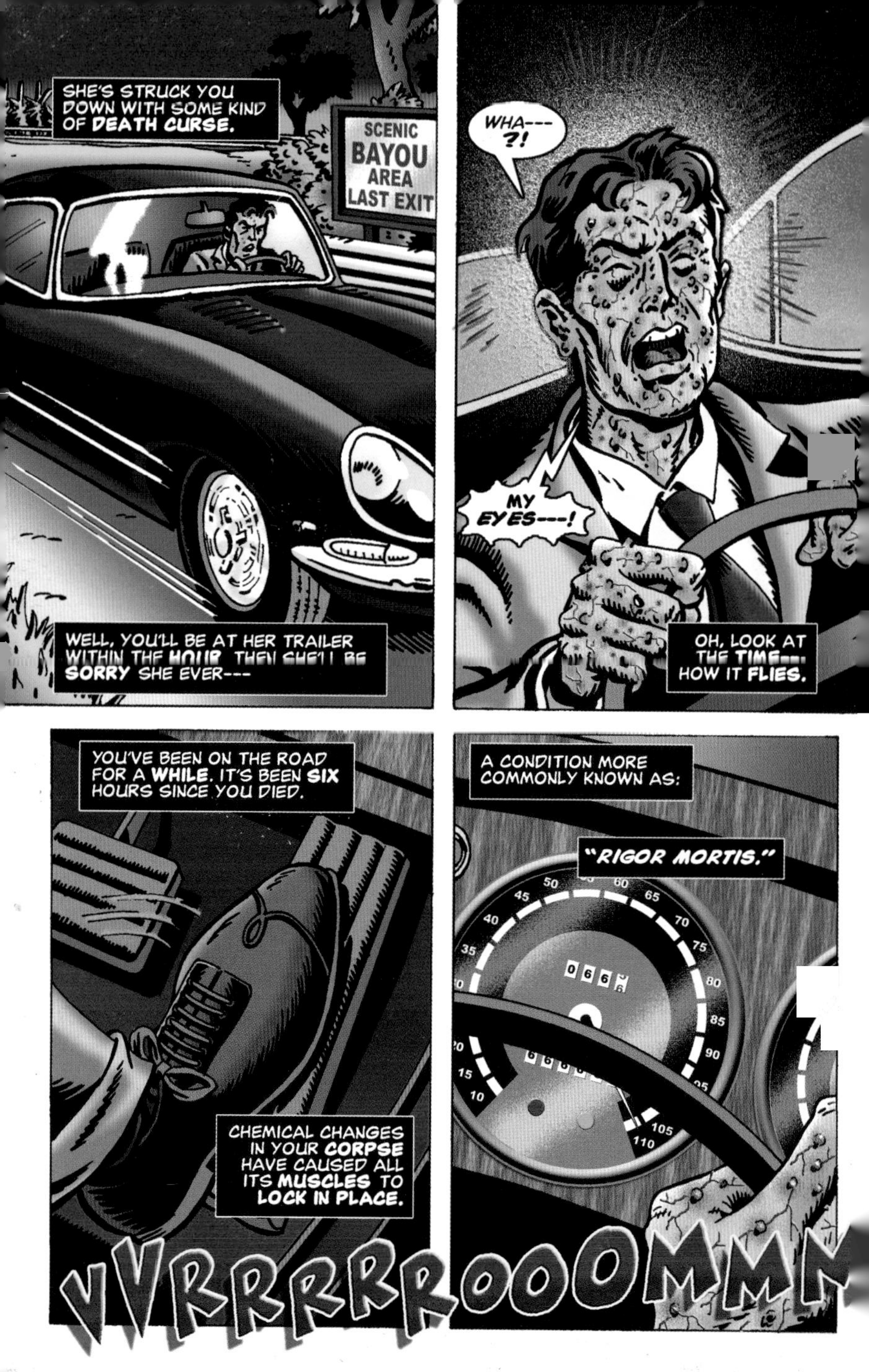

SHE'S STRUCK YOU DOWN WITH SOME KIND OF **DEATH CURSE.**
SCENIC BAYOU AREA LAST EXIT
WELL, YOU'LL BE AT HER TRAILER WITHIN THE HOUR. THEN SHE'LL BE **SORRY** SHE EVER---
WHA--- ?!
MY EYES---!
OH, LOOK AT THE **TIME**--- HOW IT **FLIES.**
YOU'VE BEEN ON THE ROAD FOR A **WHILE**. IT'S BEEN **SIX** HOURS SINCE YOU DIED.
CHEMICAL CHANGES IN YOUR **CORPSE** HAVE CAUSED ALL ITS **MUSCLES** TO **LOCK IN PLACE.**
A CONDITION MORE COMMONLY KNOWN AS:
"RIGOR MORTIS."
VVRRRRROOOOMMM

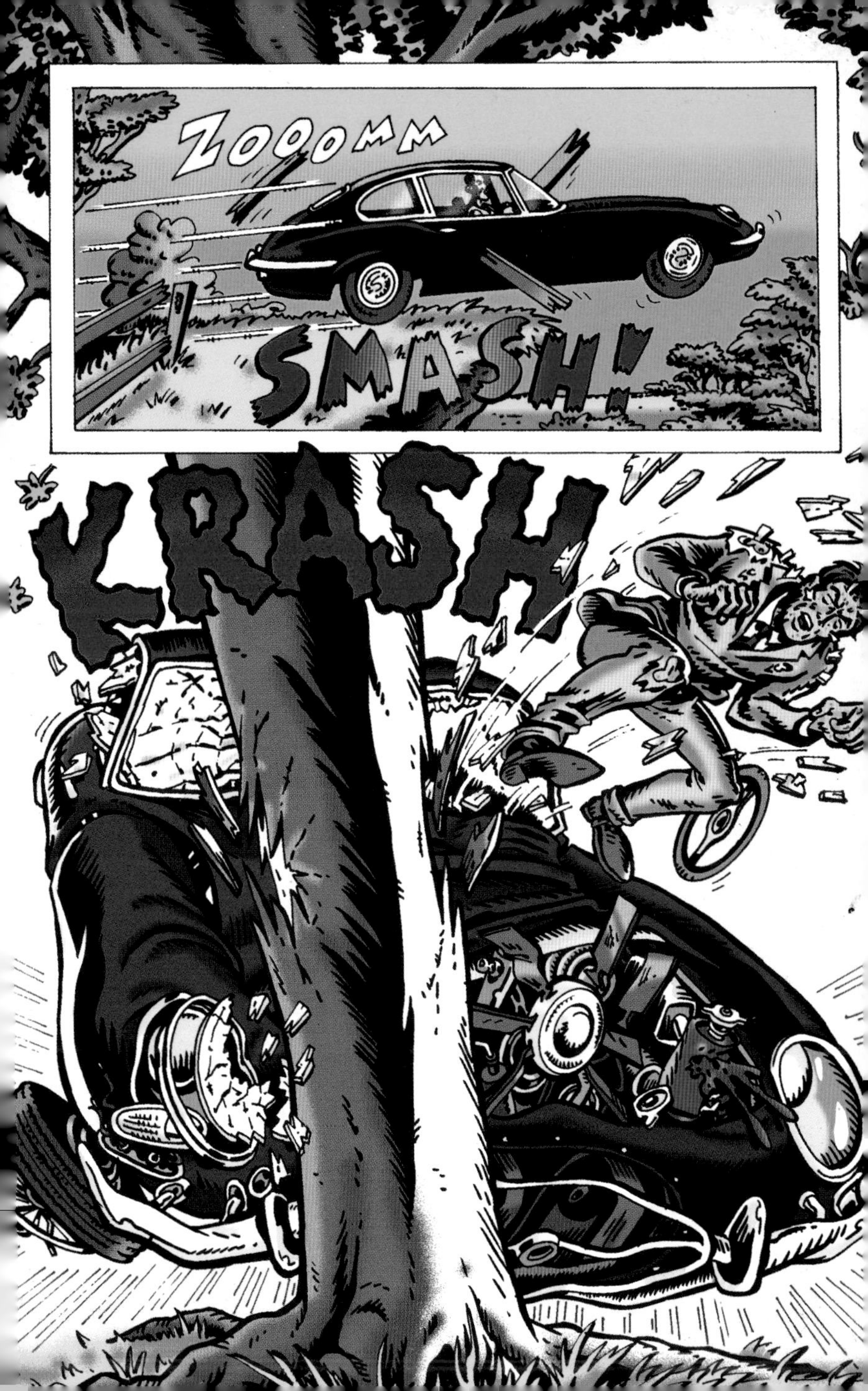
ZOOOOMM
SMASH!
KRASH

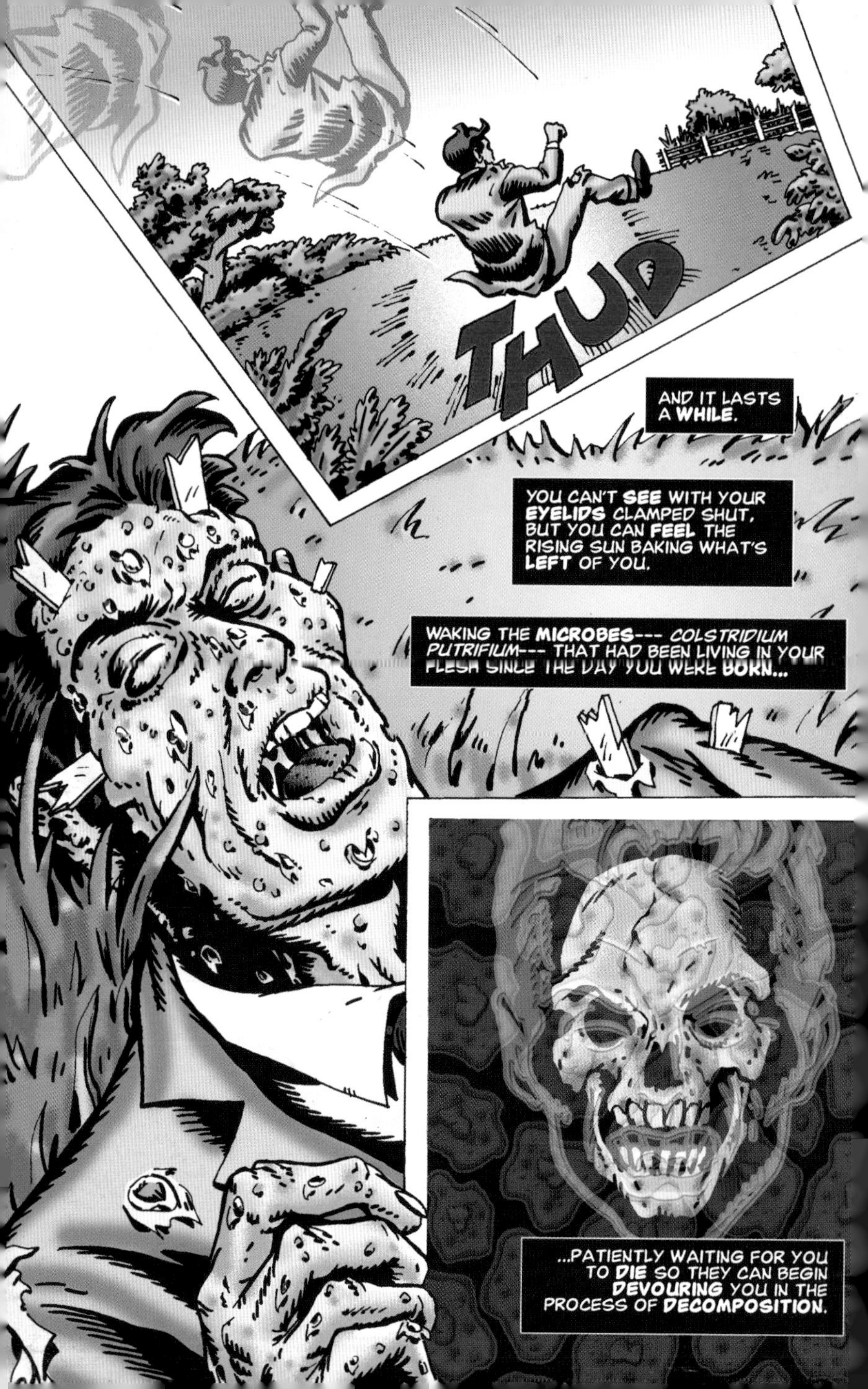
THUD
AND IT LASTS A WHILE.
YOU CAN'T SEE WITH YOUR EYELIDS CLAMPED SHUT, BUT YOU CAN FEEL THE RISING SUN BAKING WHAT'S LEFT OF YOU.
WAKING THE MICROBES--- COLSTRIDIUM PUTRIFIUM--- THAT HAD BEEN LIVING IN YOUR FLESH SINCE THE DAY YOU WERE BORN...
...PATIENTLY WAITING FOR YOU TO DIE SO THEY CAN BEGIN DEVOURING YOU IN THE PROCESS OF DECOMPOSITION.

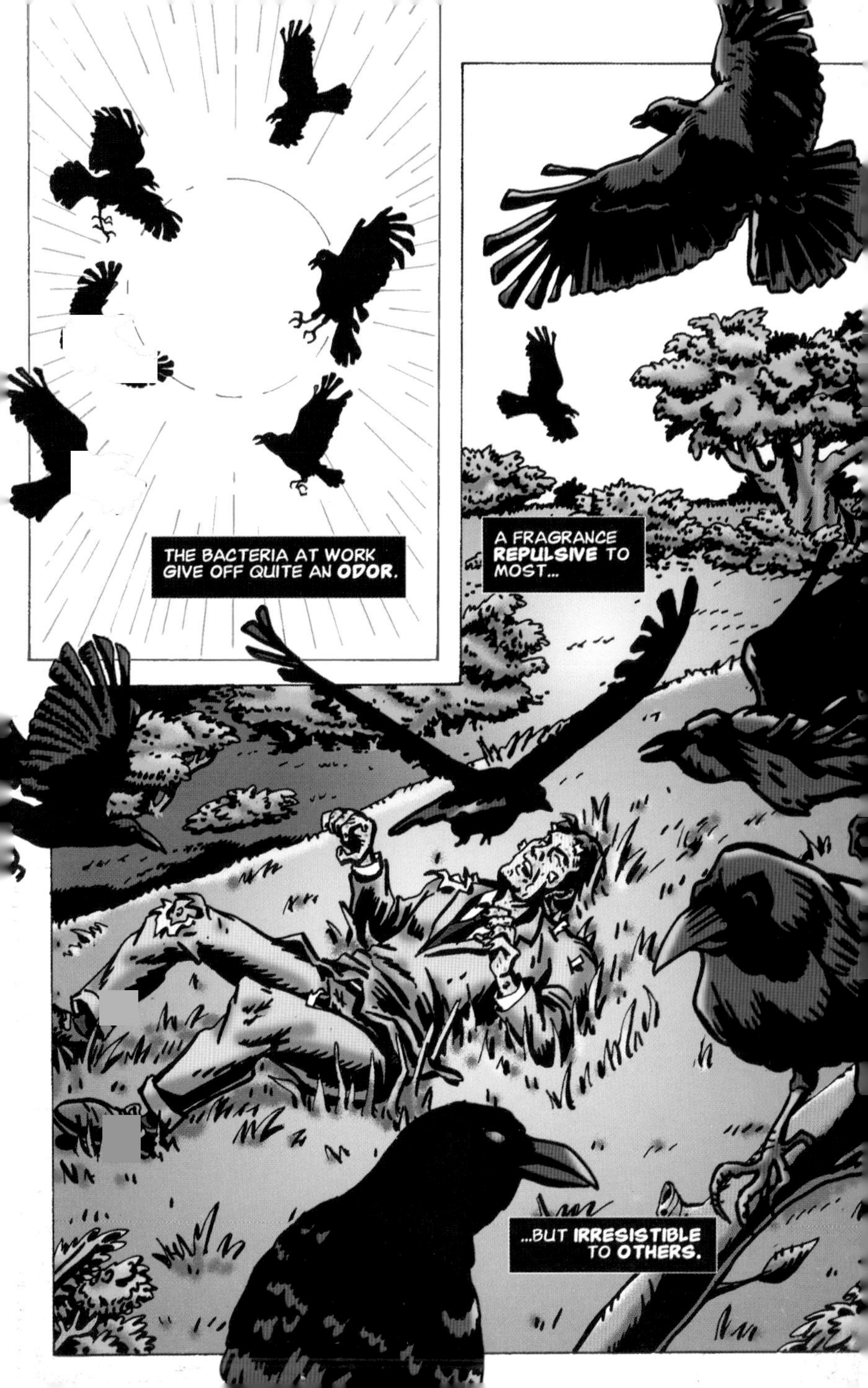
THE BACTERIA AT WORK GIVE OFF QUITE AN ODOR.
A FRAGRANCE REPULSIVE TO MOST...
...BUT IRRESISTIBLE TO OTHERS.

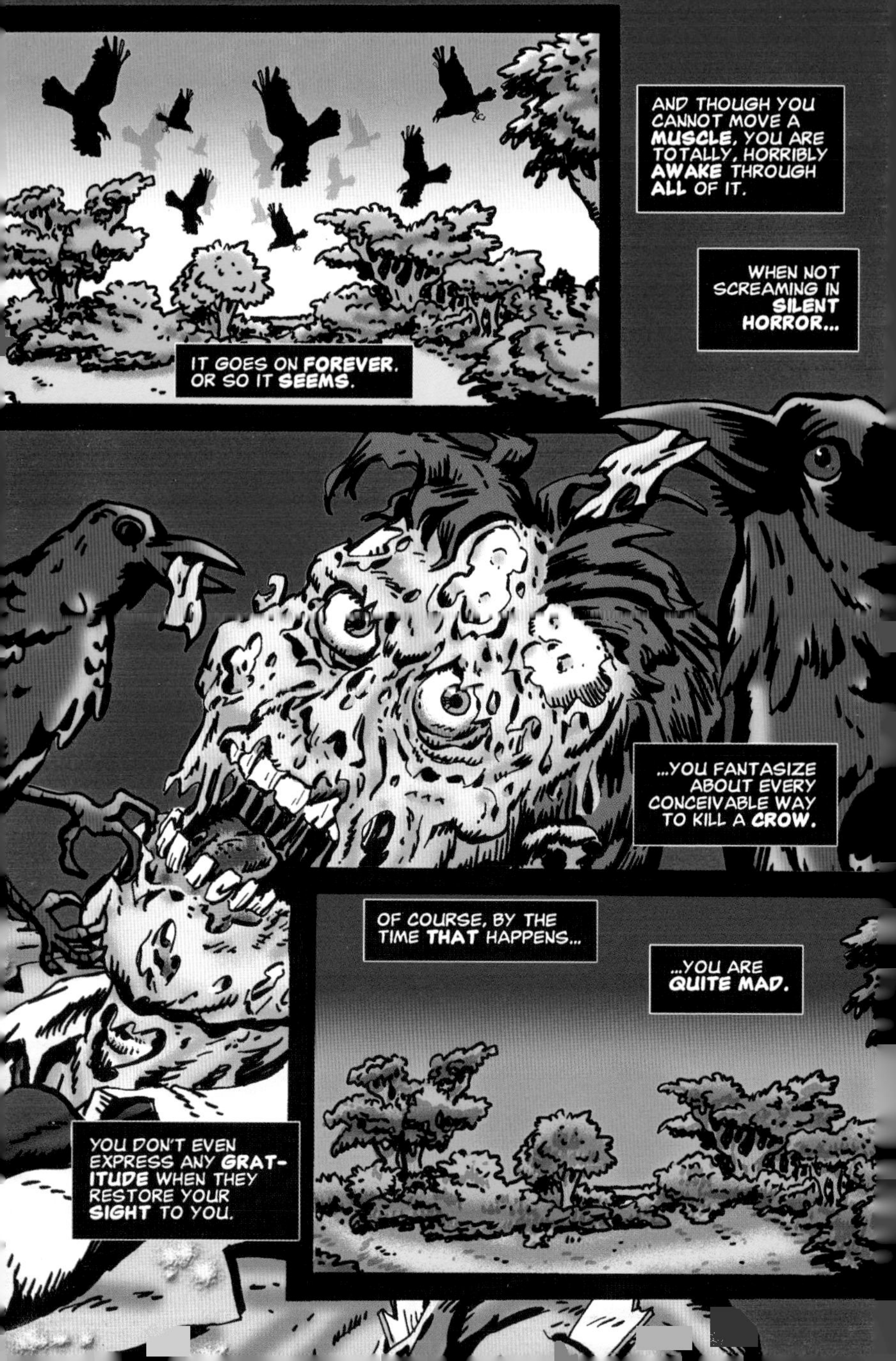
IT GOES ON **FOREVER**. OR SO IT **SEEMS**.
AND THOUGH YOU CANNOT MOVE A **MUSCLE**, YOU ARE TOTALLY, HORRIBLY **AWAKE** THROUGH **ALL** OF IT.
WHEN NOT SCREAMING IN **SILENT HORROR**...
...YOU FANTASIZE ABOUT EVERY CONCEIVABLE WAY TO KILL A **CROW**.
YOU DON'T EVEN EXPRESS ANY **GRAT-ITUDE** WHEN THEY RESTORE YOUR **SIGHT** TO YOU.
OF COURSE, BY THE TIME **THAT** HAPPENS...
...YOU ARE **QUITE MAD**.

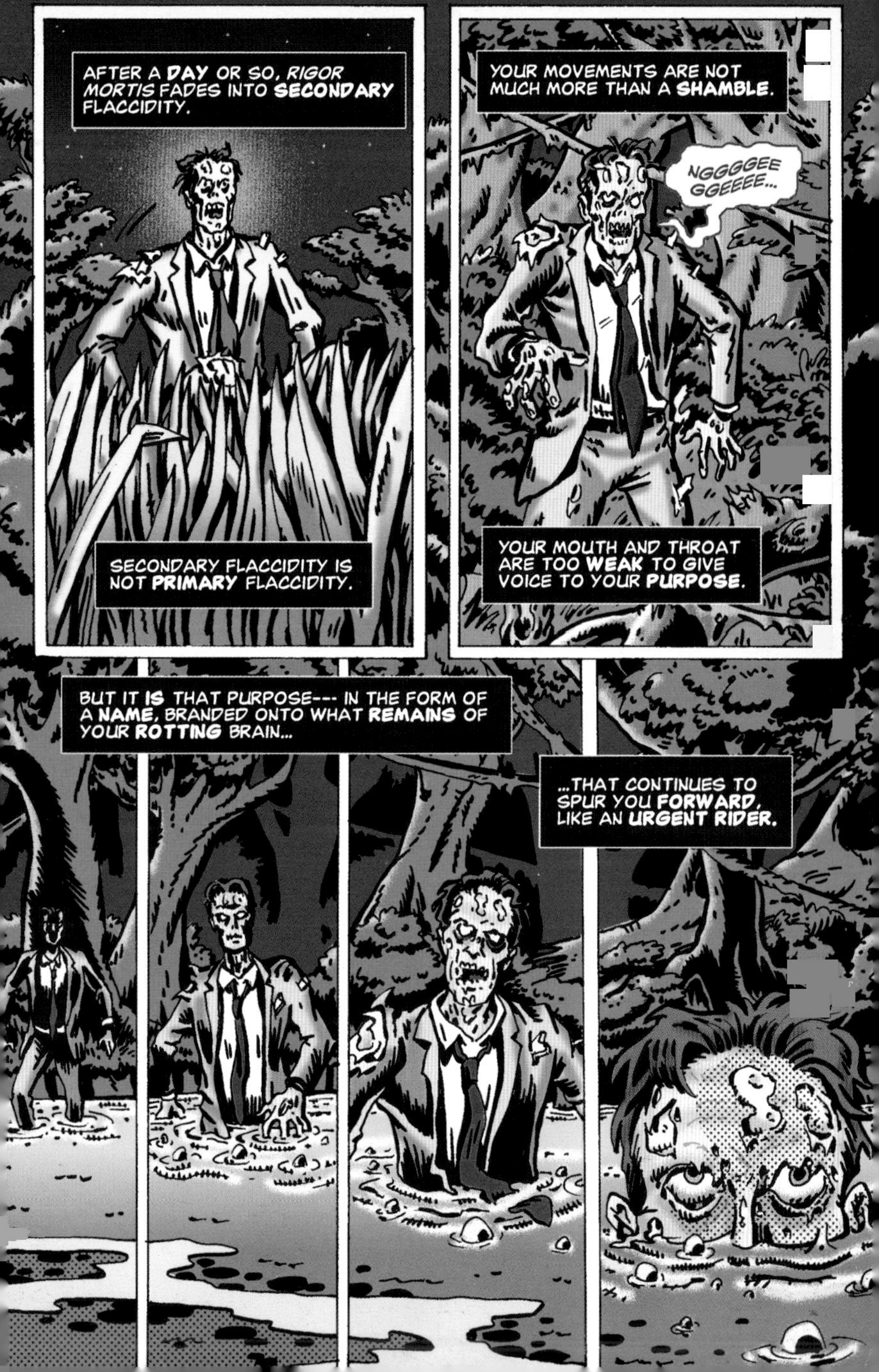
AFTER A DAY OR SO, RIGOR MORTIS FADES INTO SECONDARY FLACCIDITY.
SECONDARY FLACCIDITY IS NOT PRIMARY FLACCIDITY.
YOUR MOVEMENTS ARE NOT MUCH MORE THAN A SHAMBLE.
NGGGGEE GGEEEE...
YOUR MOUTH AND THROAT ARE TOO WEAK TO GIVE VOICE TO YOUR PURPOSE.
BUT IT IS THAT PURPOSE--- IN THE FORM OF A NAME, BRANDED ONTO WHAT REMAINS OF YOUR ROTTING BRAIN...
...THAT CONTINUES TO SPUR YOU FORWARD, LIKE AN URGENT RIDER.

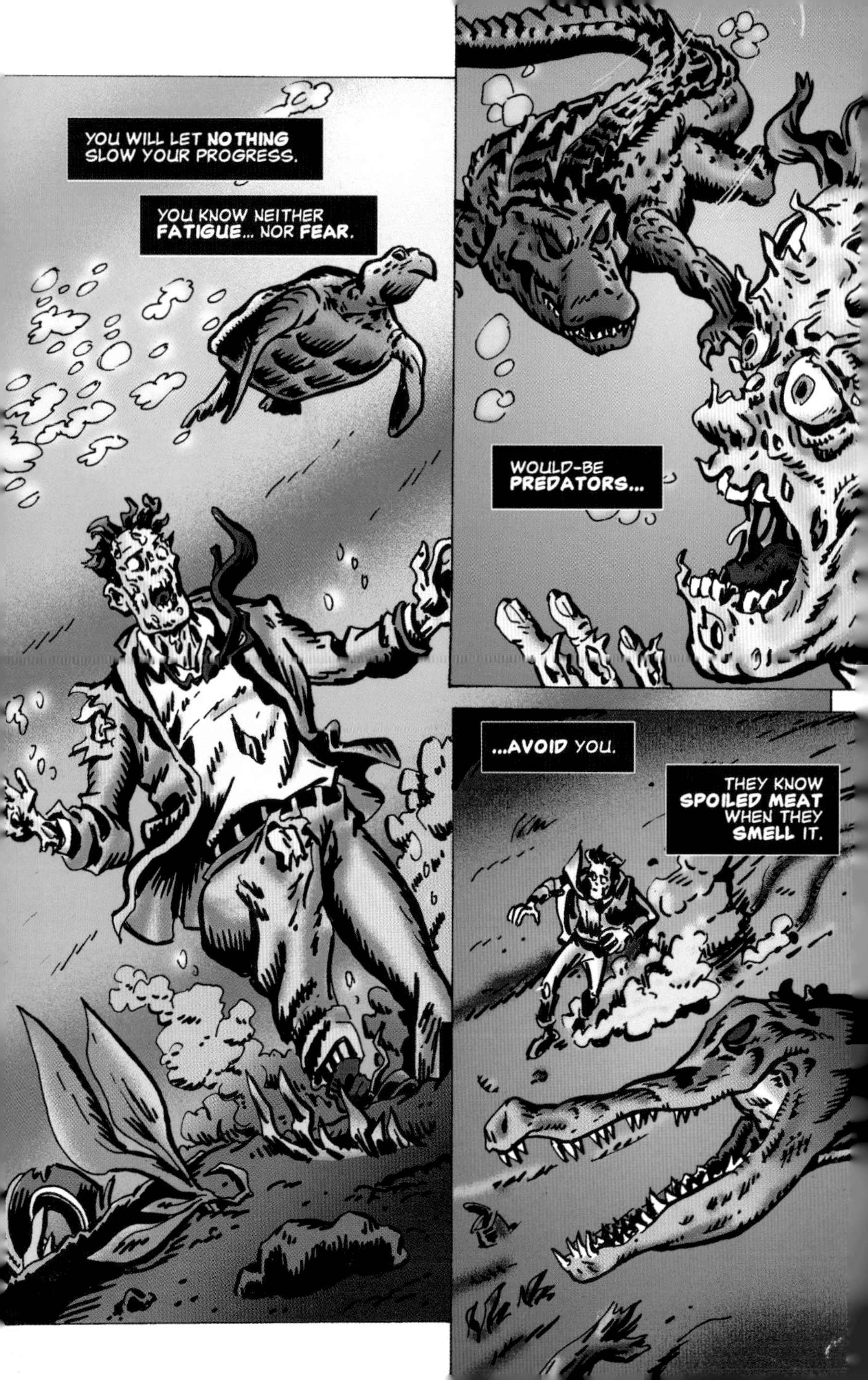
YOU WILL LET NOTHING SLOW YOUR PROGRESS.
YOU KNOW NEITHER FATIGUE... NOR FEAR.
WOULD-BE PREDATORS...
...AVOID YOU.
THEY KNOW SPOILED MEAT WHEN THEY SMELL IT.

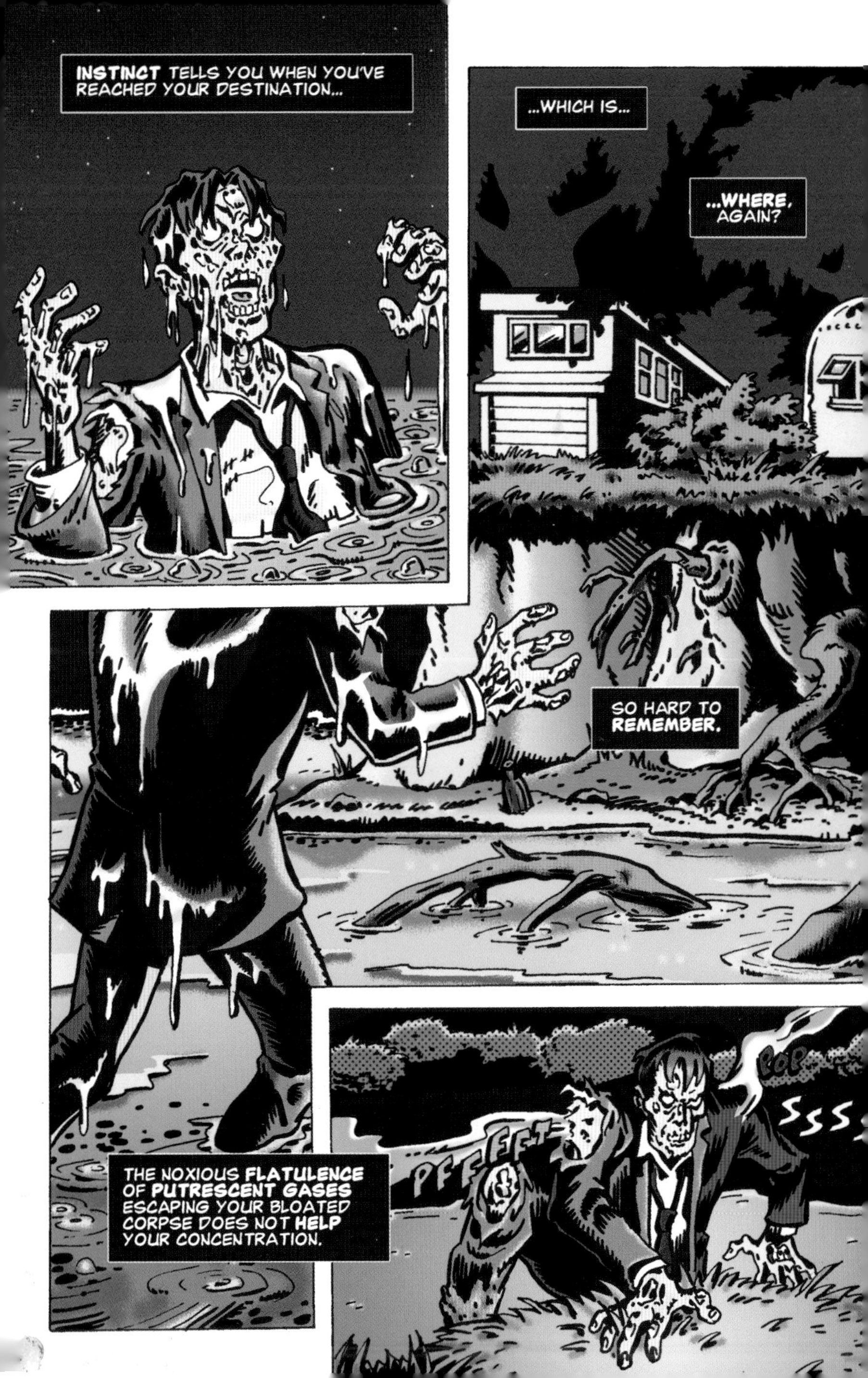

INSTINCT TELLS YOU WHEN YOU'VE REACHED YOUR DESTINATION...
...WHICH IS...
...WHERE, AGAIN?
SO HARD TO REMEMBER.
THE NOXIOUS FLATULENCE OF PUTRESCENT GASES ESCAPING YOUR BLOATED CORPSE DOES NOT HELP YOUR CONCENTRATION.
PFFFFT-
POP
SSS

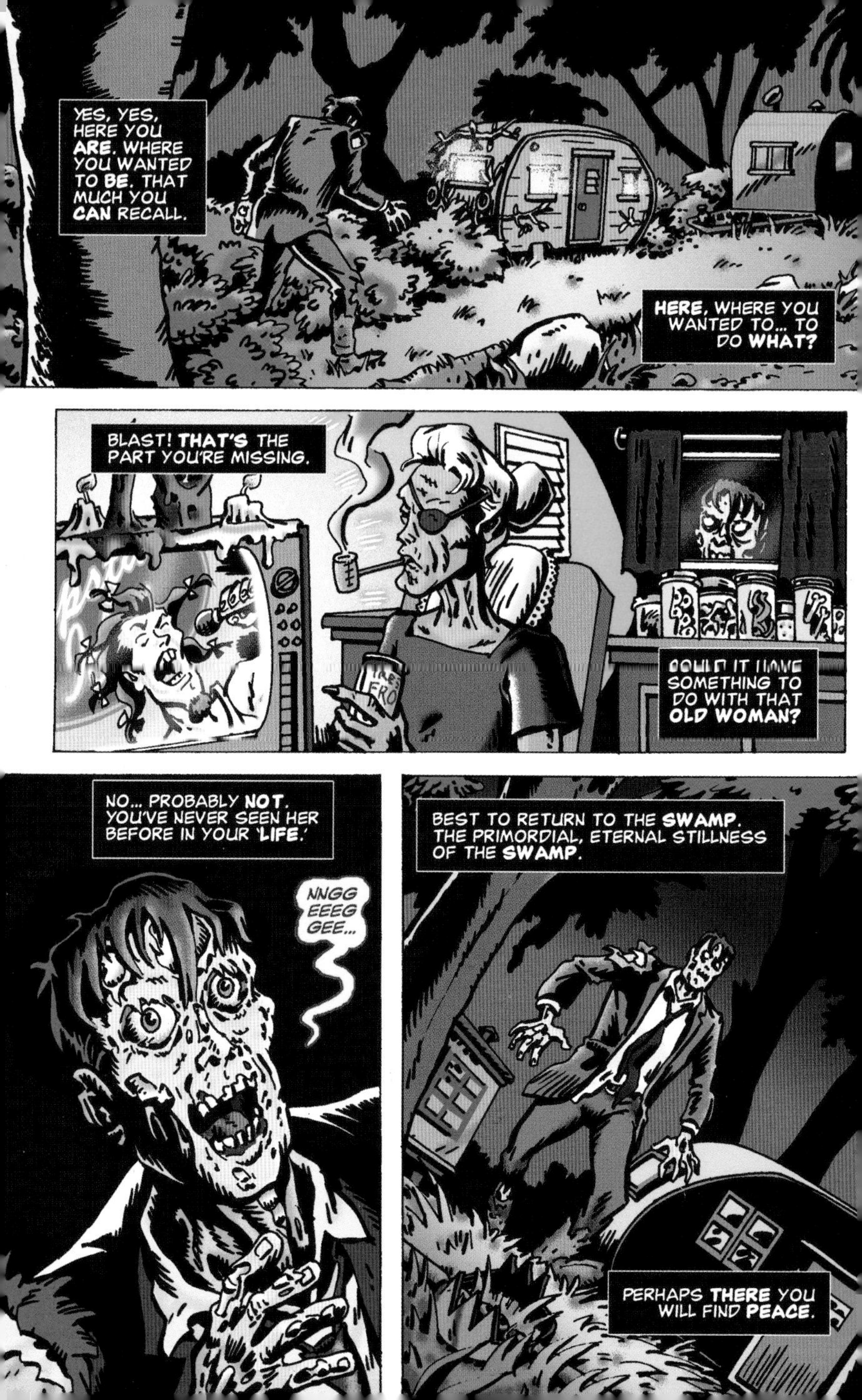
YES, YES, HERE YOU ARE. WHERE YOU WANTED TO BE. THAT MUCH YOU CAN RECALL.
HERE, WHERE YOU WANTED TO... TO DO WHAT?
BLAST! THAT'S THE PART YOU'RE MISSING.
COULD IT HAVE SOMETHING TO DO WITH THAT OLD WOMAN?
NO... PROBABLY NOT. YOU'VE NEVER SEEN HER BEFORE IN YOUR 'LIFE.'
NNGG EEEG GEE...
BEST TO RETURN TO THE SWAMP. THE PRIMORDIAL, ETERNAL STILLNESS OF THE SWAMP.
PERHAPS THERE YOU WILL FIND PEACE.

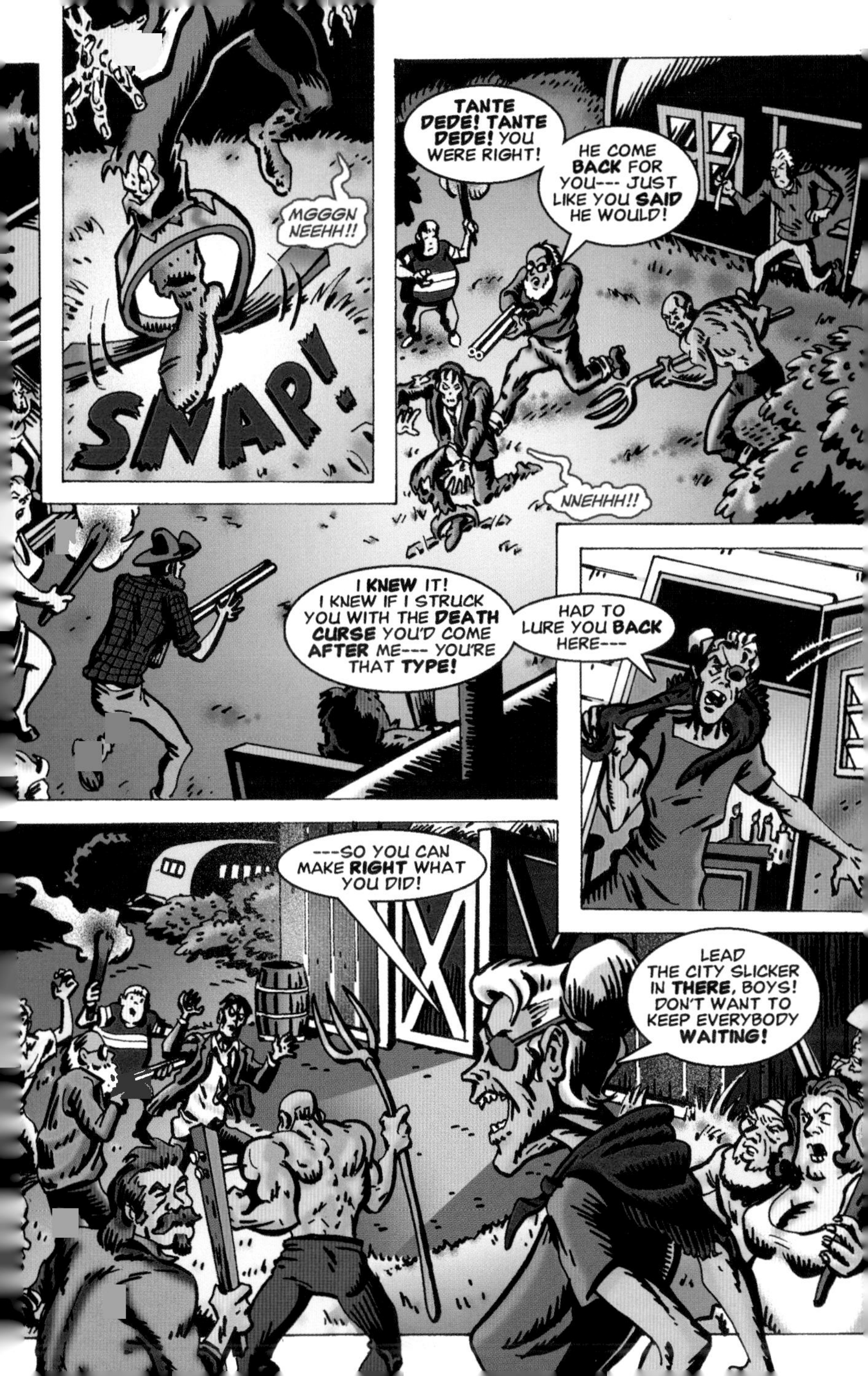
MGGGN NEEHH!!
SNAP!
TANTE DEDE! TANTE DEDE! YOU WERE RIGHT!
HE COME BACK FOR YOU--- JUST LIKE YOU SAID HE WOULD!
NNEHHH!!
I KNEW IT! I KNEW IF I STRUCK YOU WITH THE DEATH CURSE YOU'D COME AFTER ME--- YOU'RE THAT TYPE!
HAD TO LURE YOU BACK HERE---
---SO YOU CAN MAKE RIGHT WHAT YOU DID!
LEAD THE CITY SLICKER IN THERE, BOYS! DON'T WANT TO KEEP EVERYBODY WAITING!

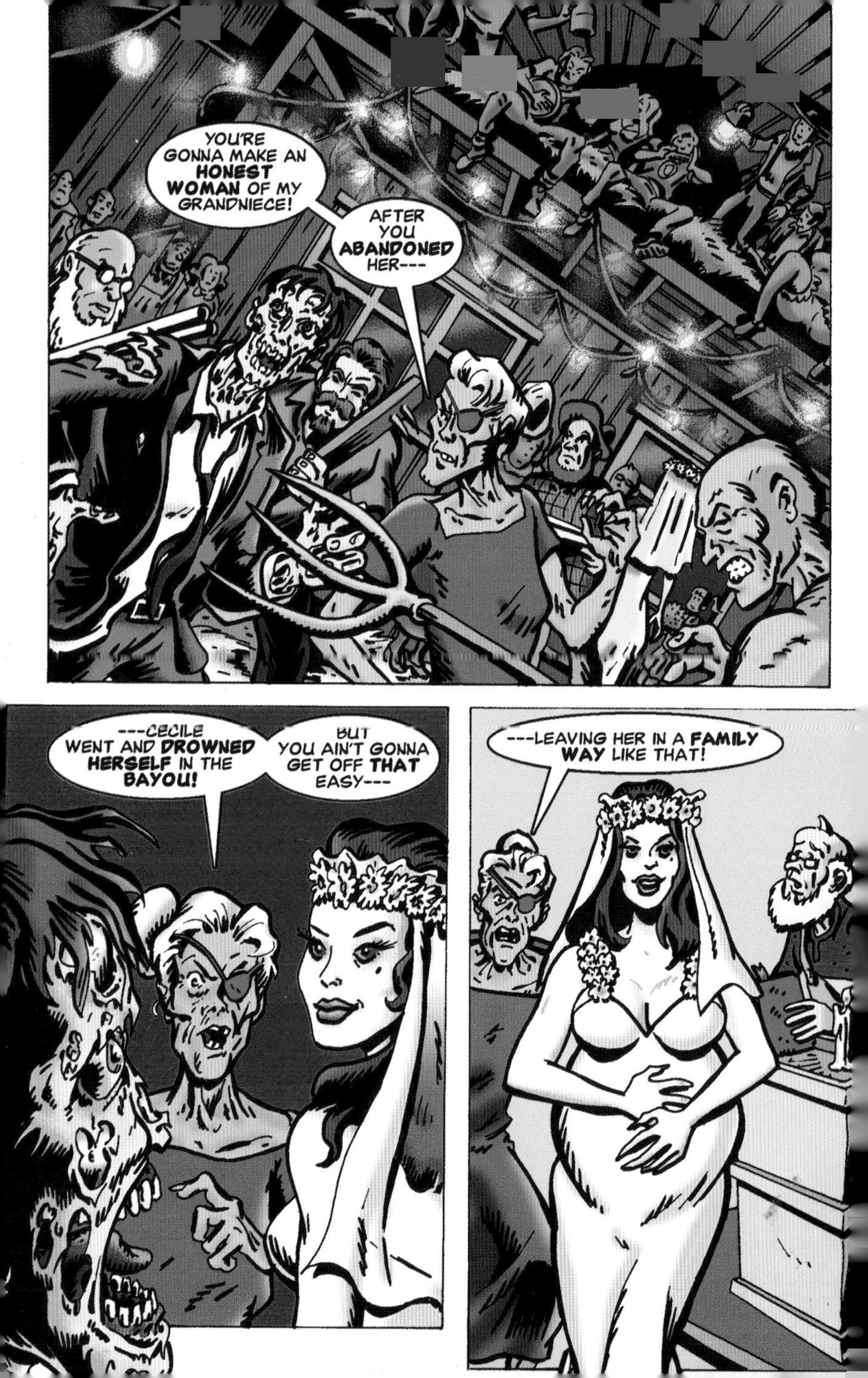
YOU'RE GONNA MAKE AN HONEST WOMAN OF MY GRANDNIECE!
AFTER YOU ABANDONED HER---
---CECILE WENT AND DROWNED HERSELF IN THE BAYOU!
BUT YOU AIN'T GONNA GET OFF THAT EASY---
---LEAVING HER IN A FAMILY WAY LIKE THAT!

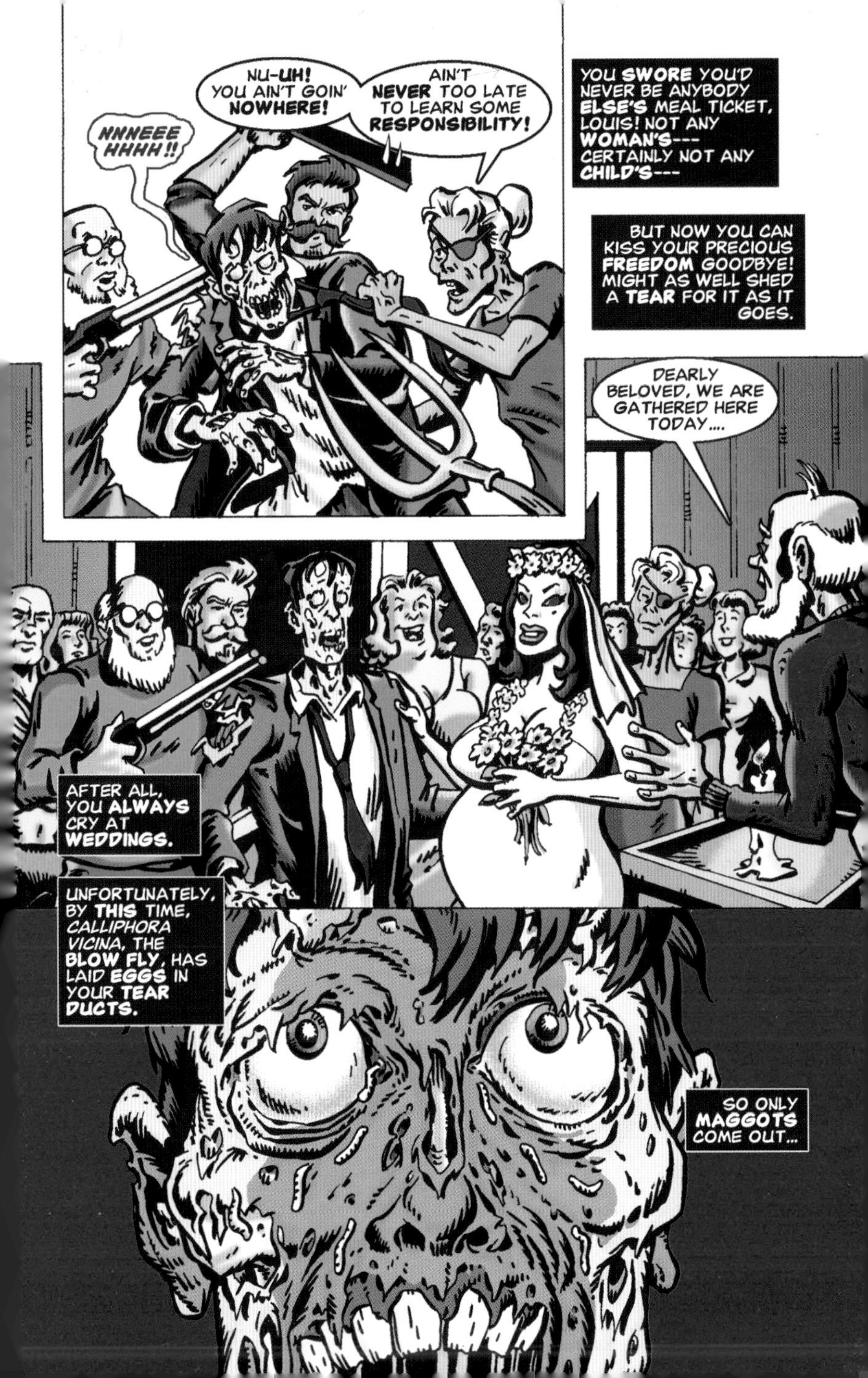
NNNEEE HHHH!!
NU-UH! YOU AIN'T GOIN' NOWHERE!
AIN'T NEVER TOO LATE TO LEARN SOME RESPONSIBILITY!
YOU SWORE YOU'D NEVER BE ANYBODY ELSE'S MEAL TICKET, LOUIS! NOT ANY WOMAN'S--- CERTAINLY NOT ANY CHILD'S---
BUT NOW YOU CAN KISS YOUR PRECIOUS FREEDOM GOODBYE! MIGHT AS WELL SHED A TEAR FOR IT AS IT GOES.
DEARLY BELOVED, WE ARE GATHERED HERE TODAY....
AFTER ALL, YOU ALWAYS CRY AT WEDDINGS.
UNFORTUNATELY, BY THIS TIME, CALLIPHORA VICINA, THE BLOW FLY, HAS LAID EGGS IN YOUR TEAR DUCTS.
SO ONLY MAGGOTS COME OUT...

WHAT'S THAT?

SOMEONE ASK FOR A NOBLE *RAT?*

I PARTICULARLY ENJOYED THAT LAST TALE – SHOWS WHAT HAPPENS WHEN FOLKS MISTREAT WITCHES!

FOLKS ARE ALWAYS SCHEMIN' TO HOLD OTHERS DOWN! LET ME TELL YOU, EVEN THE CRYPT-KEEPER AND THE VAULT-KEEPER ARE PART OF A *GHOUL-OLD BOYS CLUB* THAT LOVES KEEPING A GOOD WOMAN DOWN!

AFTER ALL, THEY'VE GOT *CRYPTS* AND *VAULTS* TO KEEP – WHAT DO I HAVE?! BUT IT'S NOT JUST WOMEN *POWER-HUNGRY PREDATORS PREY* UPON! ANYONE THEY DEEM TO BE *WEAK* IS *FAIR GAME!*

TAKE *STANLEY POTTS,* FOR EXAMPLE! ALL HE HAD WAS A SIMPLE DREAM, AND AN OPPORTUNISTIC CO-WORKER STOLE IT! IT'S ALL LOVINGLY LAID OUT IN...

VIRTUAL HOO DOO

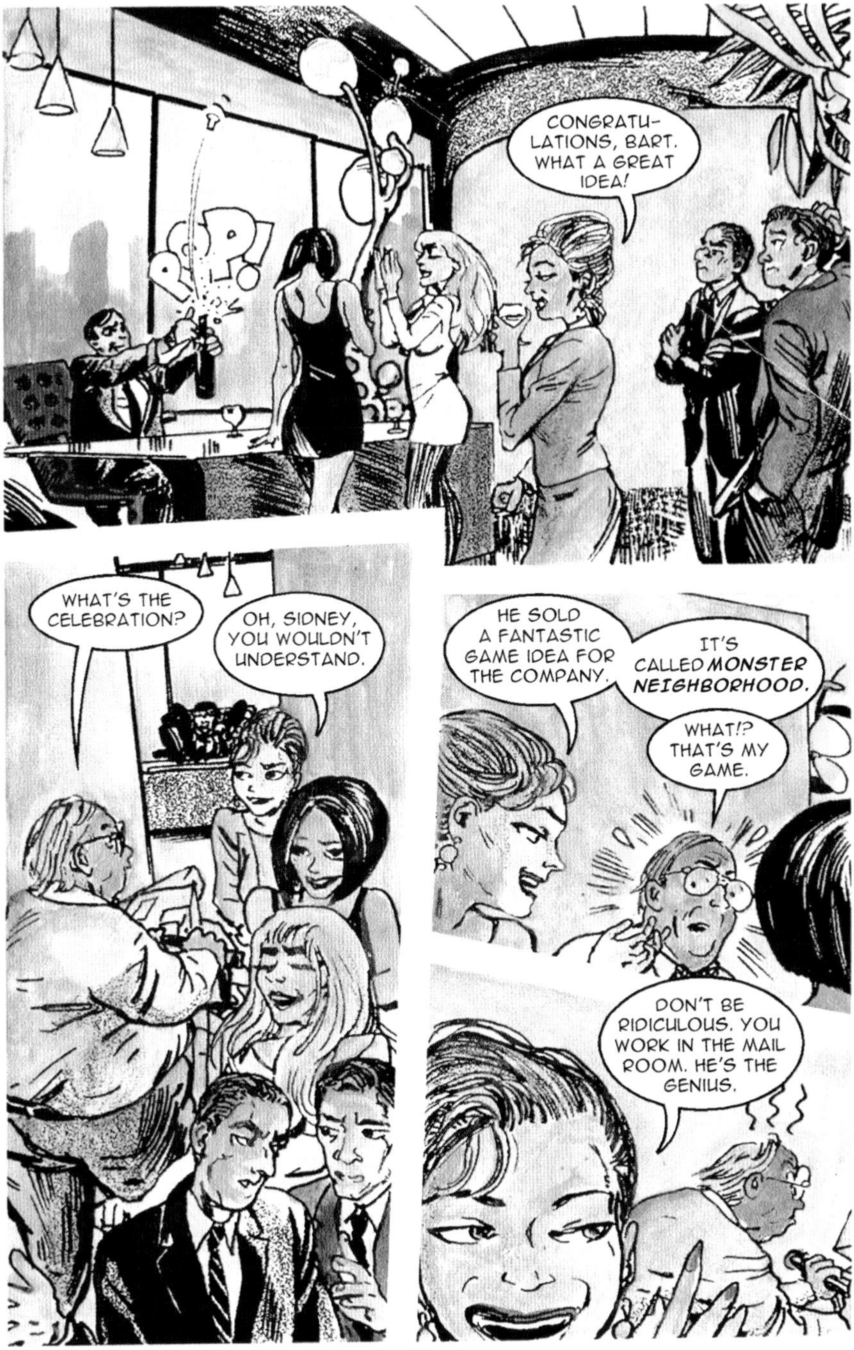

POP!
CONGRATULATIONS, BART. WHAT A GREAT IDEA!
WHAT'S THE CELEBRATION?
OH, SIDNEY, YOU WOULDN'T UNDERSTAND.
HE SOLD A FANTASTIC GAME IDEA FOR THE COMPANY.
IT'S CALLED ***MONSTER NEIGHBORHOOD.***
WHAT!? THAT'S MY GAME.
DON'T BE RIDICULOUS. YOU WORK IN THE MAIL ROOM. HE'S THE GENIUS.

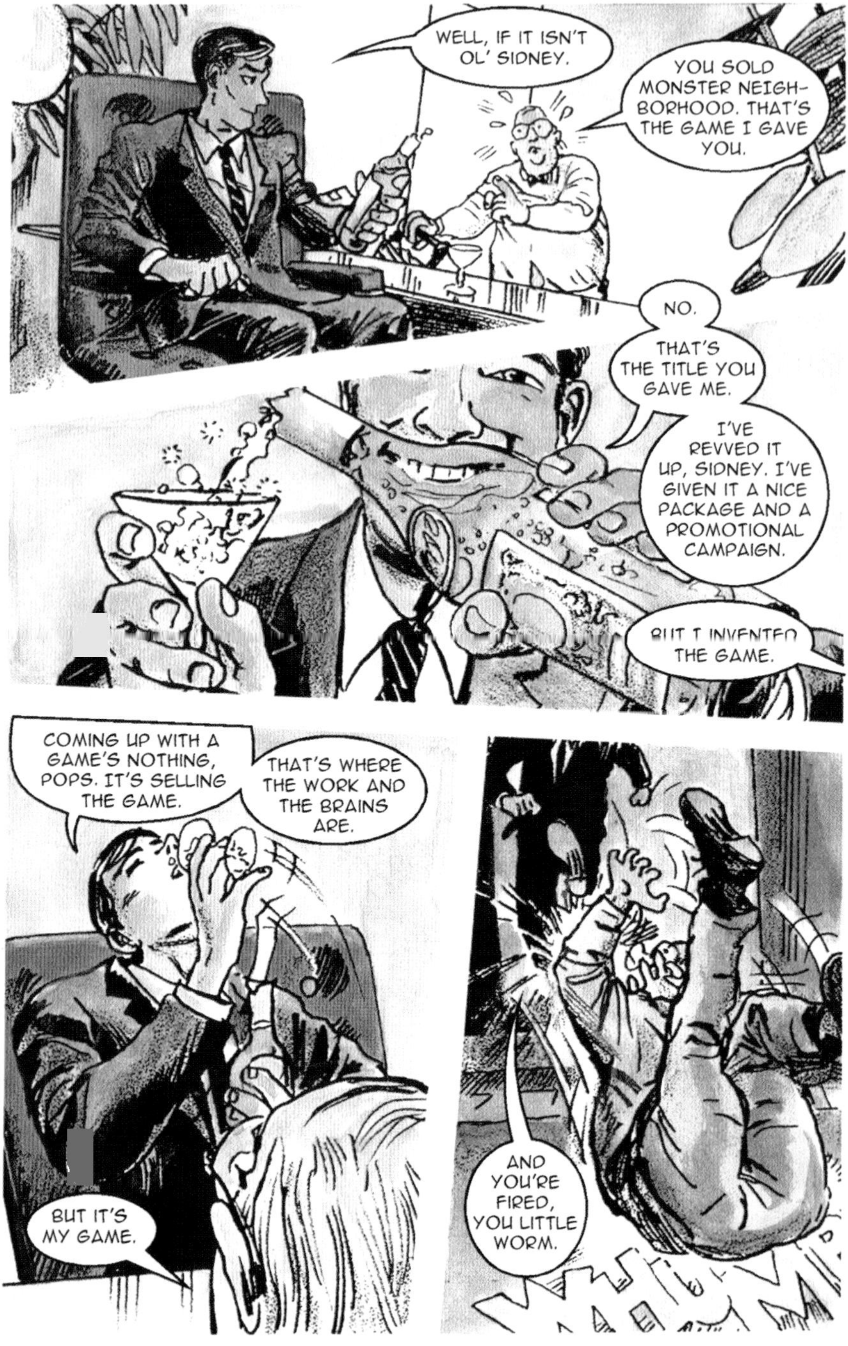
WELL, IF IT ISN'T OL' SIDNEY.
YOU SOLD MONSTER NEIGH-BORHOOD. THAT'S THE GAME I GAVE YOU.
NO.
THAT'S THE TITLE YOU GAVE ME.
I'VE REVVED IT UP, SIDNEY. I'VE GIVEN IT A NICE PACKAGE AND A PROMOTIONAL CAMPAIGN.
BUT I INVENTED THE GAME.
COMING UP WITH A GAME'S NOTHING, POPS. IT'S SELLING THE GAME.
THAT'S WHERE THE WORK AND THE BRAINS ARE.
BUT IT'S MY GAME.
AND YOU'RE FIRED, YOU LITTLE WORM.

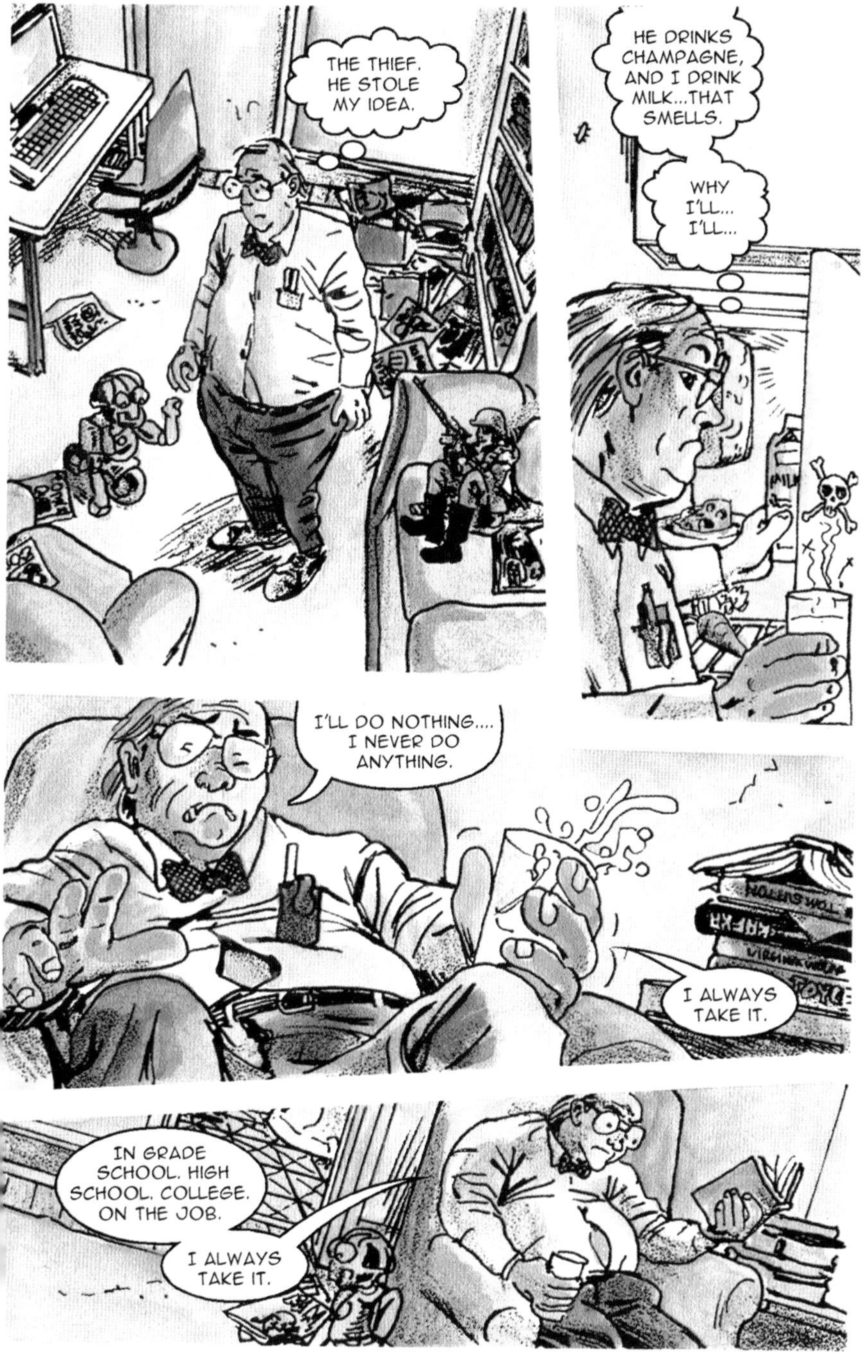
THE THIEF. HE STOLE MY IDEA.
HE DRINKS CHAMPAGNE, AND I DRINK MILK...THAT SMELLS.
WHY I'LL... I'LL...
I'LL DO NOTHING.... I NEVER DO ANYTHING.
I ALWAYS TAKE IT.
IN GRADE SCHOOL. HIGH SCHOOL. COLLEGE. ON THE JOB.
I ALWAYS TAKE IT.

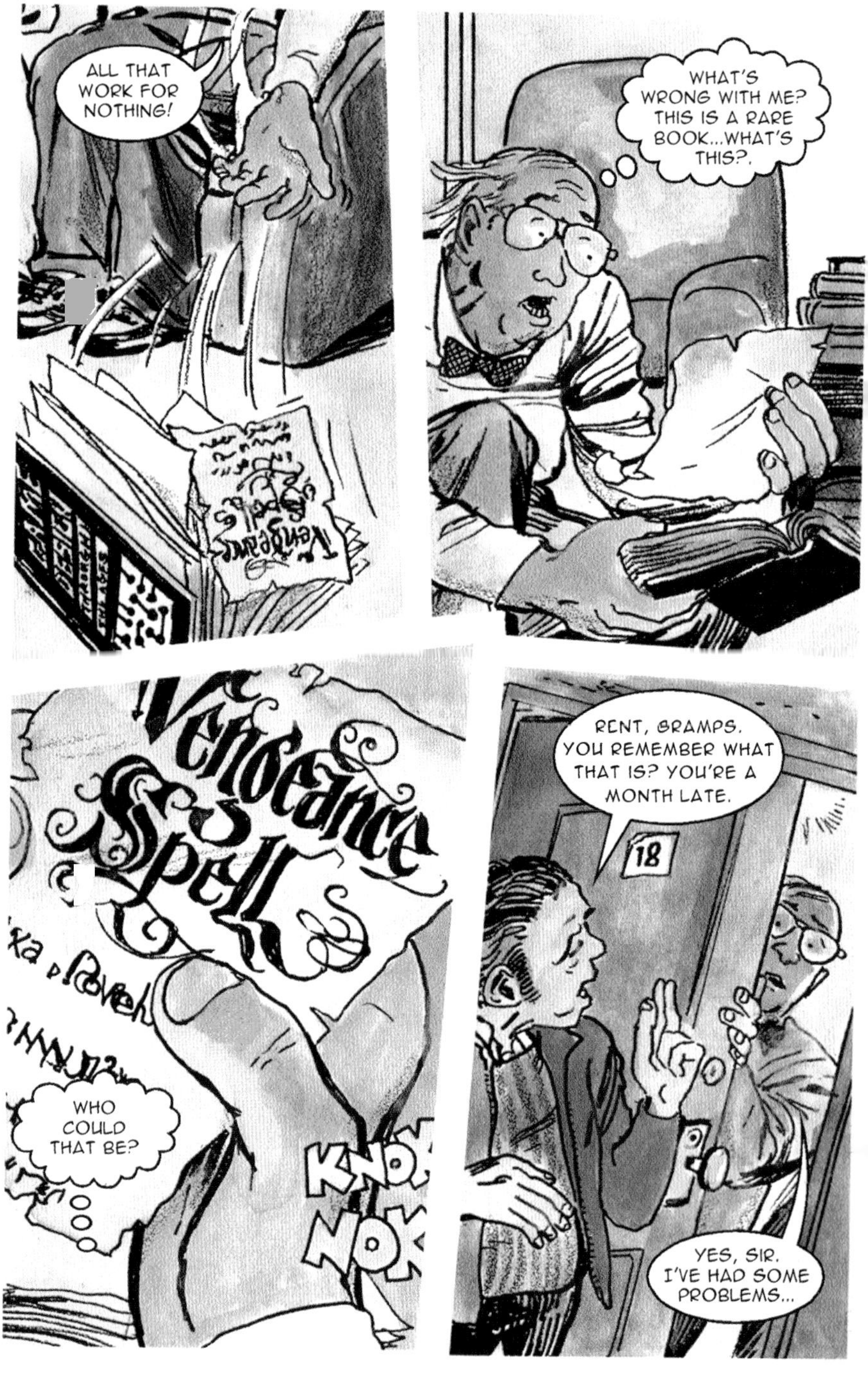
ALL THAT WORK FOR NOTHING!
WHAT'S WRONG WITH ME? THIS IS A RARE BOOK...WHAT'S THIS?.
Vengeance Spell
WHO COULD THAT BE?
KNO
NOK
RENT, GRAMPS. YOU REMEMBER WHAT THAT IS? YOU'RE A MONTH LATE.
18
YES, SIR. I'VE HAD SOME PROBLEMS...

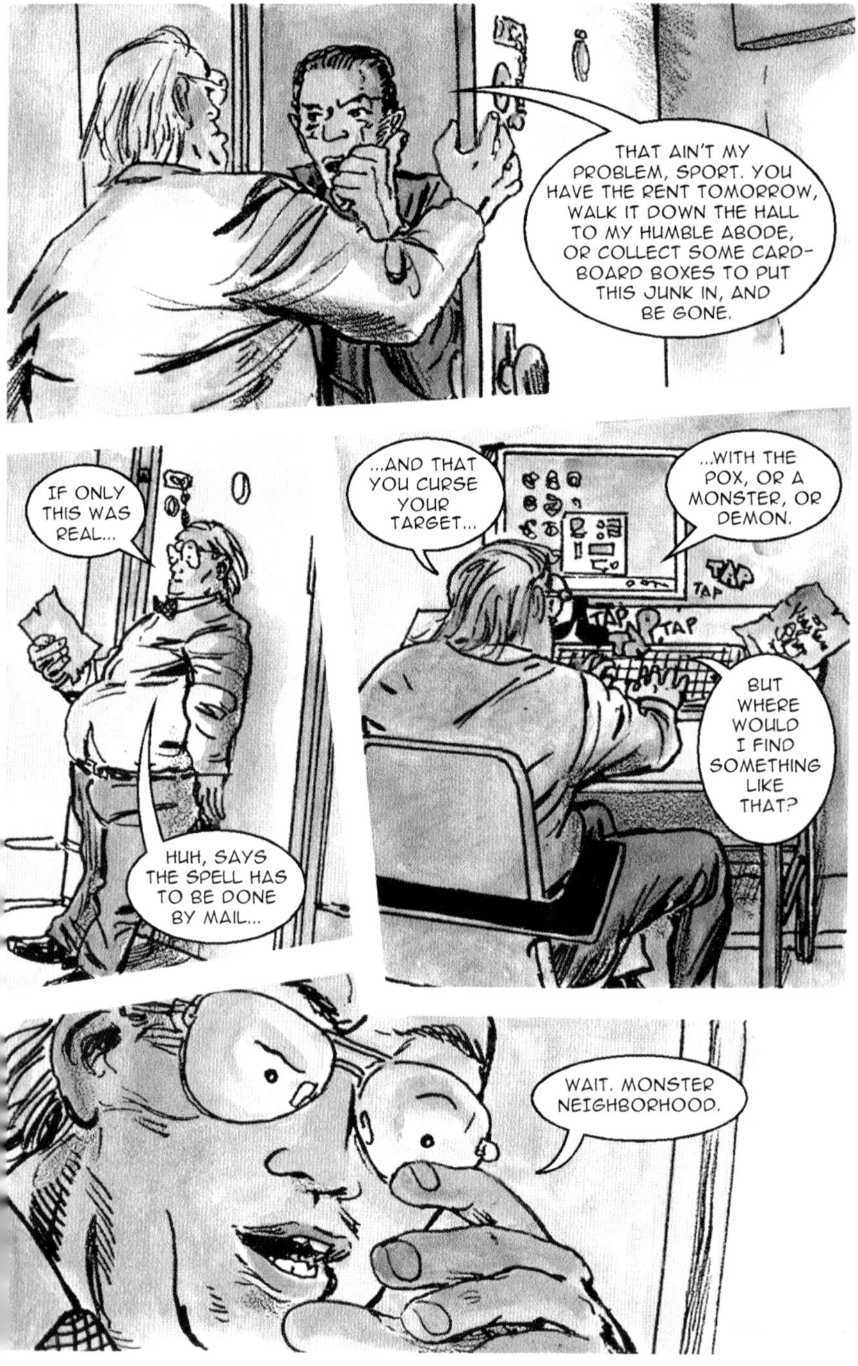
THAT AIN'T MY PROBLEM, SPORT. YOU HAVE THE RENT TOMORROW, WALK IT DOWN THE HALL TO MY HUMBLE ABODE, OR COLLECT SOME CARD-BOARD BOXES TO PUT THIS JUNK IN, AND BE GONE.
IF ONLY THIS WAS REAL...
HUH, SAYS THE SPELL HAS TO BE DONE BY MAIL...
...AND THAT YOU CURSE YOUR TARGET...
...WITH THE POX, OR A MONSTER, OR DEMON.
TAP
TAP
TAP
TAP
BUT WHERE WOULD I FIND SOMETHING LIKE THAT?
WAIT. MONSTER NEIGHBORHOOD.

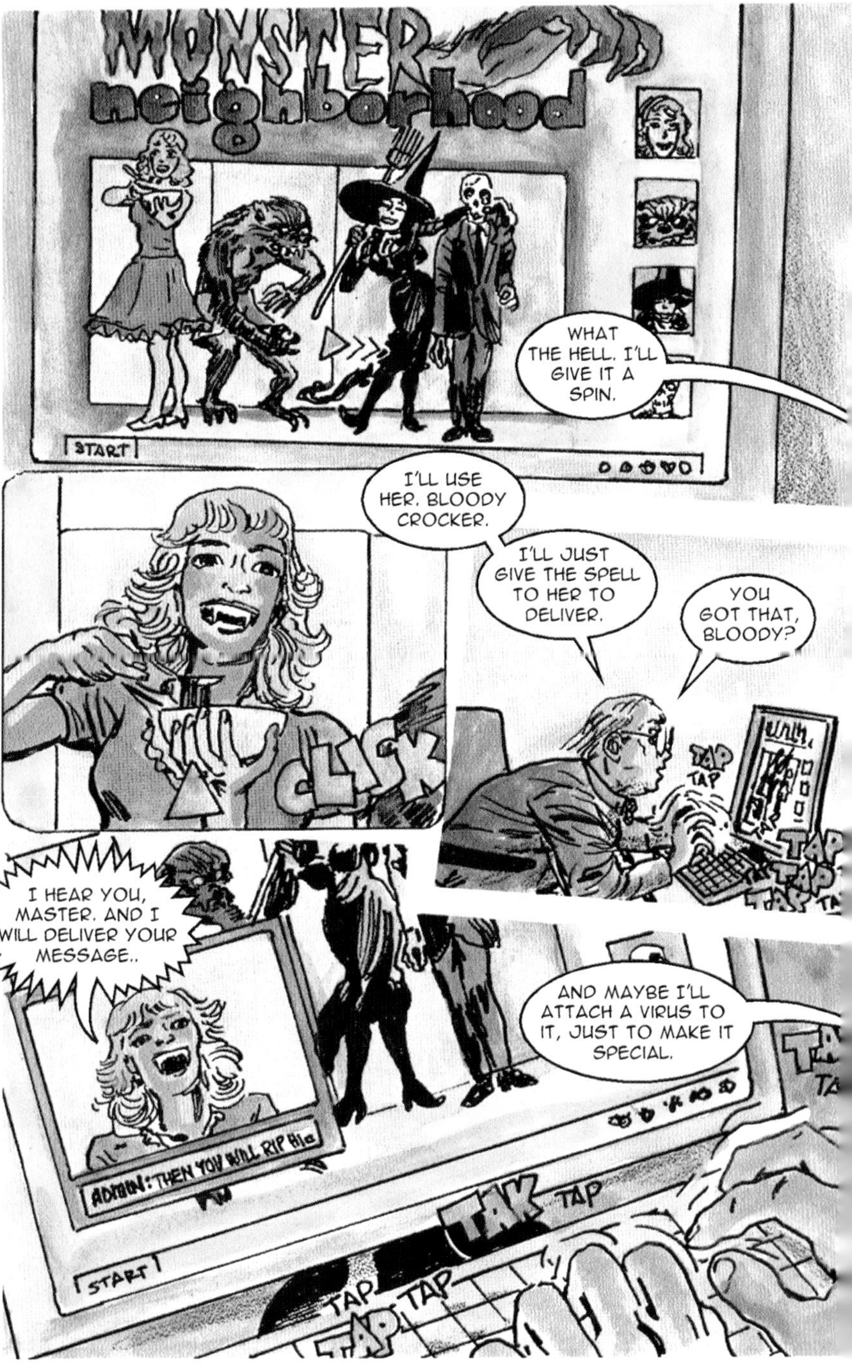
MONSTER neighborhood
START
WHAT THE HELL. I'LL GIVE IT A SPIN.
I'LL USE HER. BLOODY CROCKER.
I'LL JUST GIVE THE SPELL TO HER TO DELIVER.
YOU GOT THAT, BLOODY?
CLICK
TAP TAP
TAP TAP
I HEAR YOU, MASTER. AND I WILL DELIVER YOUR MESSAGE..
AND MAYBE I'LL ATTACH A VIRUS TO IT, JUST TO MAKE IT SPECIAL.
ADMIN: THEN YOU WILL RIP HIS
START
TAK TAP
TAP TAP TAP

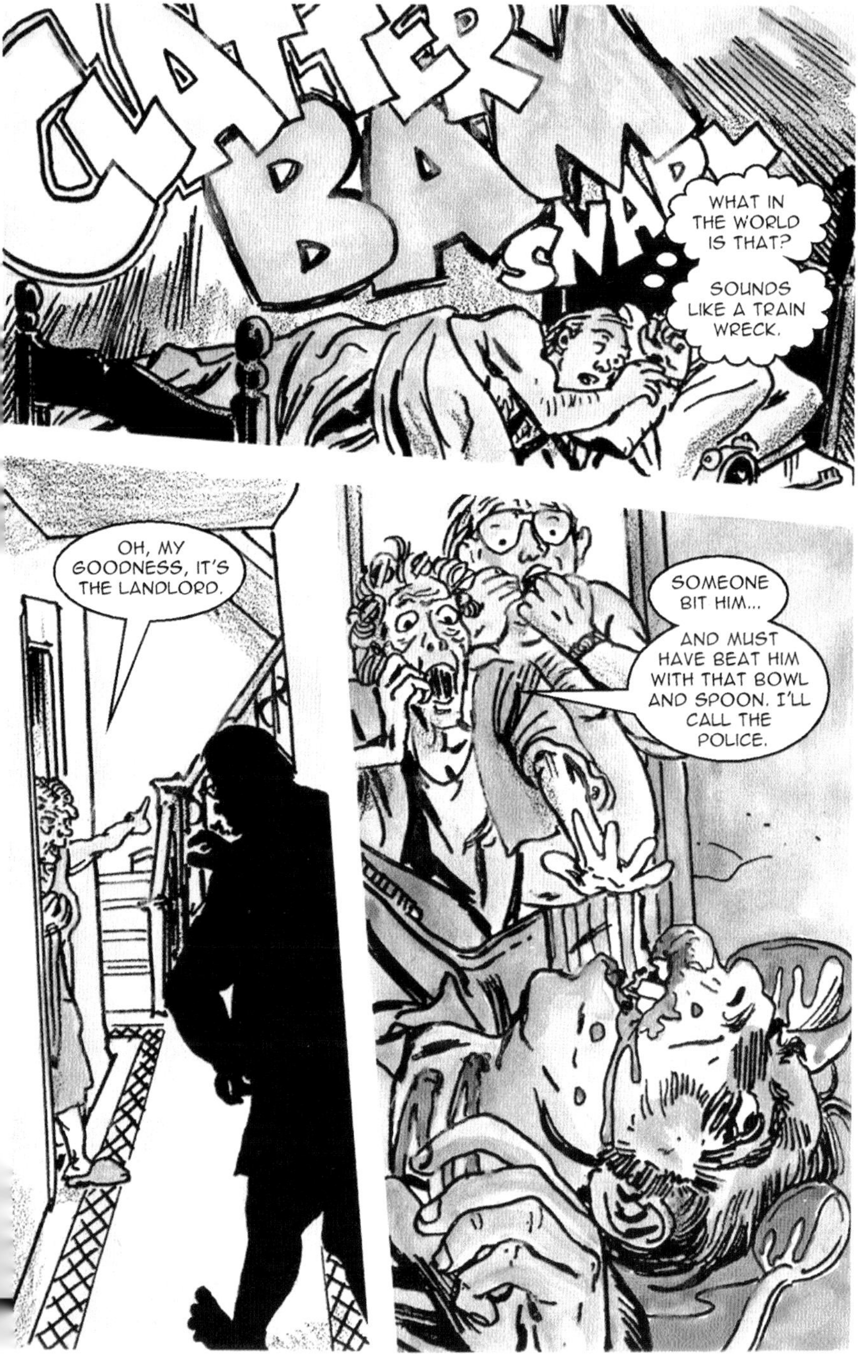
WHAT IN THE WORLD IS THAT?
SOUNDS LIKE A TRAIN WRECK.
OH, MY GOODNESS, IT'S THE LANDLORD.
SOMEONE BIT HIM...
AND MUST HAVE BEAT HIM WITH THAT BOWL AND SPOON. I'LL CALL THE POLICE.

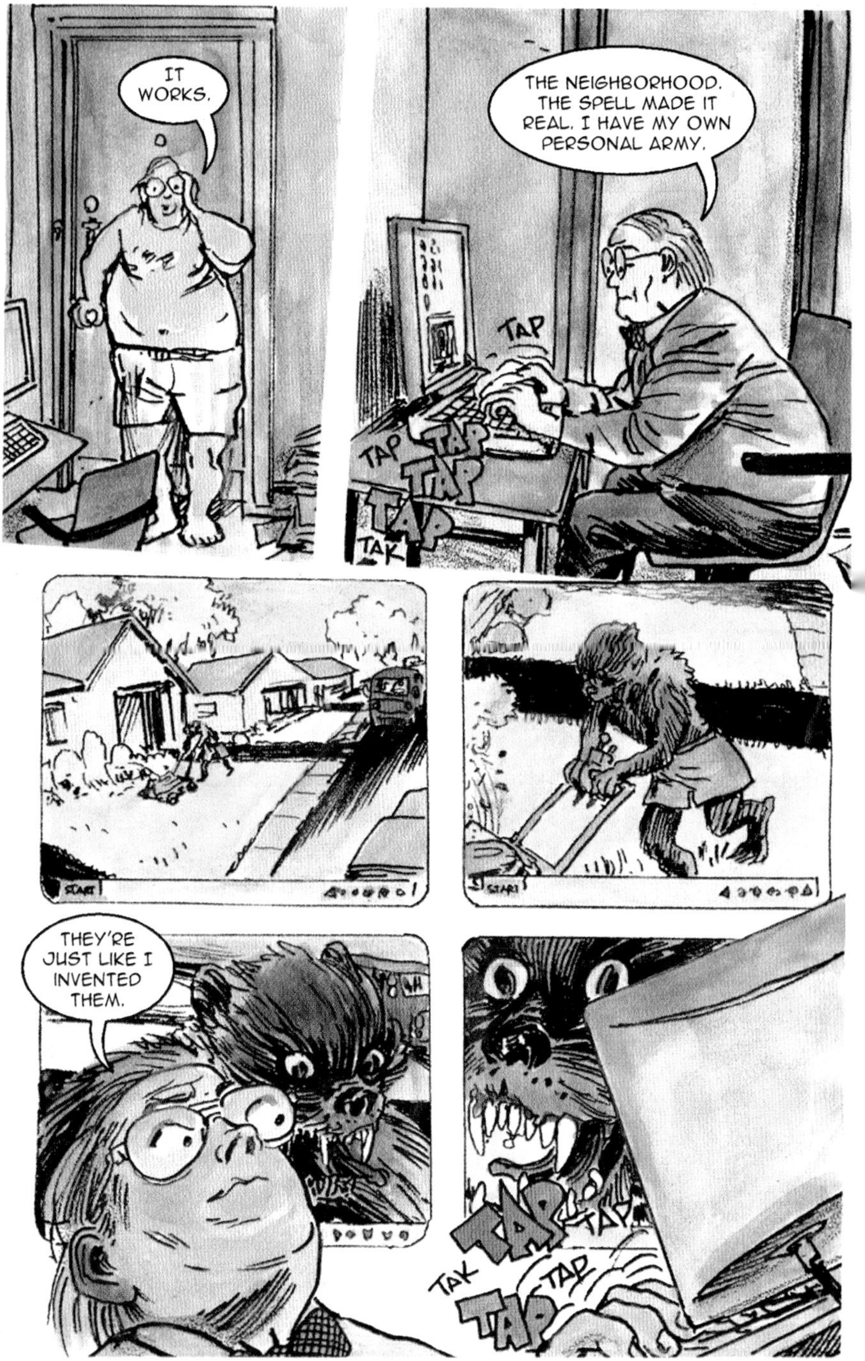
IT WORKS.
THE NEIGHBORHOOD. THE SPELL MADE IT REAL. I HAVE MY OWN PERSONAL ARMY.
TAP
TAP TAP TAP TAP TAK
THEY'RE JUST LIKE I INVENTED THEM.
TAP TAP TAK TAP TAP

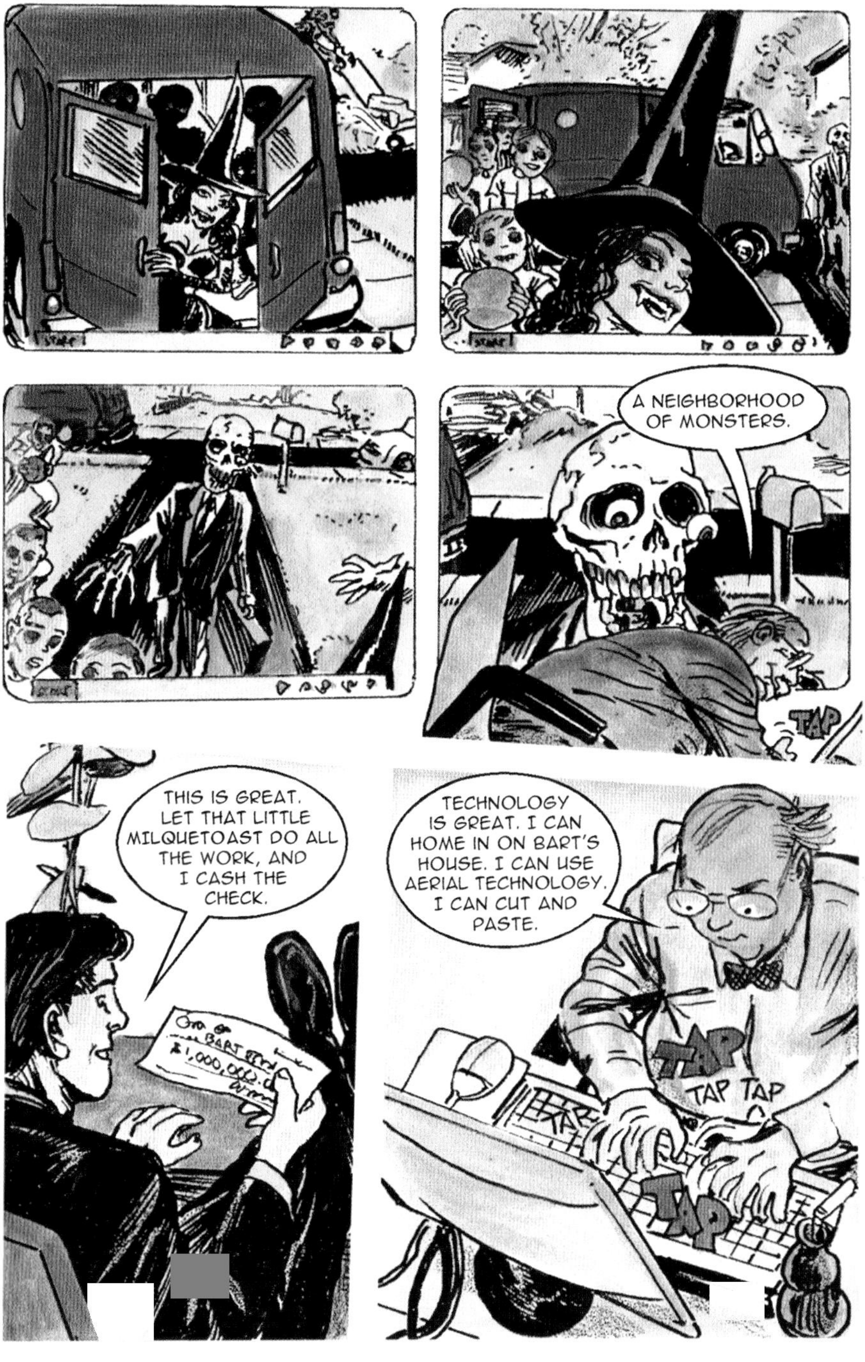
A NEIGHBORHOOD OF MONSTERS.
TAP
THIS IS GREAT. LET THAT LITTLE MILQUETOAST DO ALL THE WORK, AND I CASH THE CHECK.
TECHNOLOGY IS GREAT. I CAN HOME IN ON BART'S HOUSE. I CAN USE AERIAL TECHNOLOGY. I CAN CUT AND PASTE.
TAP
TAP TAP
TAP
TAP

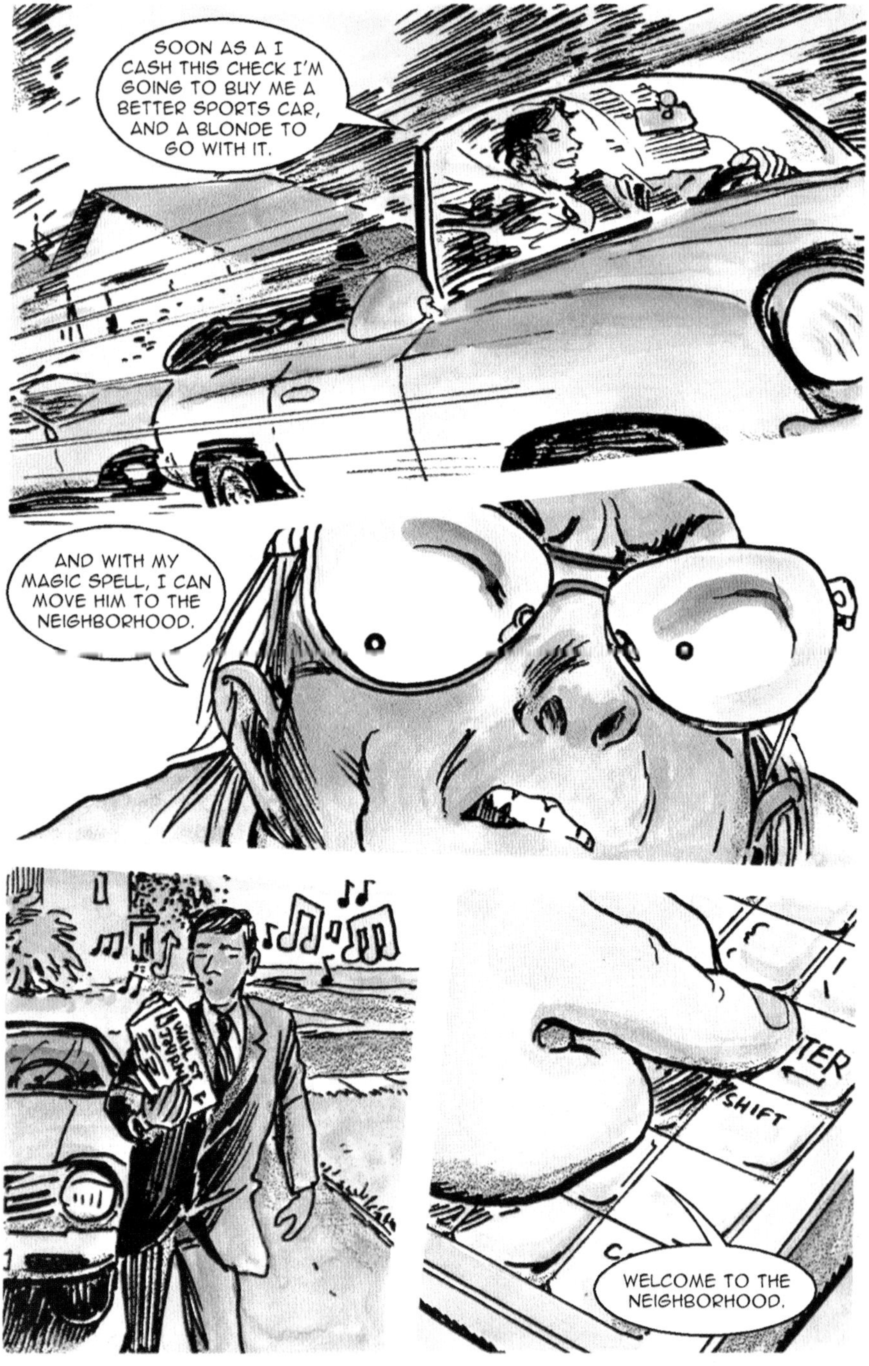
SOON AS A I CASH THIS CHECK I'M GOING TO BUY ME A BETTER SPORTS CAR, AND A BLONDE TO GO WITH IT.
AND WITH MY MAGIC SPELL, I CAN MOVE HIM TO THE NEIGHBORHOOD.
WALL ST JOURNAL
SHIFT
WELCOME TO THE NEIGHBORHOOD.

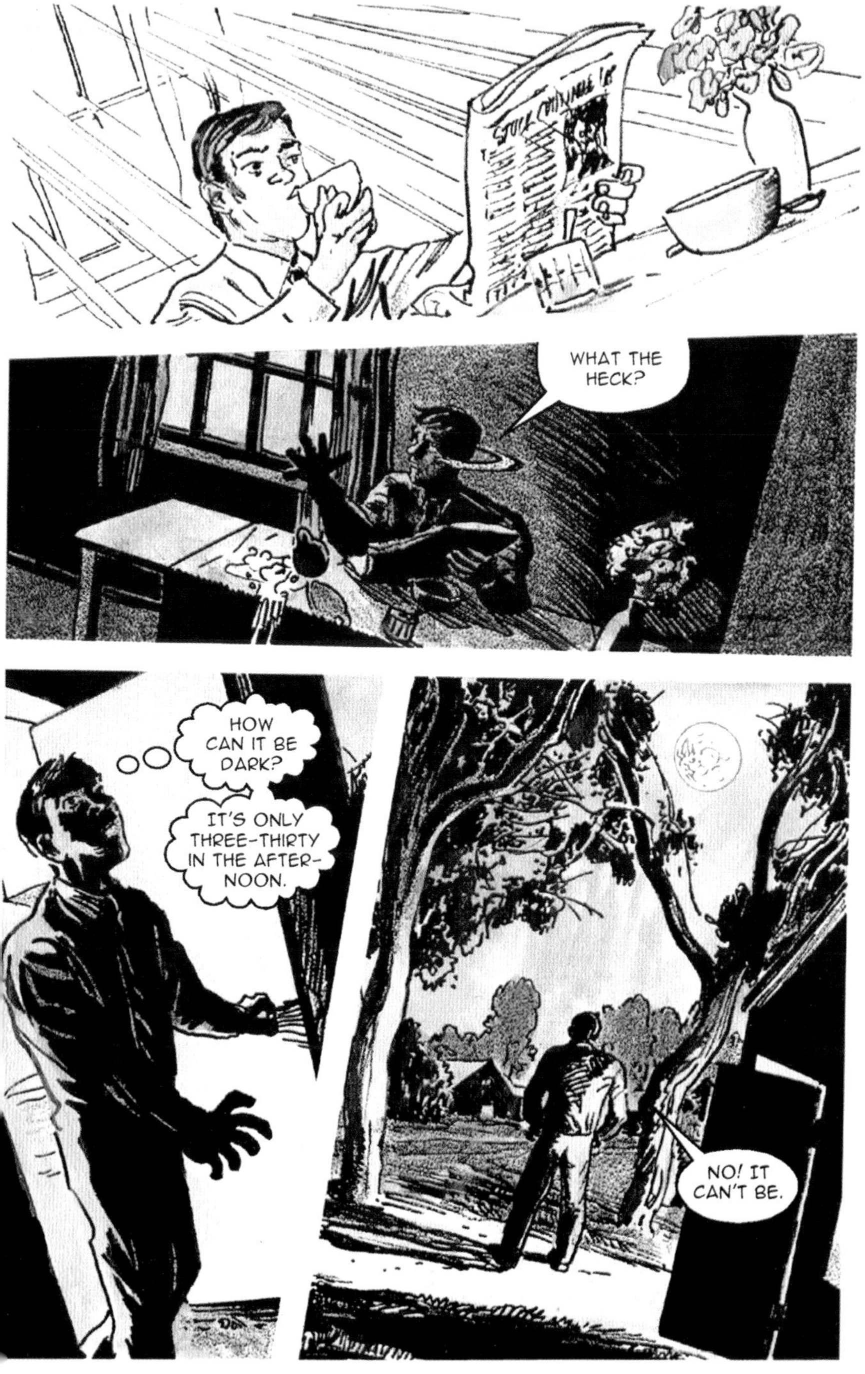
WHAT THE HECK?
HOW CAN IT BE DARK?
IT'S ONLY THREE-THIRTY IN THE AFTER-NOON.
NO! IT CAN'T BE.

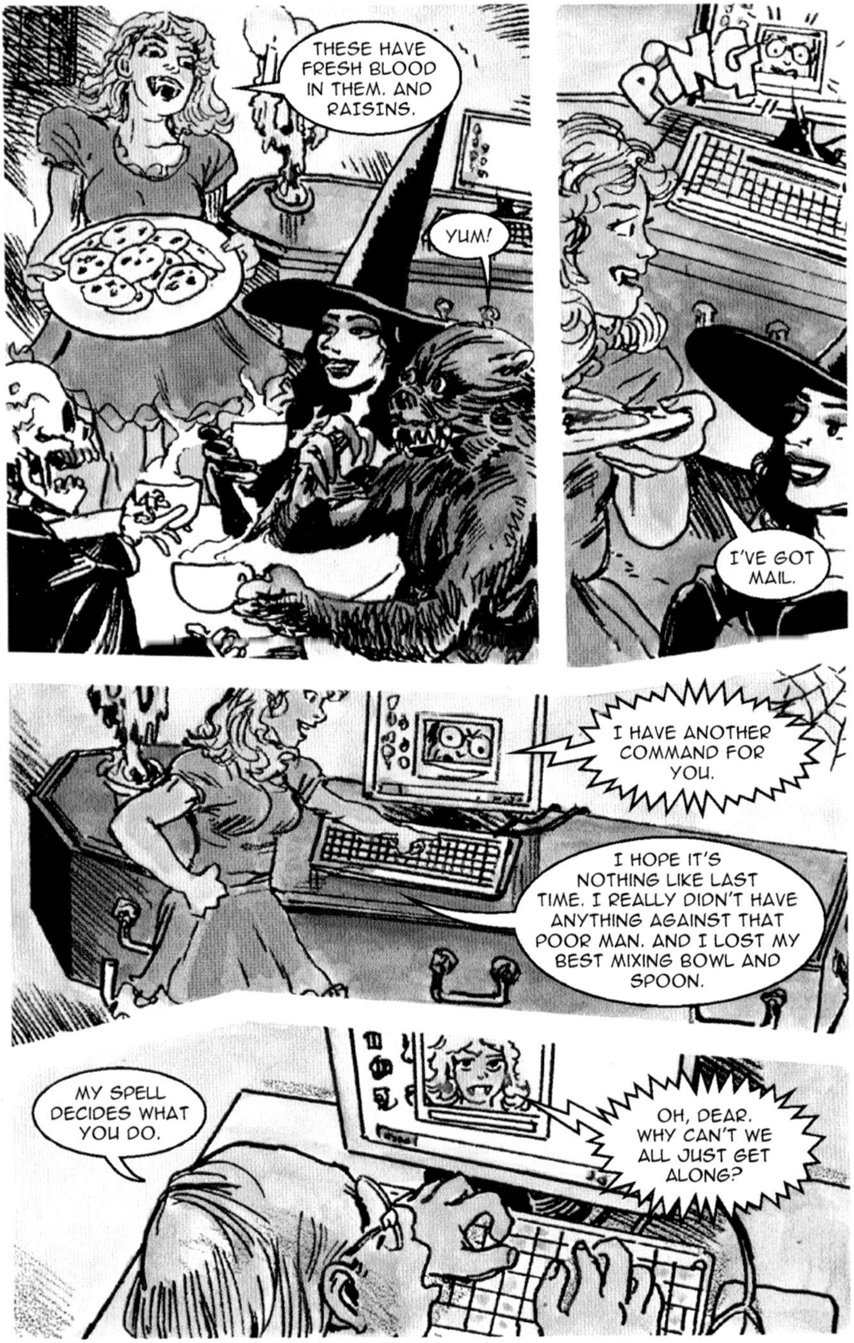
THESE HAVE FRESH BLOOD IN THEM. AND RAISINS.
YUM!
PING
I'VE GOT MAIL.
I HAVE ANOTHER COMMAND FOR YOU.
I HOPE IT'S NOTHING LIKE LAST TIME. I REALLY DIDN'T HAVE ANYTHING AGAINST THAT POOR MAN. AND I LOST MY BEST MIXING BOWL AND SPOON.
MY SPELL DECIDES WHAT YOU DO.
OH, DEAR. WHY CAN'T WE ALL JUST GET ALONG?

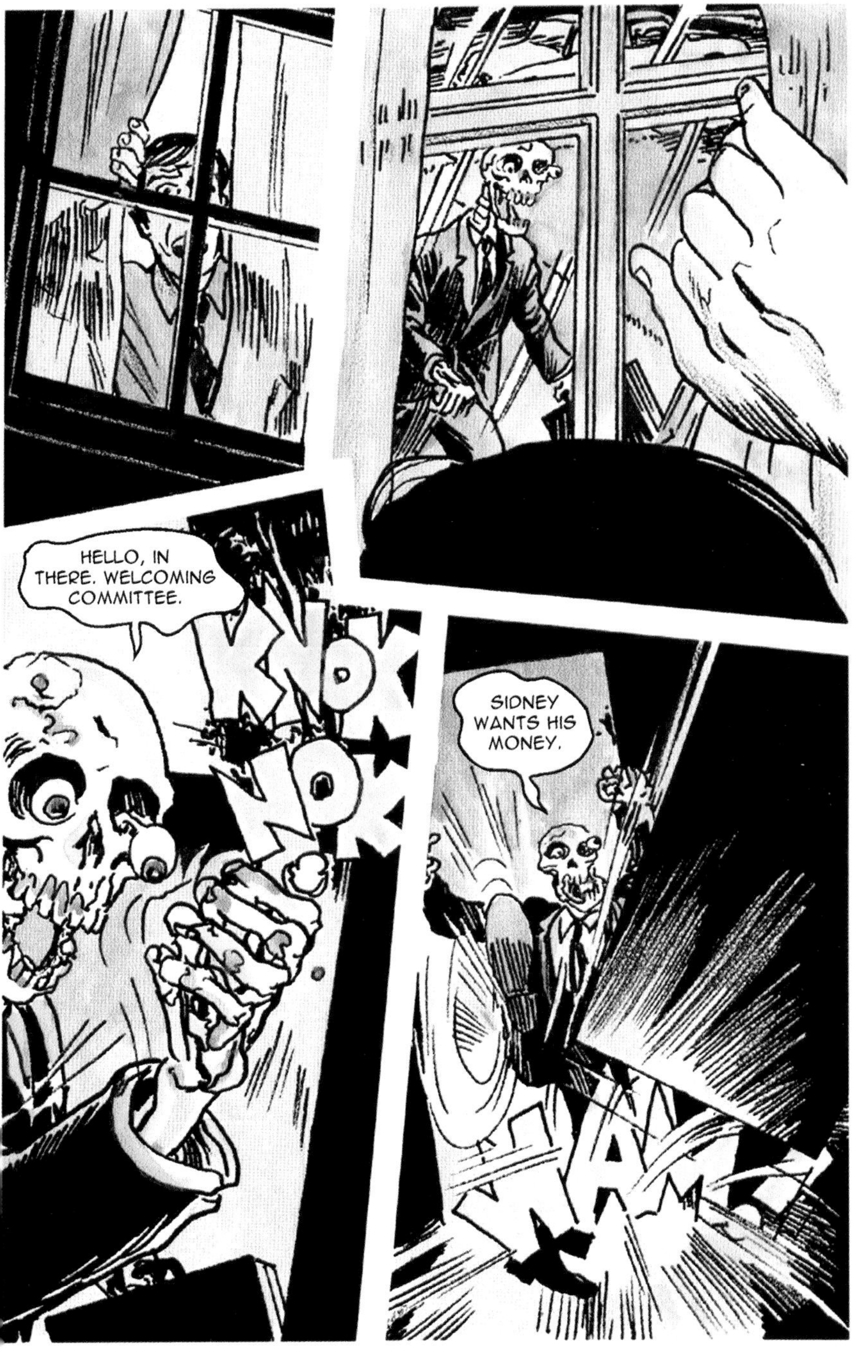
HELLO, IN THERE. WELCOMING COMMITTEE.
SIDNEY WANTS HIS MONEY.

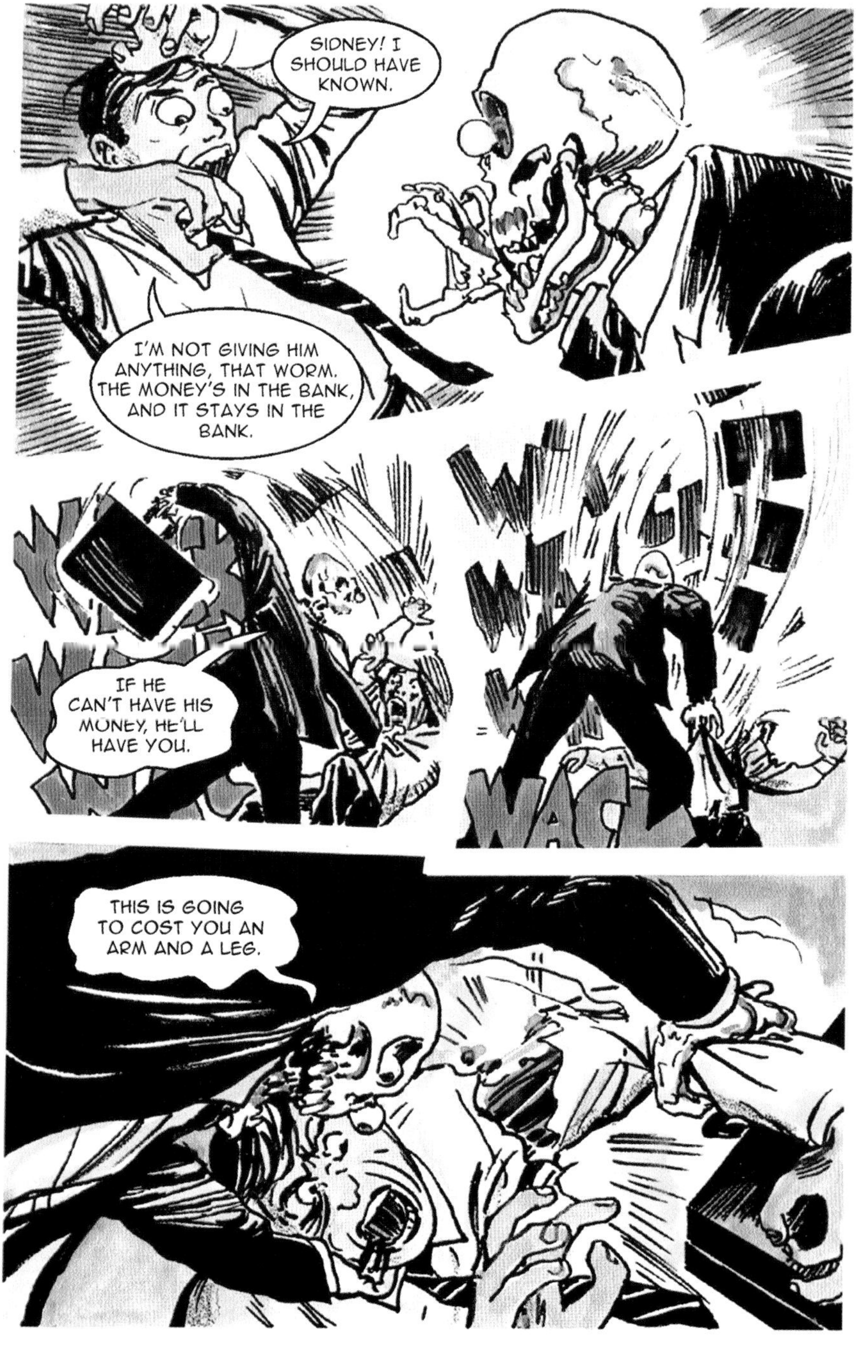
SIDNEY! I SHOULD HAVE KNOWN.
I'M NOT GIVING HIM ANYTHING, THAT WORM. THE MONEY'S IN THE BANK, AND IT STAYS IN THE BANK.
IF HE CAN'T HAVE HIS MONEY, HE'LL HAVE YOU.
THIS IS GOING TO COST YOU AN ARM AND A LEG.

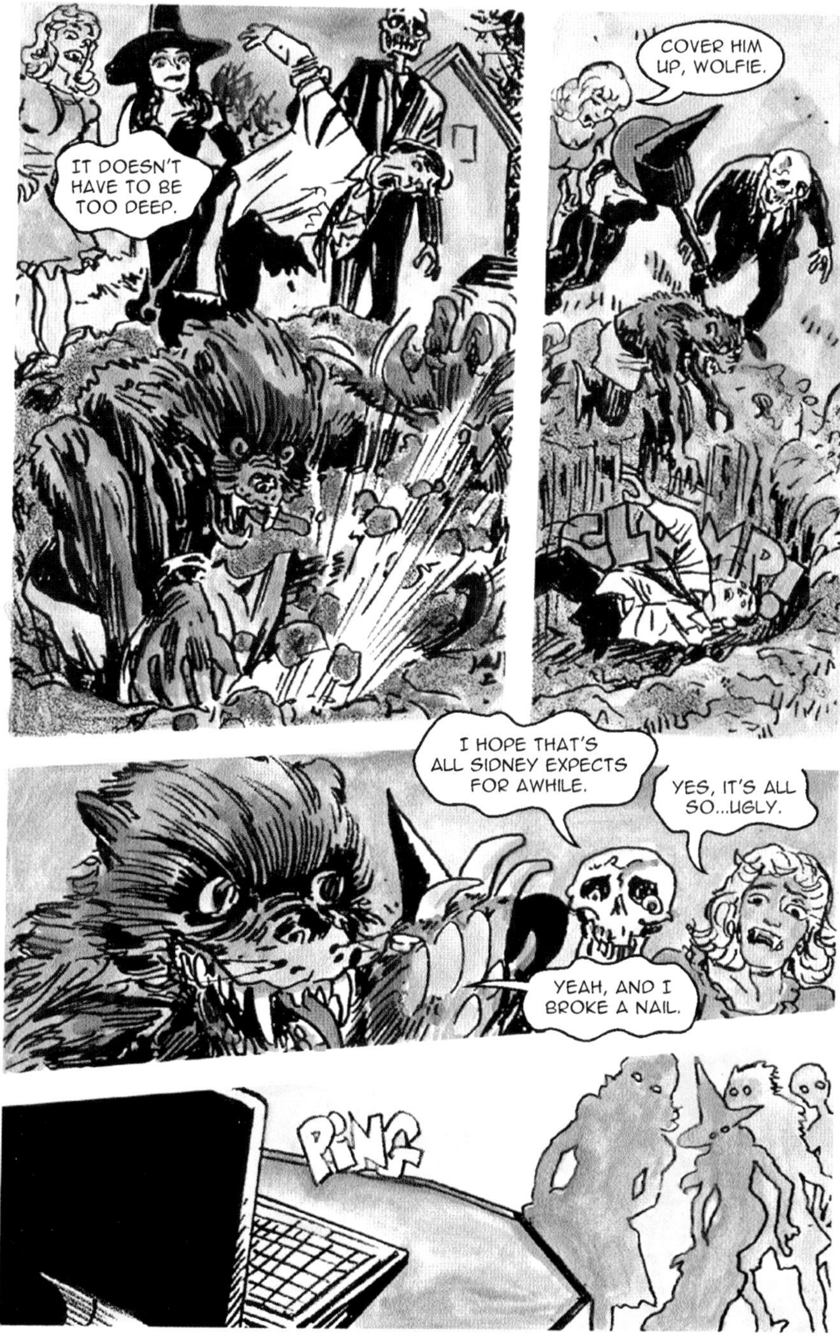
IT DOESN'T HAVE TO BE TOO DEEP.
COVER HIM UP, WOLFIE.
CLUMP
I HOPE THAT'S ALL SIDNEY EXPECTS FOR AWHILE.
YES, IT'S ALL SO...UGLY.
YEAH, AND I BROKE A NAIL.
PING

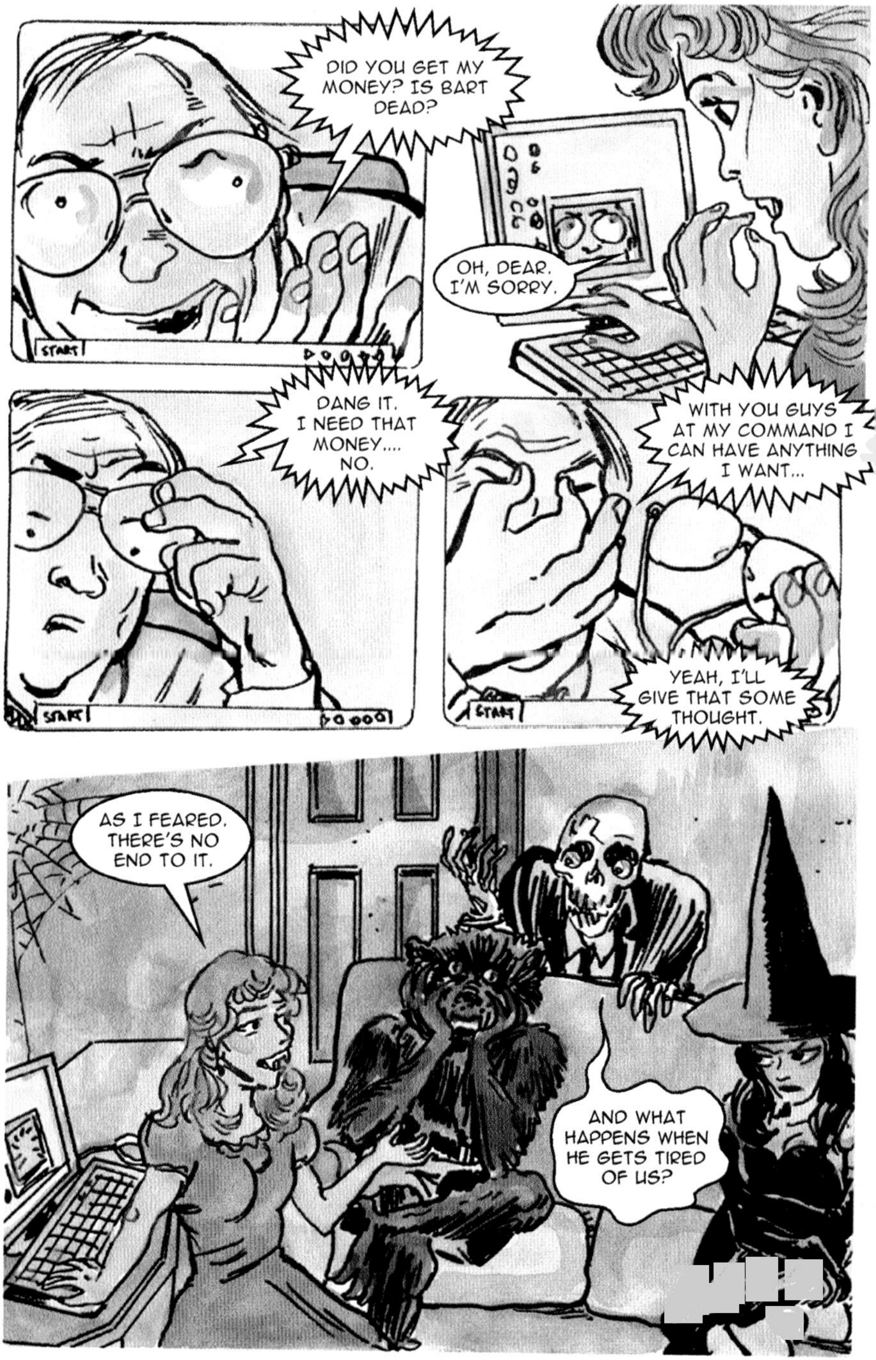
DID YOU GET MY MONEY? IS BART DEAD?
OH, DEAR. I'M SORRY.
START
DANG IT. I NEED THAT MONEY.... NO.
START
WITH YOU GUYS AT MY COMMAND I CAN HAVE ANYTHING I WANT...
YEAH, I'LL GIVE THAT SOME THOUGHT.
START
AS I FEARED. THERE'S NO END TO IT.
AND WHAT HAPPENS WHEN HE GETS TIRED OF US?

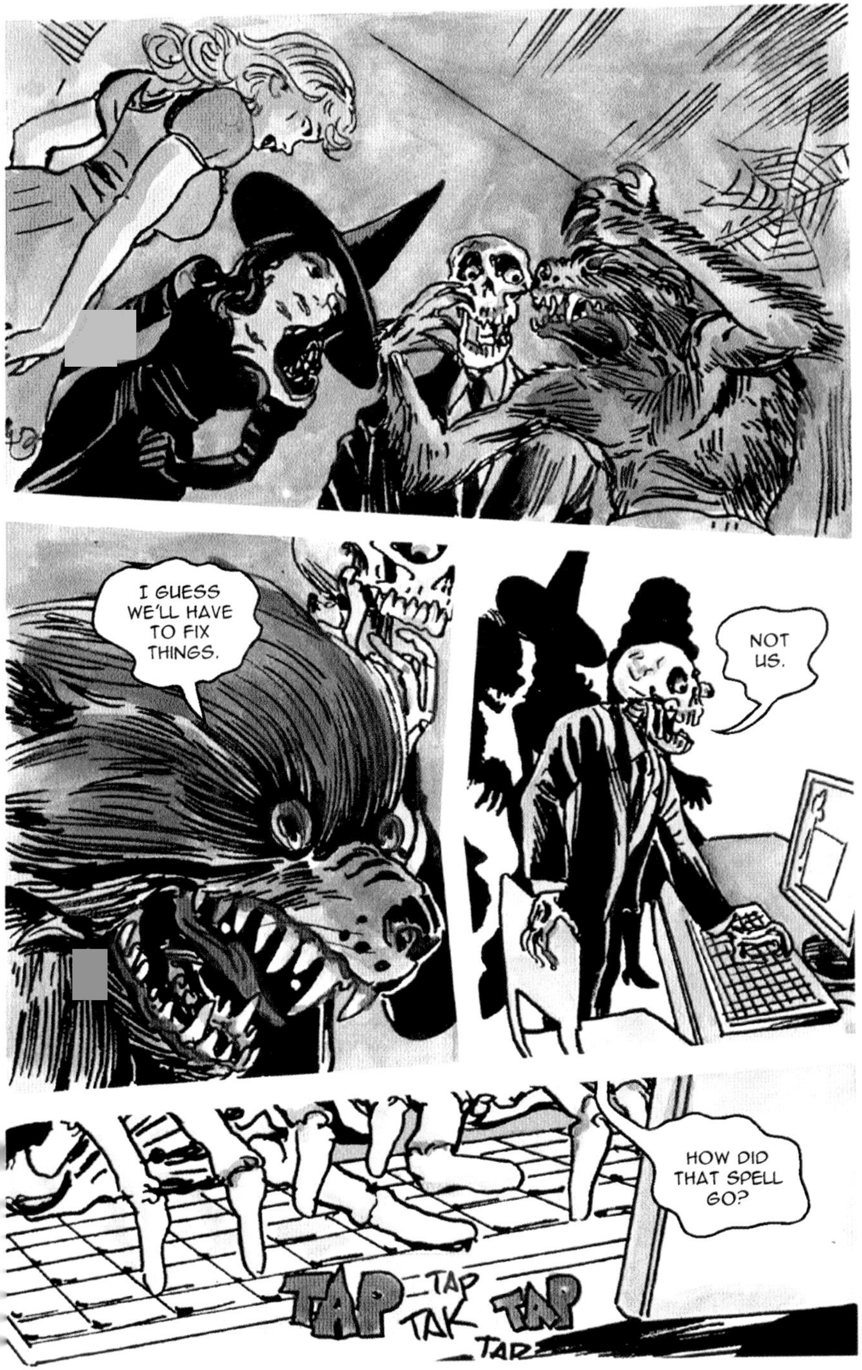
I GUESS WE'LL HAVE TO FIX THINGS.
NOT US.
HOW DID THAT SPELL GO?
TAP TAP
TAK
TAP

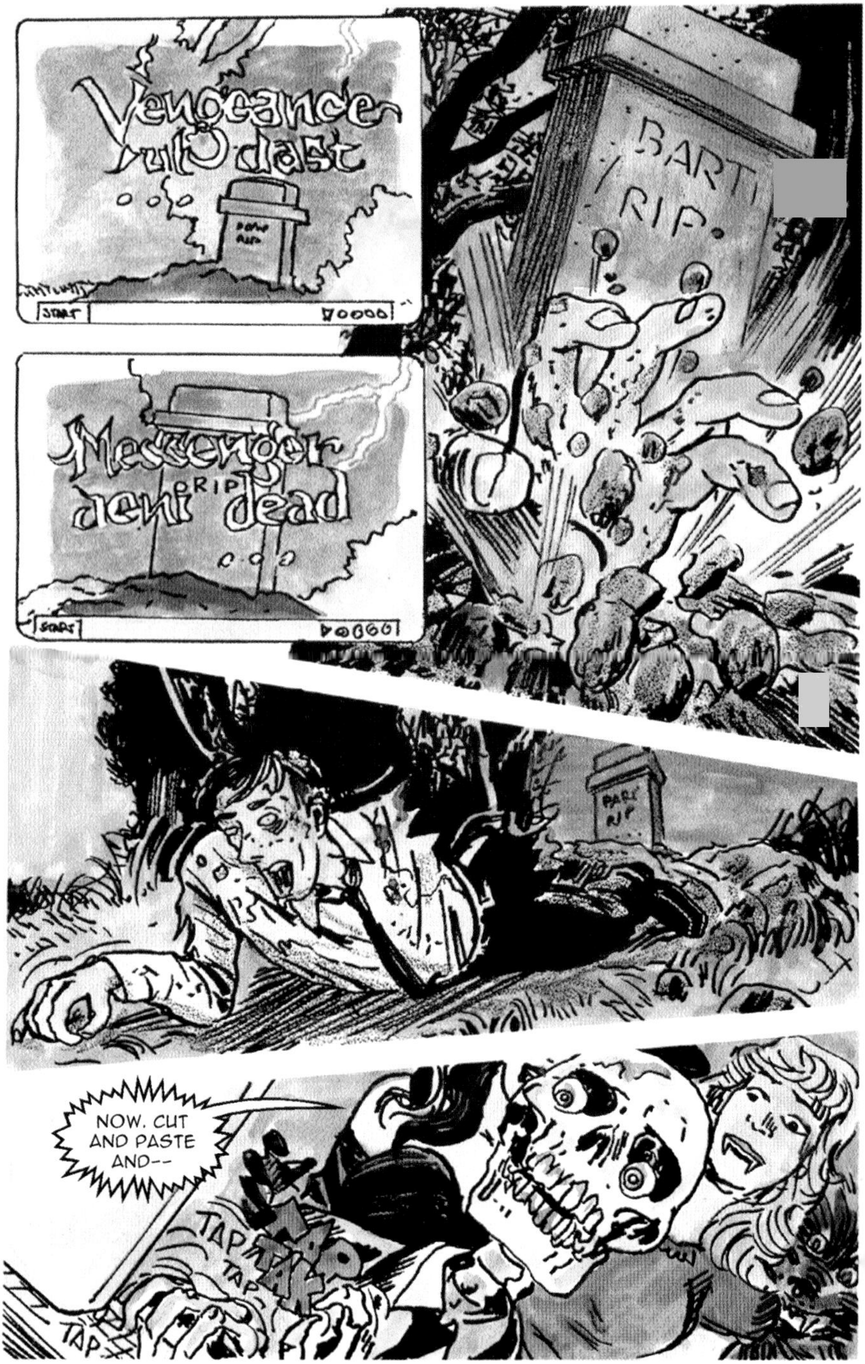
Vengeance
START
Messenger
RIP
dead
BART
RIP
NOW, CUT AND PASTE AND--
TAP
TAP
TAP

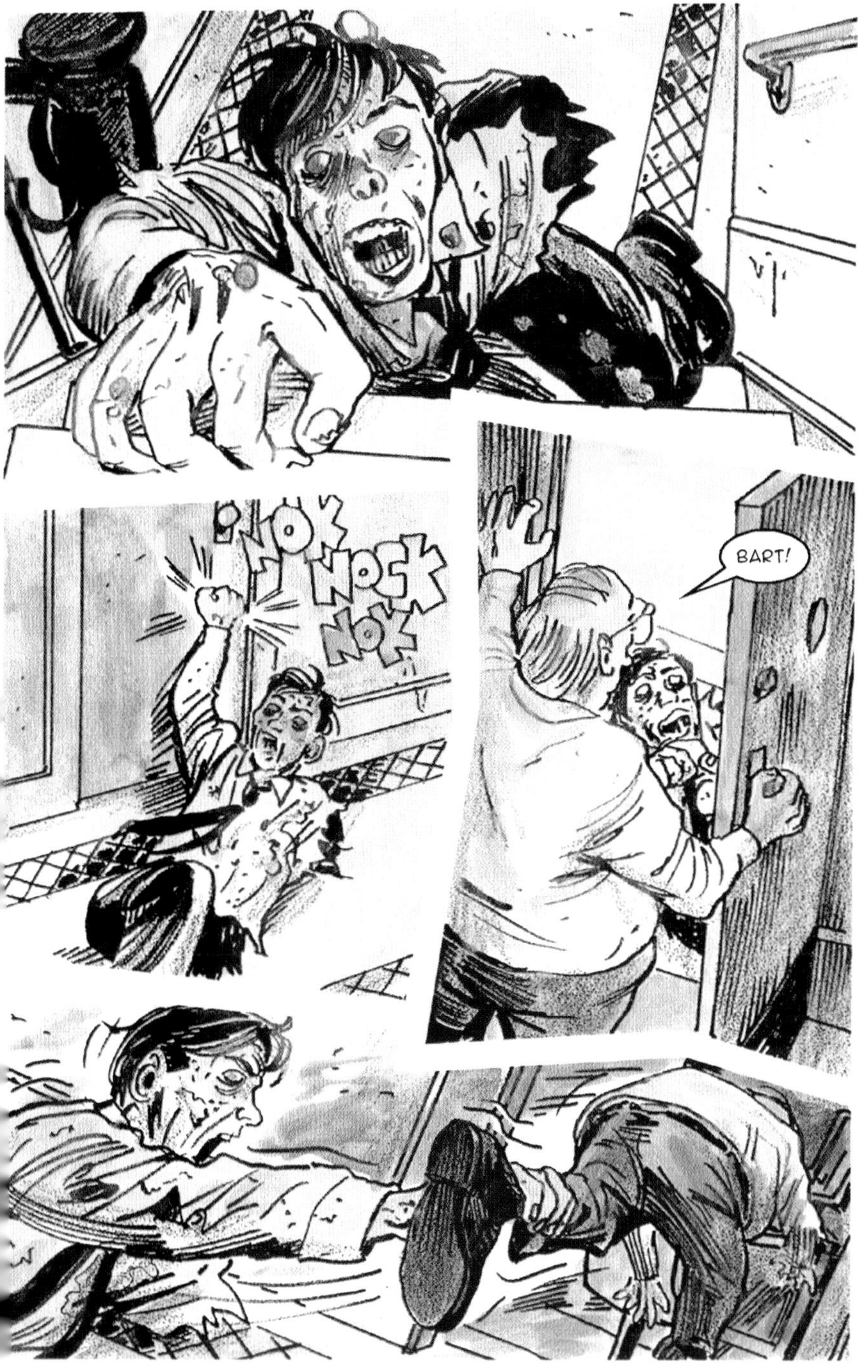
NOK NOCK NOK
BART!

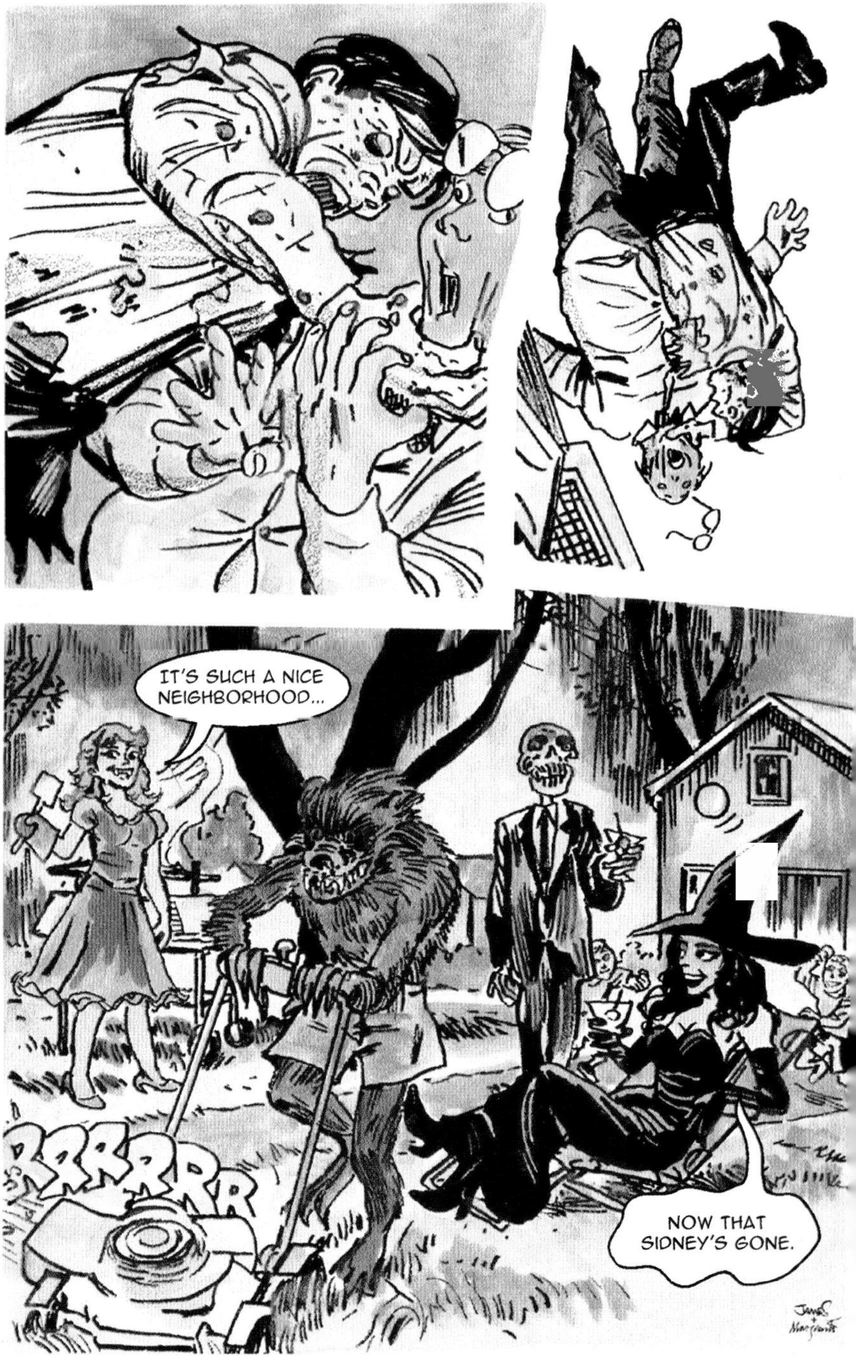
IT'S SUCH A NICE NEIGHBORHOOD...
NOW THAT SIDNEY'S GONE.

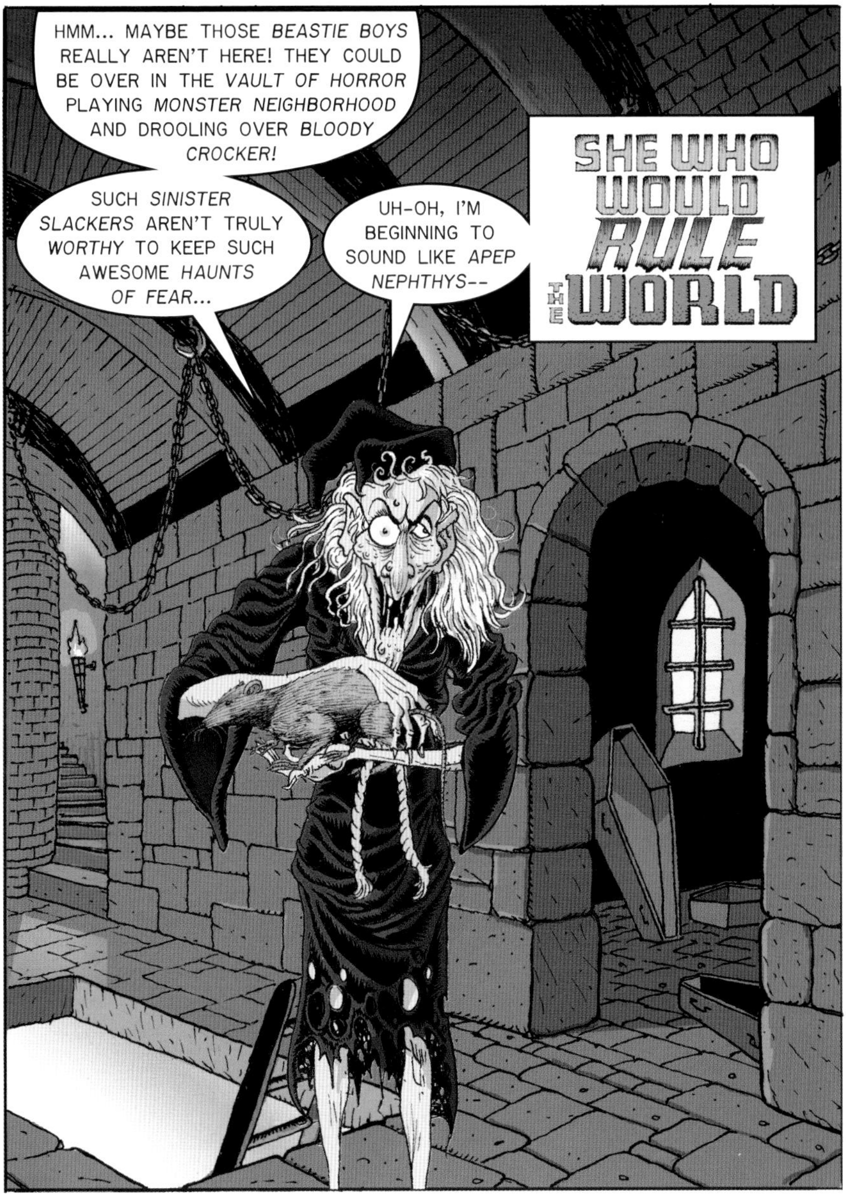
HMM... MAYBE THOSE *BEASTIE BOYS* REALLY AREN'T HERE! THEY COULD BE OVER IN THE *VAULT OF HORROR* PLAYING *MONSTER NEIGHBORHOOD* AND DROOLING OVER *BLOODY CROCKER!*
SUCH *SINISTER SLACKERS* AREN'T TRULY *WORTHY* TO KEEP SUCH AWESOME *HAUNTS OF FEAR...*
UH-OH, I'M BEGINNING TO SOUND LIKE *APEP NEPHTHYS--*
SHE WHO WOULD RULE THE WORLD

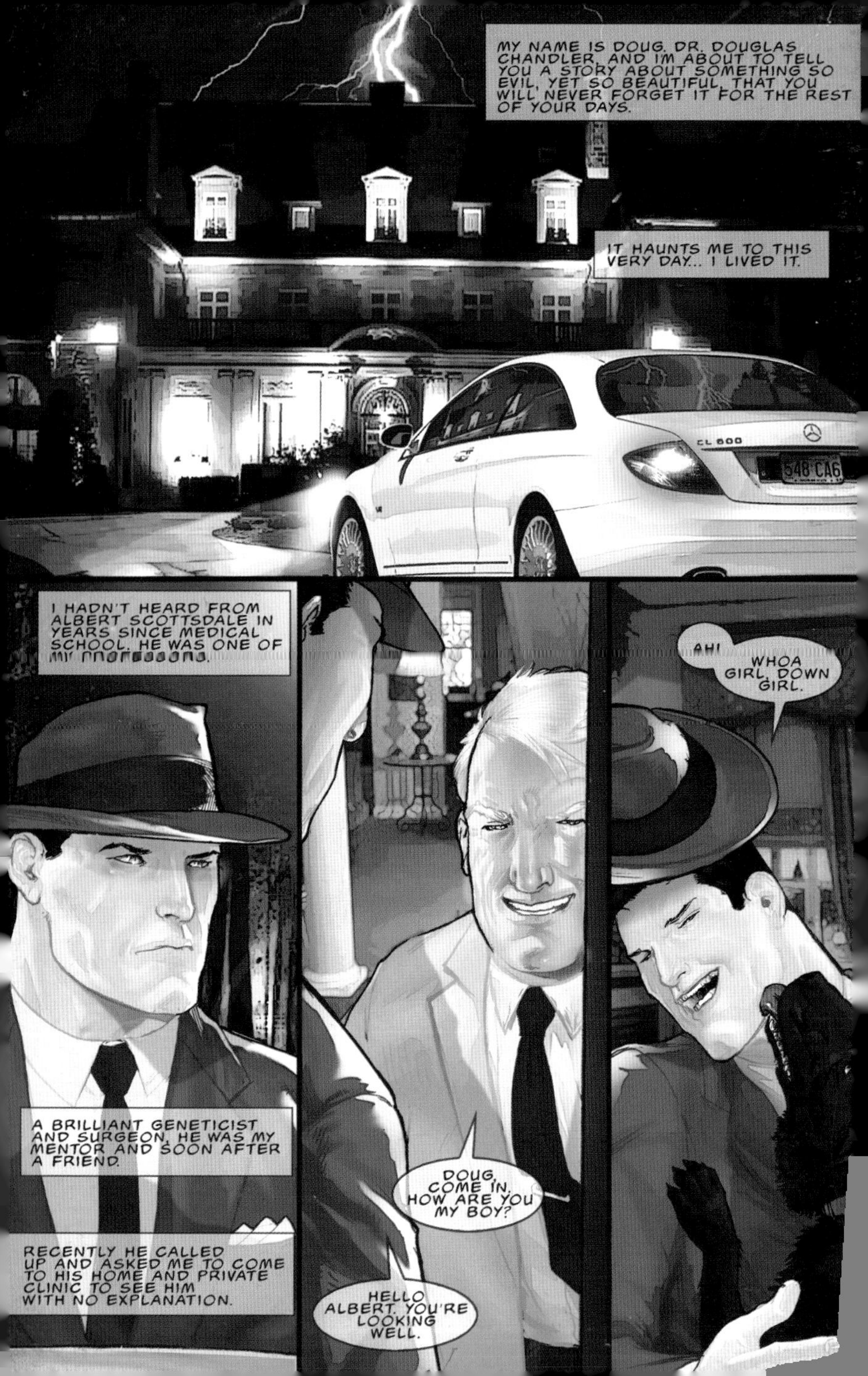

MY NAME IS DOUG. DR. DOUGLAS CHANDLER, AND I'M ABOUT TO TELL YOU A STORY ABOUT SOMETHING SO EVIL, YET SO BEAUTIFUL, THAT YOU WILL NEVER FORGET IT FOR THE REST OF YOUR DAYS.
IT HAUNTS ME TO THIS VERY DAY... I LIVED IT.
CL 500
548 CA6
I HADN'T HEARD FROM ALBERT SCOTTSDALE IN YEARS SINCE MEDICAL SCHOOL. HE WAS ONE OF
A BRILLIANT GENETICIST AND SURGEON, HE WAS MY MENTOR AND SOON AFTER A FRIEND.
RECENTLY HE CALLED UP AND ASKED ME TO COME TO HIS HOME AND PRIVATE CLINIC TO SEE HIM WITH NO EXPLANATION.
DOUG, COME IN. HOW ARE YOU MY BOY?
HELLO ALBERT. YOU'RE LOOKING WELL.
AH!
WHOA GIRL, DOWN GIRL.

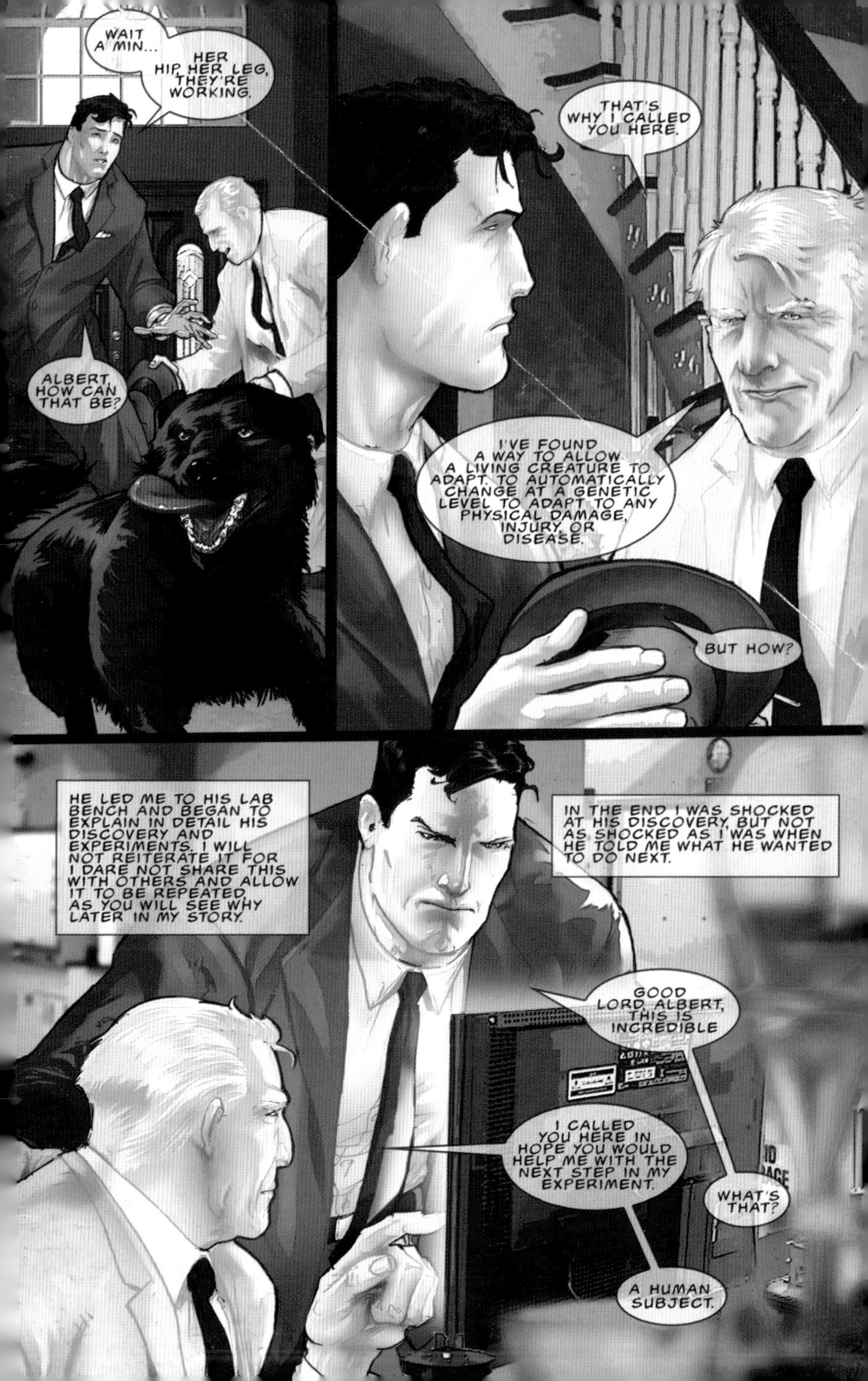
WAIT A MIN...
HER HIP, HER LEG, THEY'RE WORKING.
ALBERT, HOW CAN THAT BE?
THAT'S WHY I CALLED YOU HERE.
I'VE FOUND A WAY TO ALLOW A LIVING CREATURE TO ADAPT, TO AUTOMATICALLY CHANGE AT A GENETIC LEVEL TO ADAPT TO ANY PHYSICAL DAMAGE, INJURY, OR DISEASE.
BUT HOW?
HE LED ME TO HIS LAB BENCH AND BEGAN TO EXPLAIN IN DETAIL HIS DISCOVERY AND EXPERIMENTS. I WILL NOT REITERATE IT FOR I DARE NOT SHARE THIS WITH OTHERS AND ALLOW IT TO BE REPEATED, AS YOU WILL SEE WHY LATER IN MY STORY.
IN THE END I WAS SHOCKED AT HIS DISCOVERY, BUT NOT AS SHOCKED AS I WAS WHEN HE TOLD ME WHAT HE WANTED TO DO NEXT.
GOOD LORD, ALBERT, THIS IS INCREDIBLE
I CALLED YOU HERE IN HOPE YOU WOULD HELP ME WITH THE NEXT STEP IN MY EXPERIMENT.
WHAT'S THAT?
A HUMAN SUBJECT.

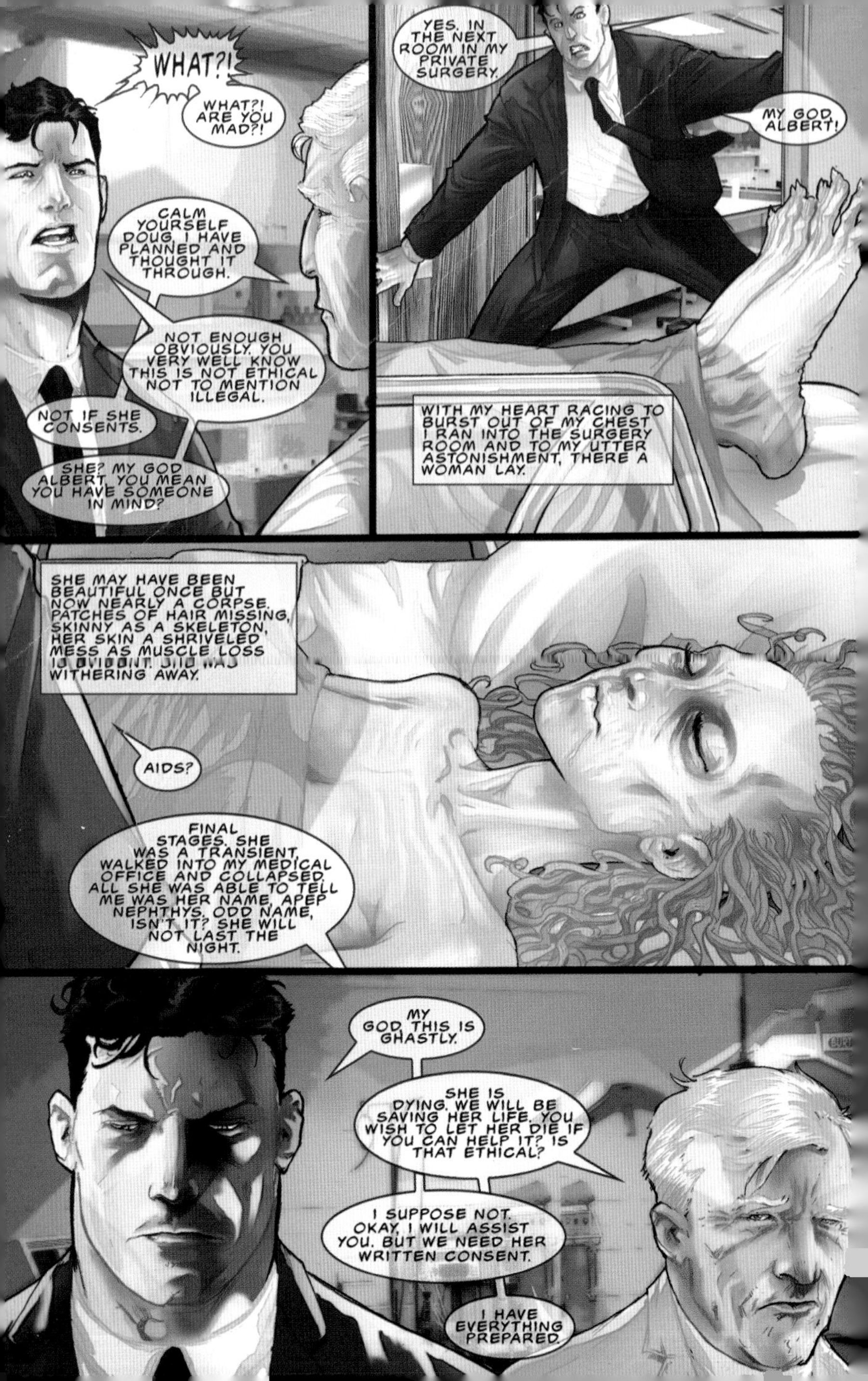
WHAT?!
WHAT?! ARE YOU MAD?!
CALM YOURSELF DOUG, I HAVE PLANNED AND THOUGHT IT THROUGH.
NOT ENOUGH OBVIOUSLY. YOU VERY WELL KNOW THIS IS NOT ETHICAL NOT TO MENTION ILLEGAL.
NOT IF SHE CONSENTS.
SHE? MY GOD ALBERT, YOU MEAN YOU HAVE SOMEONE IN MIND?
YES. IN THE NEXT ROOM IN MY PRIVATE SURGERY.
MY GOD, ALBERT!
WITH MY HEART RACING TO BURST OUT OF MY CHEST I RAN INTO THE SURGERY ROOM AND TO MY UTTER ASTONISHMENT, THERE A WOMAN LAY.
SHE MAY HAVE BEEN BEAUTIFUL ONCE BUT NOW NEARLY A CORPSE. PATCHES OF HAIR MISSING, SKINNY AS A SKELETON, HER SKIN A SHRIVELED MESS AS MUSCLE LOSS
WITHERING AWAY.
AIDS?
FINAL STAGES. SHE WAS A TRANSIENT, WALKED INTO MY MEDICAL OFFICE AND COLLAPSED. ALL SHE WAS ABLE TO TELL ME WAS HER NAME, APEP NEPHTHYS. ODD NAME, ISN'T IT? SHE WILL NOT LAST THE NIGHT.
MY GOD THIS IS GHASTLY.
SHE IS DYING. WE WILL BE SAVING HER LIFE. YOU WISH TO LET HER DIE IF YOU CAN HELP IT? IS THAT ETHICAL?
I SUPPOSE NOT. OKAY, I WILL ASSIST YOU. BUT WE NEED HER WRITTEN CONSENT.
I HAVE EVERYTHING PREPARED.

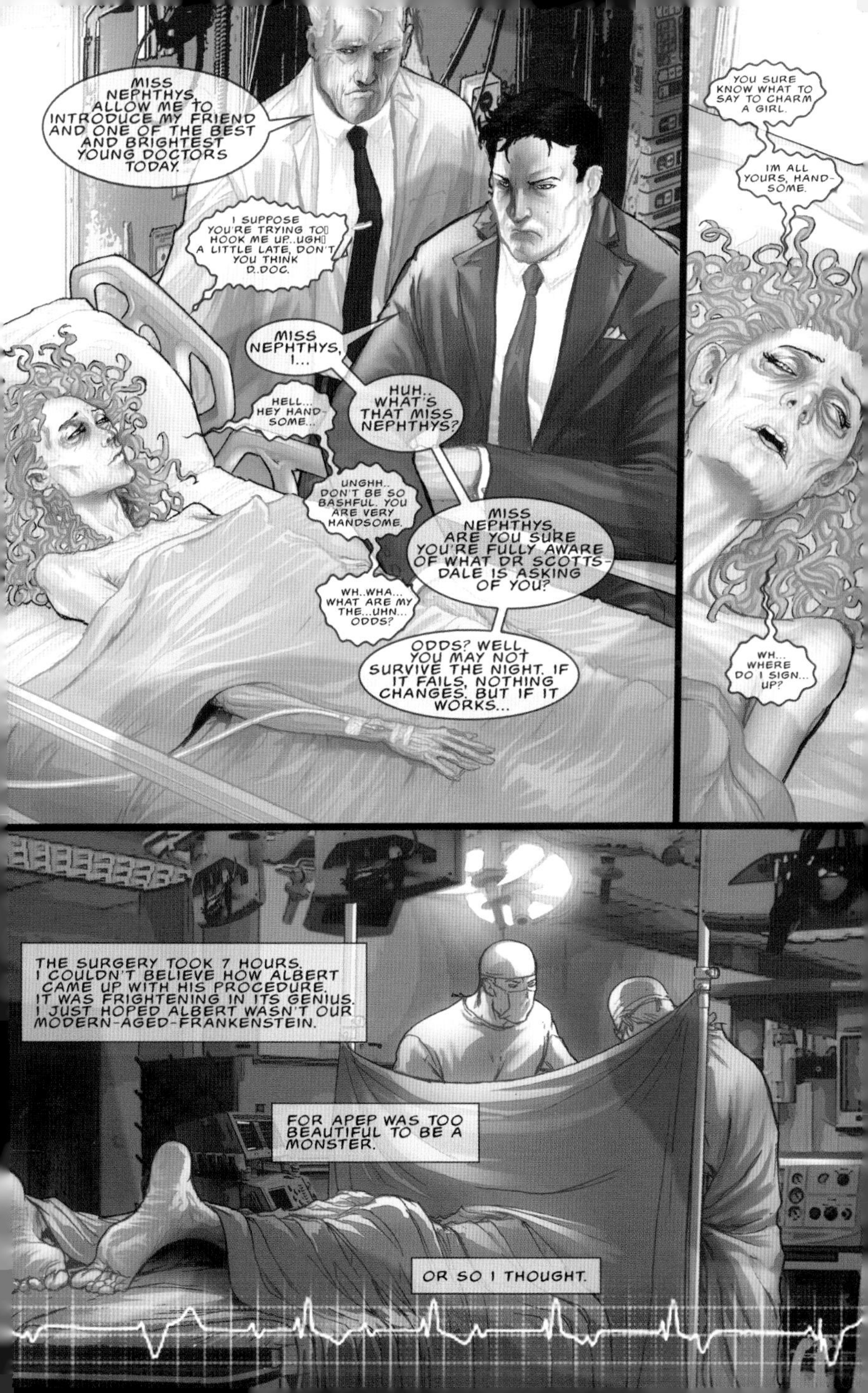
MISS NEPHTHYS, ALLOW ME TO INTRODUCE MY FRIEND AND ONE OF THE BEST AND BRIGHTEST YOUNG DOCTORS TODAY.
I SUPPOSE YOU'RE TRYING TO HOOK ME UP...UGH A LITTLE LATE, DON'T YOU THINK D..DOC.
MISS NEPHTHYS, I...
HELL... HEY HANDSOME...
HUH.. WHAT'S THAT MISS NEPHTHYS?
UNGHH.. DON'T BE SO BASHFUL. YOU ARE VERY HANDSOME.
MISS NEPHTHYS, ARE YOU SURE YOU'RE FULLY AWARE OF WHAT DR SCOTTSDALE IS ASKING OF YOU?
WH..WHA... WHAT ARE MY THE...UHN... ODDS?
ODDS? WELL, YOU MAY NOT SURVIVE THE NIGHT. IF IT FAILS, NOTHING CHANGES. BUT IF IT WORKS...
YOU SURE KNOW WHAT TO SAY TO CHARM A GIRL.
IM ALL YOURS, HANDSOME.
WH... WHERE DO I SIGN... UP?
THE SURGERY TOOK 7 HOURS. I COULDN'T BELIEVE HOW ALBERT CAME UP WITH HIS PROCEDURE. IT WAS FRIGHTENING IN ITS GENIUS. I JUST HOPED ALBERT WASN'T OUR MODERN-AGED-FRANKENSTEIN.
FOR APEP WAS TOO BEAUTIFUL TO BE A MONSTER.
OR SO I THOUGHT.

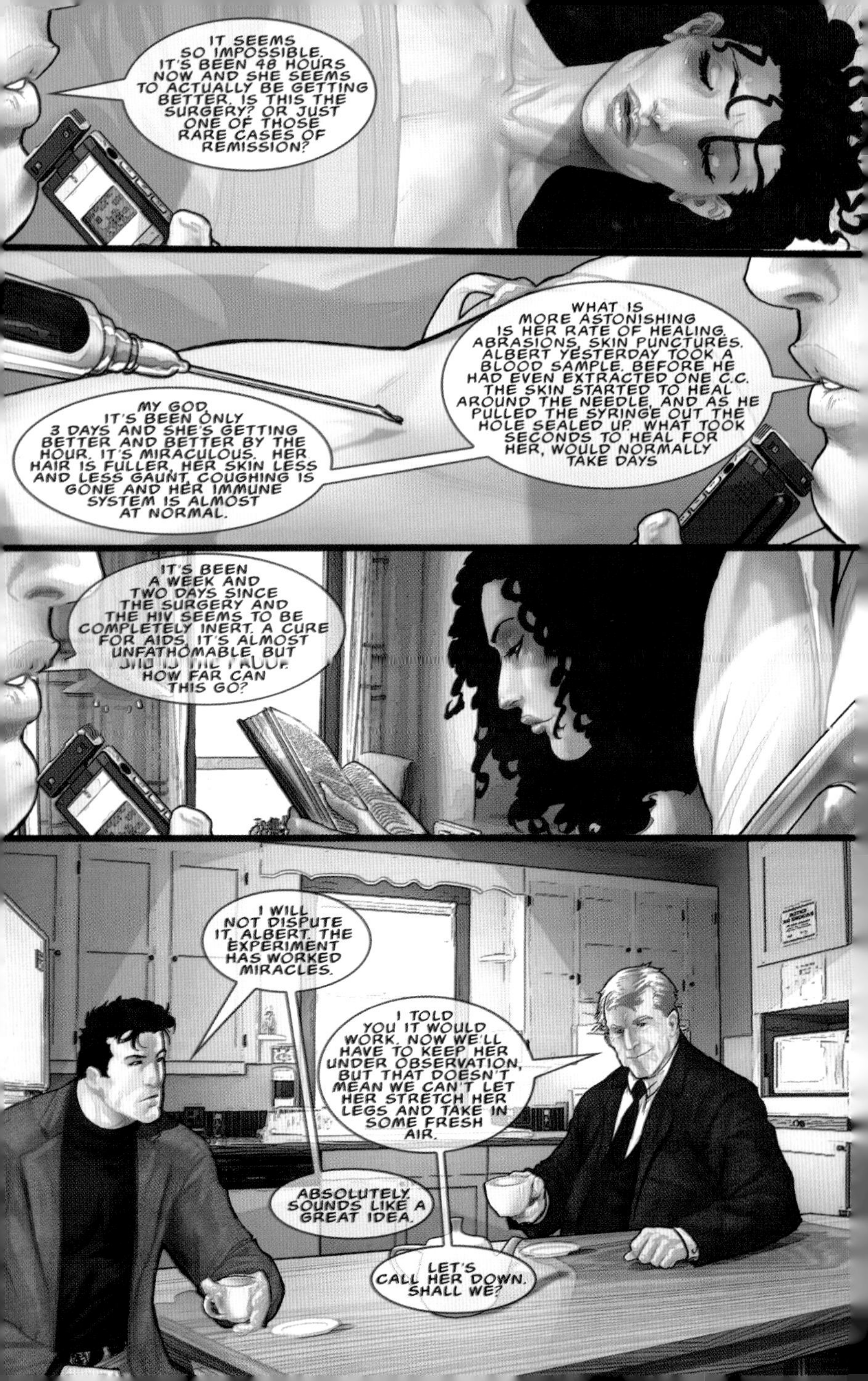
IT'S SEEMS SO IMPOSSIBLE. IT'S BEEN 48 HOURS NOW AND SHE SEEMS TO ACTUALLY BE GETTING BETTER. IS THIS THE SURGERY? OR JUST ONE OF THOSE RARE CASES OF REMISSION?
MY GOD. IT'S BEEN ONLY 3 DAYS AND SHE'S GETTING BETTER AND BETTER BY THE HOUR. IT'S MIRACULOUS. HER HAIR IS FULLER, HER SKIN LESS AND LESS GAUNT, COUGHING IS GONE AND HER IMMUNE SYSTEM IS ALMOST AT NORMAL.
WHAT IS MORE ASTONISHING IS HER RATE OF HEALING. ABRASIONS, SKIN PUNCTURES. ALBERT YESTERDAY TOOK A BLOOD SAMPLE. BEFORE HE HAD EVEN EXTRACTED ONE C.C. THE SKIN STARTED TO HEAL AROUND THE NEEDLE, AND AS HE PULLED THE SYRINGE OUT THE HOLE SEALED UP. WHAT TOOK SECONDS TO HEAL FOR HER, WOULD NORMALLY TAKE DAYS
IT'S BEEN A WEEK AND TWO DAYS SINCE THE SURGERY AND THE HIV SEEMS TO BE COMPLETELY INERT. A CURE FOR AIDS. IT'S ALMOST UNFATHOMABLE. BUT
HOW FAR CAN THIS GO?
I WILL NOT DISPUTE IT, ALBERT. THE EXPERIMENT HAS WORKED MIRACLES.
I TOLD YOU IT WOULD WORK. NOW WE'LL HAVE TO KEEP HER UNDER OBSERVATION, BUT THAT DOESN'T MEAN WE CAN'T LET HER STRETCH HER LEGS AND TAKE IN SOME FRESH AIR.
ABSOLUTELY. SOUNDS LIKE A GREAT IDEA.
LET'S CALL HER DOWN. SHALL WE?

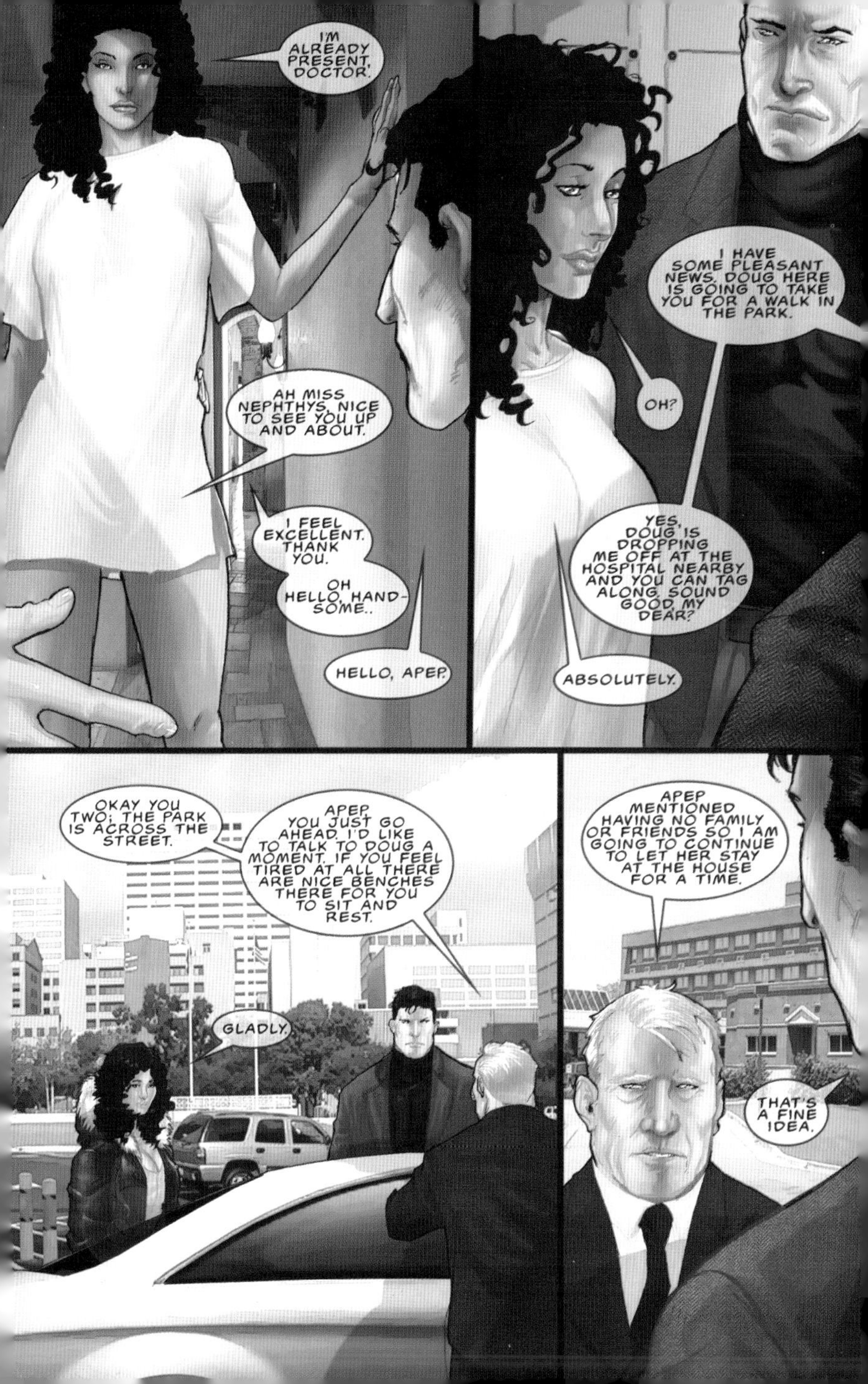
I'M ALREADY PRESENT, DOCTOR.
AH MISS NEPHTHYS, NICE TO SEE YOU UP AND ABOUT.
I FEEL EXCELLENT. THANK YOU.
OH HELLO, HAND-SOME..
HELLO, APEP.
I HAVE SOME PLEASANT NEWS. DOUG HERE IS GOING TO TAKE YOU FOR A WALK IN THE PARK.
OH?
YES, DOUG IS DROPPING ME OFF AT THE HOSPITAL NEARBY AND YOU CAN TAG ALONG. SOUND GOOD, MY DEAR?
ABSOLUTELY.
OKAY YOU TWO; THE PARK IS ACROSS THE STREET.
APEP YOU JUST GO AHEAD. I'D LIKE TO TALK TO DOUG A MOMENT. IF YOU FEEL TIRED AT ALL THERE ARE NICE BENCHES THERE FOR YOU TO SIT AND REST.
GLADLY.
APEP MENTIONED HAVING NO FAMILY OR FRIENDS SO I AM GOING TO CONTINUE TO LET HER STAY AT THE HOUSE FOR A TIME.
THAT'S A FINE IDEA.

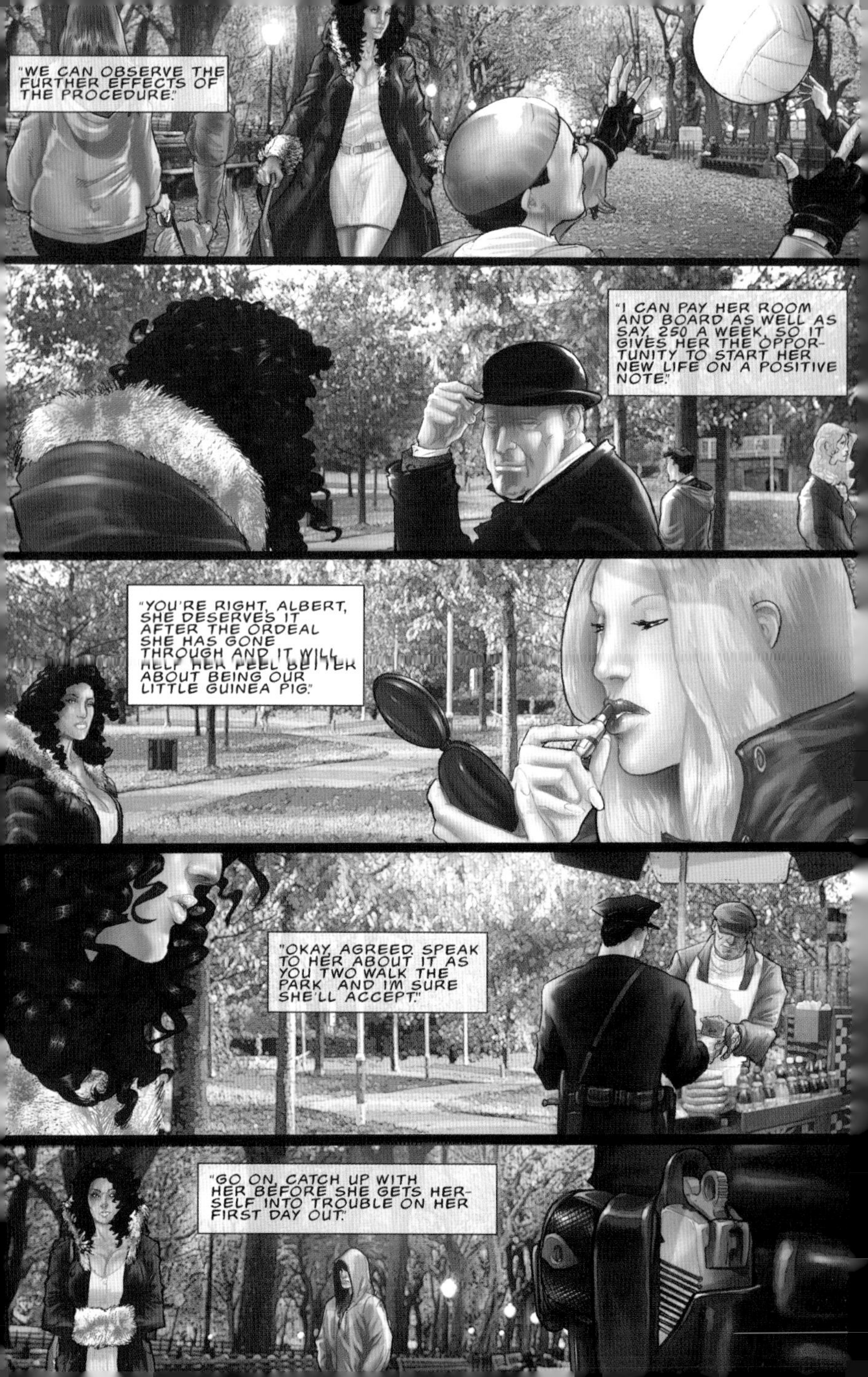
"WE CAN OBSERVE THE FURTHER EFFECTS OF THE PROCEDURE."
"I CAN PAY HER ROOM AND BOARD AS WELL AS SAY, 250 A WEEK, SO IT GIVES HER THE OPPORTUNITY TO START HER NEW LIFE ON A POSITIVE NOTE."
"YOU'RE RIGHT, ALBERT, SHE DESERVES IT AFTER THE ORDEAL SHE HAS GONE THROUGH AND IT WILL HELP HER FEEL BETTER ABOUT BEING OUR LITTLE GUINEA PIG."
"OKAY, AGREED. SPEAK TO HER ABOUT IT AS YOU TWO WALK THE PARK AND I'M SURE SHE'LL ACCEPT."
"GO ON, CATCH UP WITH HER BEFORE SHE GETS HERSELF INTO TROUBLE ON HER FIRST DAY OUT."

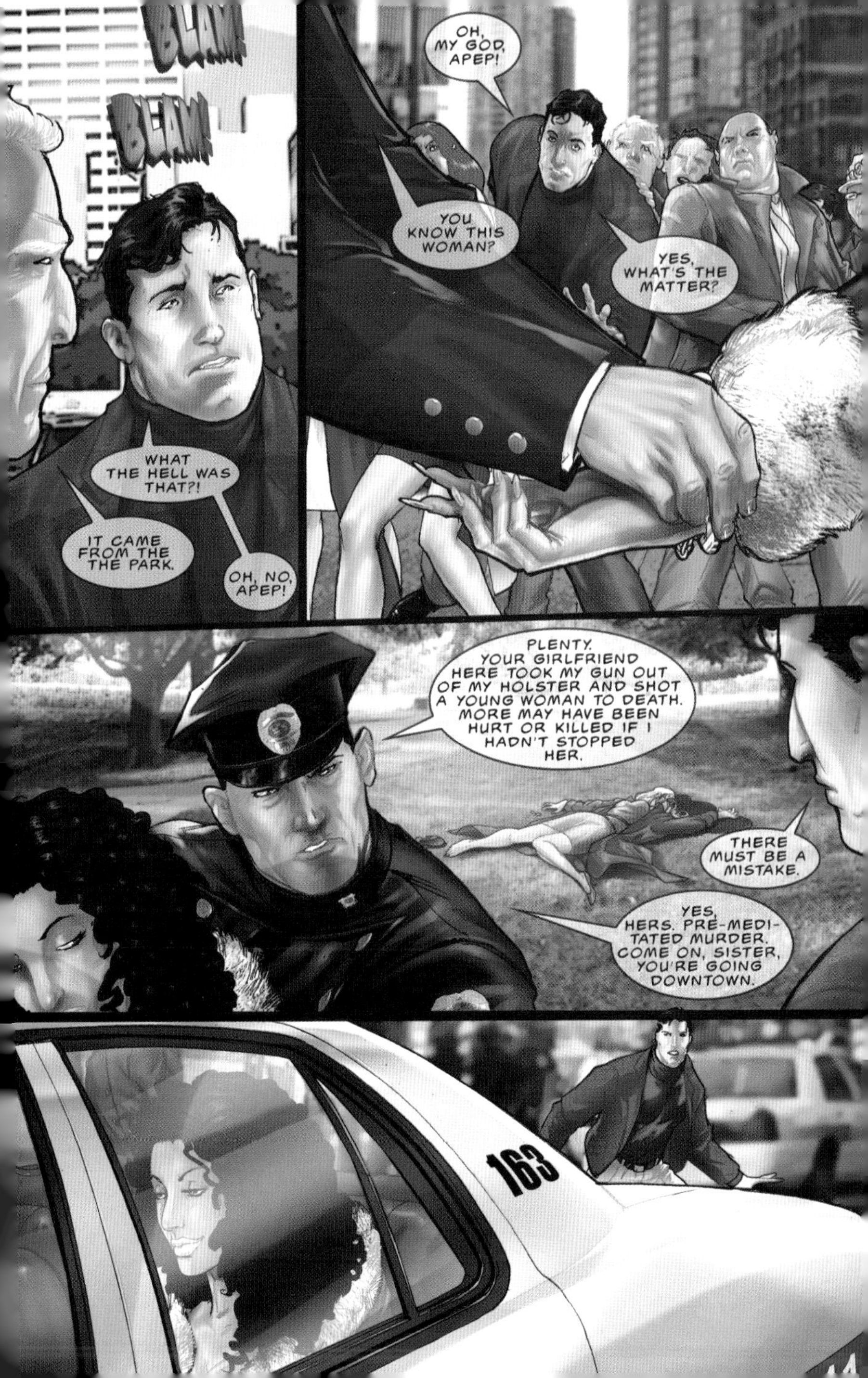
BLAM!
BLAM!
WHAT THE HELL WAS THAT?!
IT CAME FROM THE THE PARK.
OH, NO, APEP!
OH, MY GOD, APEP!
YOU KNOW THIS WOMAN?
YES, WHAT'S THE MATTER?
PLENTY. YOUR GIRLFRIEND HERE TOOK MY GUN OUT OF MY HOLSTER AND SHOT A YOUNG WOMAN TO DEATH. MORE MAY HAVE BEEN HURT OR KILLED IF I HADN'T STOPPED HER.
THERE MUST BE A MISTAKE.
YES, HERS. PRE-MEDITATED MURDER. COME ON, SISTER, YOU'RE GOING DOWNTOWN.
163

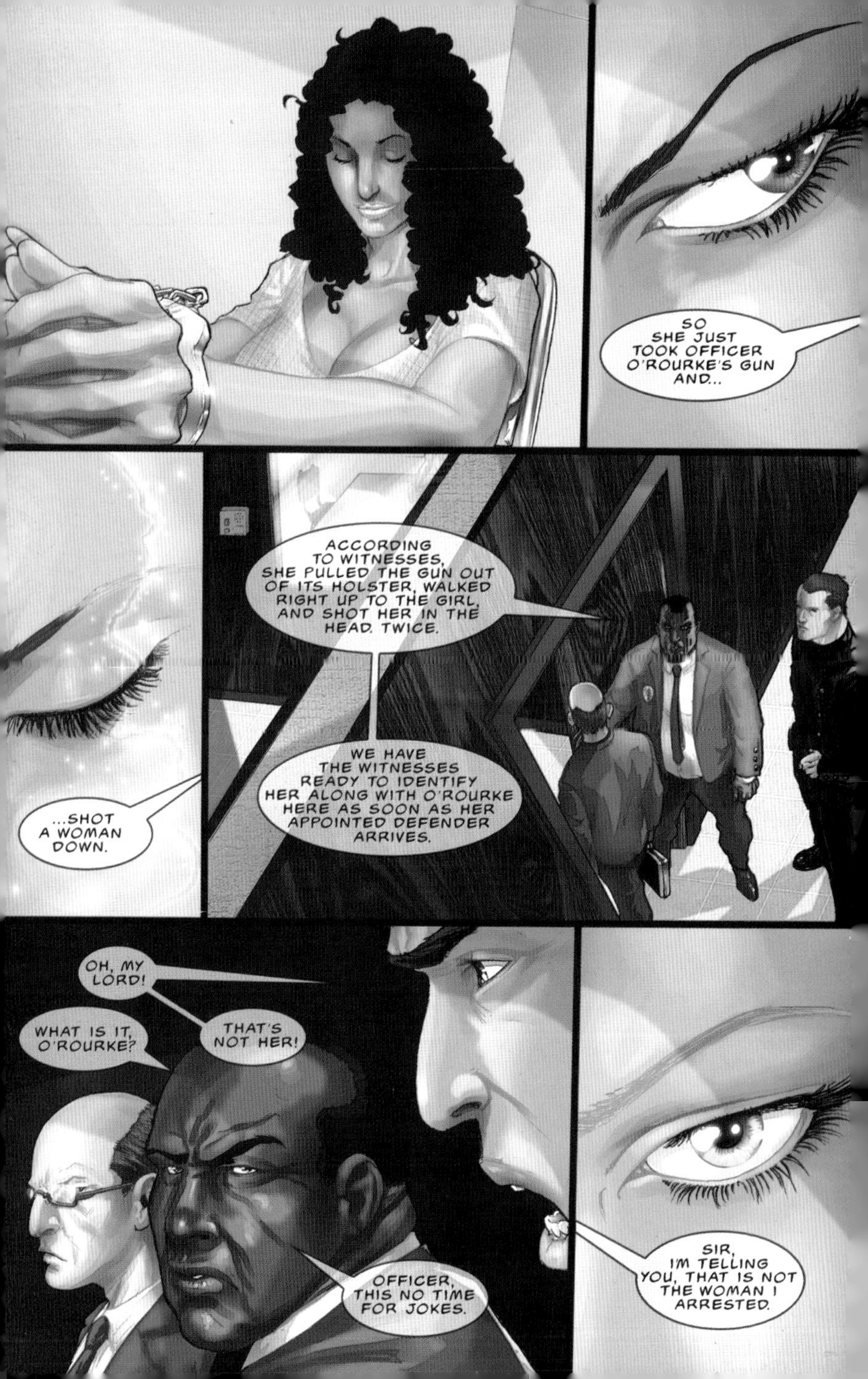
SO SHE JUST TOOK OFFICER O'ROURKE'S GUN AND...
...SHOT A WOMAN DOWN.
ACCORDING TO WITNESSES, SHE PULLED THE GUN OUT OF ITS HOLSTER, WALKED RIGHT UP TO THE GIRL, AND SHOT HER IN THE HEAD. TWICE.
WE HAVE THE WITNESSES READY TO IDENTIFY HER ALONG WITH O'ROURKE HERE AS SOON AS HER APPOINTED DEFENDER ARRIVES.
OH, MY LORD!
THAT'S NOT HER!
WHAT IS IT, O'ROURKE?
OFFICER, THIS NO TIME FOR JOKES.
SIR, I'M TELLING YOU, THAT IS NOT THE WOMAN I ARRESTED.

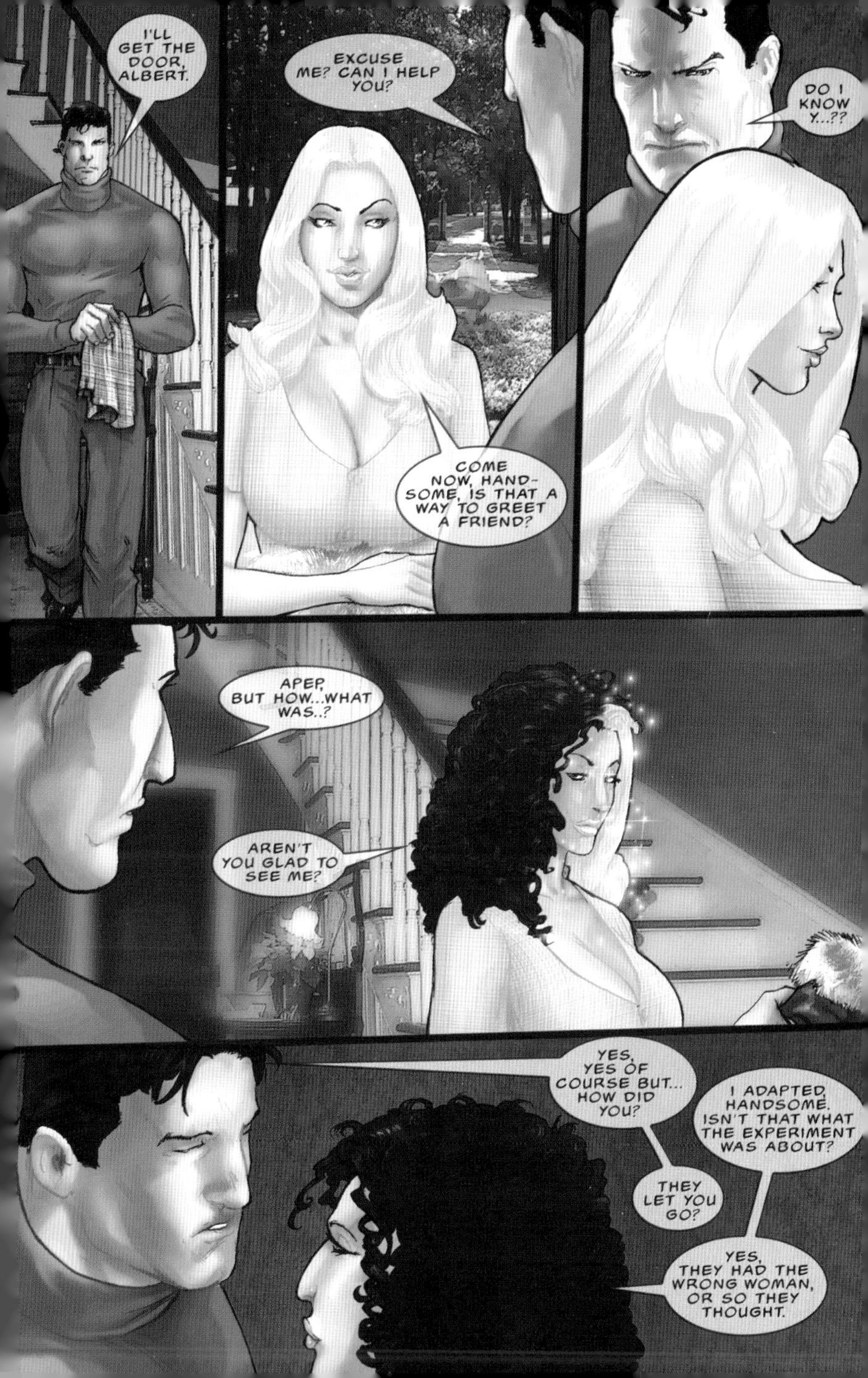
I'LL GET THE DOOR, ALBERT.
EXCUSE ME? CAN I HELP YOU?
COME NOW, HANDSOME, IS THAT A WAY TO GREET A FRIEND?
DO I KNOW Y...??
APEP, BUT HOW...WHAT WAS..?
AREN'T YOU GLAD TO SEE ME?
YES, YES OF COURSE BUT... HOW DID YOU?
THEY LET YOU GO?
I ADAPTED, HANDSOME. ISN'T THAT WHAT THE EXPERIMENT WAS ABOUT?
YES, THEY HAD THE WRONG WOMAN, OR SO THEY THOUGHT.

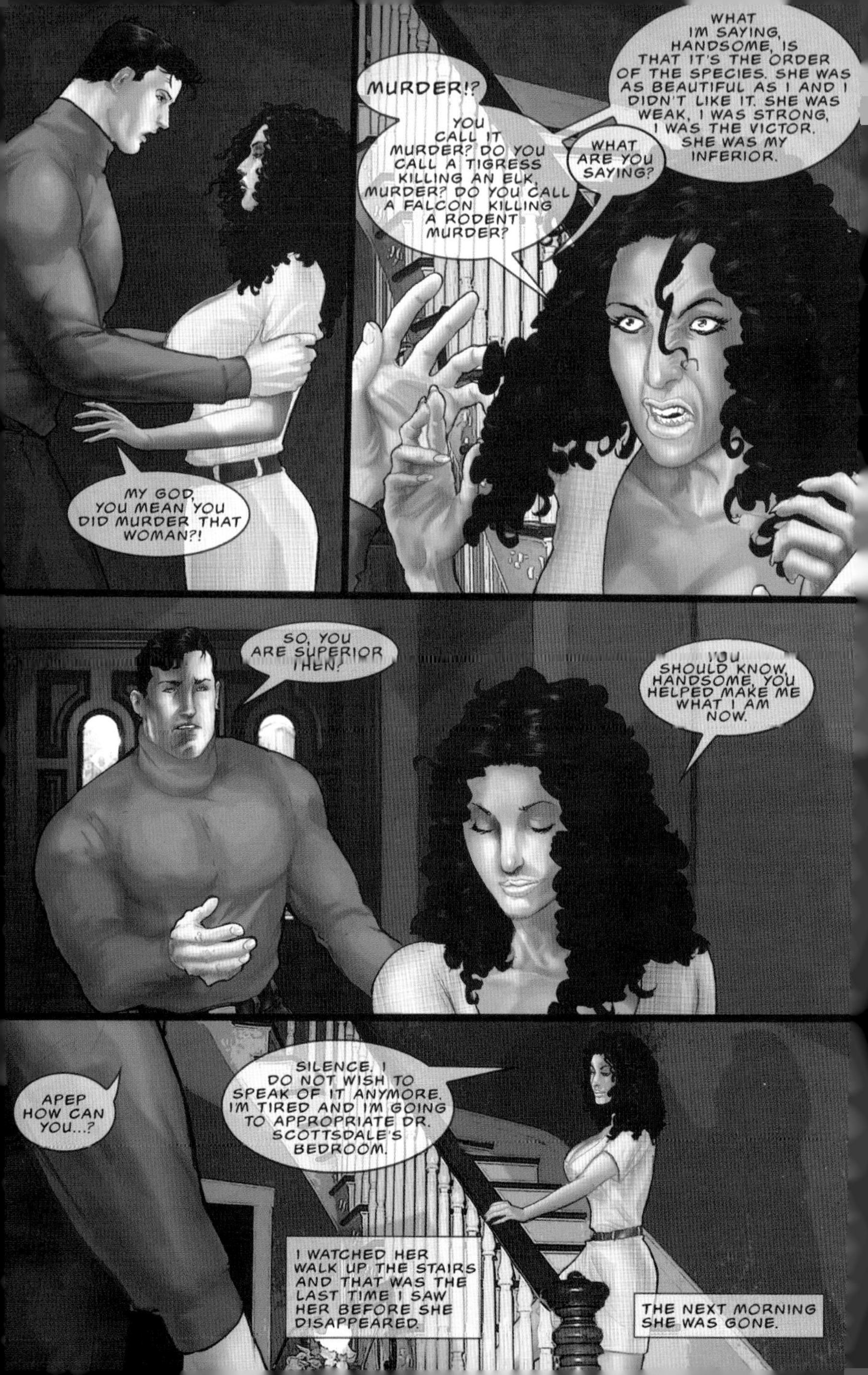
MY GOD, YOU MEAN YOU DID MURDER THAT WOMAN?!
MURDER!?
YOU CALL IT MURDER? DO YOU CALL A TIGRESS KILLING AN ELK, MURDER? DO YOU CALL A FALCON KILLING A RODENT MURDER?
WHAT ARE YOU SAYING?
WHAT IM SAYING, HANDSOME, IS THAT IT'S THE ORDER OF THE SPECIES. SHE WAS AS BEAUTIFUL AS I AND I DIDN'T LIKE IT. SHE WAS WEAK, I WAS STRONG, I WAS THE VICTOR. SHE WAS MY INFERIOR.
SO, YOU ARE SUPERIOR THEN?
YOU SHOULD KNOW, HANDSOME, YOU HELPED MAKE ME WHAT I AM NOW.
APEP HOW CAN YOU...?
SILENCE. I DO NOT WISH TO SPEAK OF IT ANYMORE. IM TIRED AND IM GOING TO APPROPRIATE DR. SCOTTSDALE'S BEDROOM.
I WATCHED HER WALK UP THE STAIRS AND THAT WAS THE LAST TIME I SAW HER BEFORE SHE DISAPPEARED.
THE NEXT MORNING SHE WAS GONE.

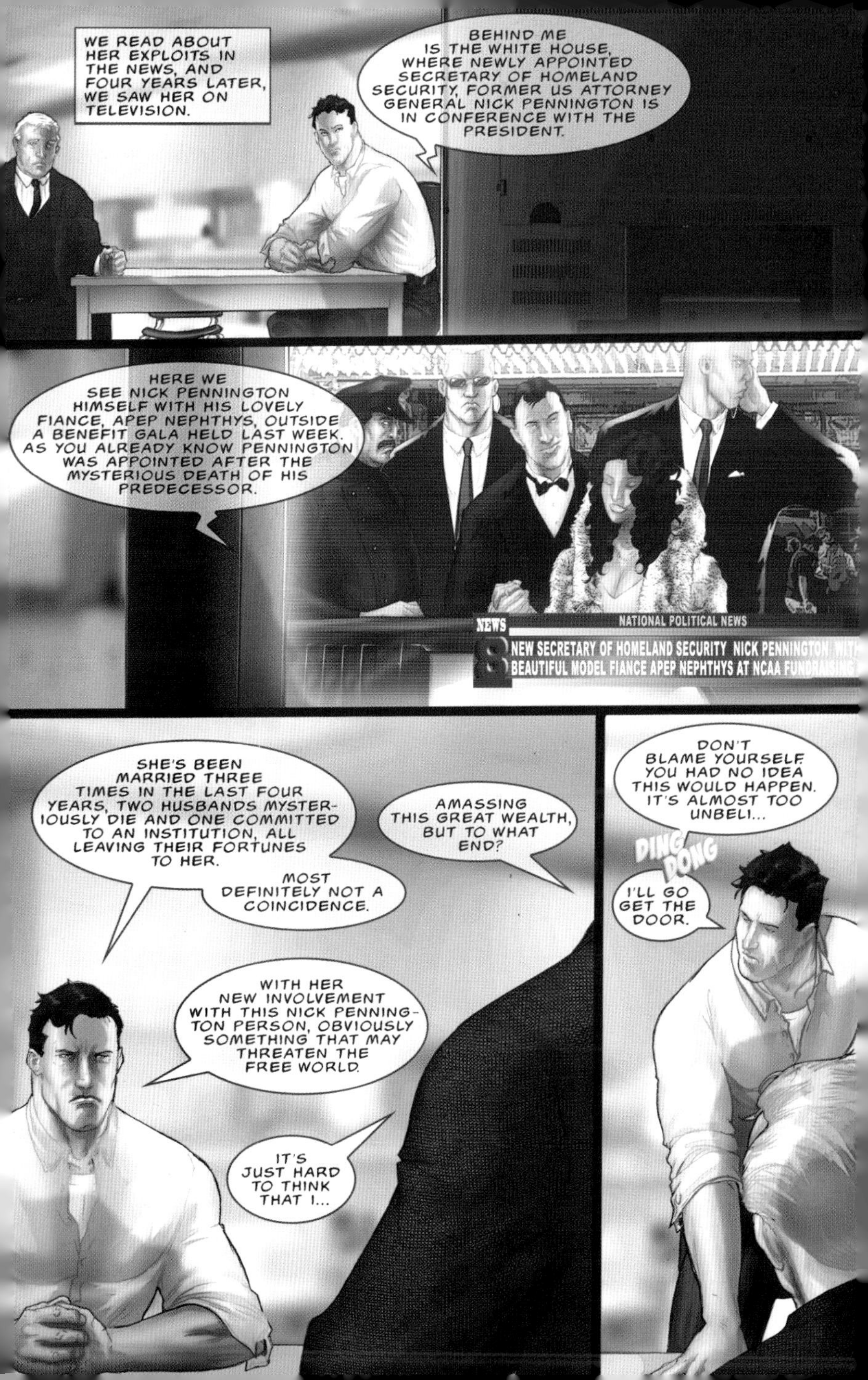
WE READ ABOUT HER EXPLOITS IN THE NEWS, AND FOUR YEARS LATER, WE SAW HER ON TELEVISION.
BEHIND ME IS THE WHITE HOUSE, WHERE NEWLY APPOINTED SECRETARY OF HOMELAND SECURITY, FORMER US ATTORNEY GENERAL NICK PENNINGTON IS IN CONFERENCE WITH THE PRESIDENT.
HERE WE SEE NICK PENNINGTON HIMSELF WITH HIS LOVELY FIANCE, APEP NEPHTHYS, OUTSIDE A BENEFIT GALA HELD LAST WEEK. AS YOU ALREADY KNOW PENNINGTON WAS APPOINTED AFTER THE MYSTERIOUS DEATH OF HIS PREDECESSOR.
NEWS
NATIONAL POLITICAL NEWS
8
NEW SECRETARY OF HOMELAND SECURITY NICK PENNINGTON WITH
BEAUTIFUL MODEL FIANCE APEP NEPHTHYS AT NCAA FUNDRAISING
SHE'S BEEN MARRIED THREE TIMES IN THE LAST FOUR YEARS, TWO HUSBANDS MYSTERIOUSLY DIE AND ONE COMMITTED TO AN INSTITUTION, ALL LEAVING THEIR FORTUNES TO HER.
MOST DEFINITELY NOT A COINCIDENCE.
AMASSING THIS GREAT WEALTH, BUT TO WHAT END?
WITH HER NEW INVOLVEMENT WITH THIS NICK PENNINGTON PERSON, OBVIOUSLY SOMETHING THAT MAY THREATEN THE FREE WORLD.
IT'S JUST HARD TO THINK THAT I...
DON'T BLAME YOURSELF. YOU HAD NO IDEA THIS WOULD HAPPEN. IT'S ALMOST TOO UNBELI...
DING DONG
I'LL GO GET THE DOOR.

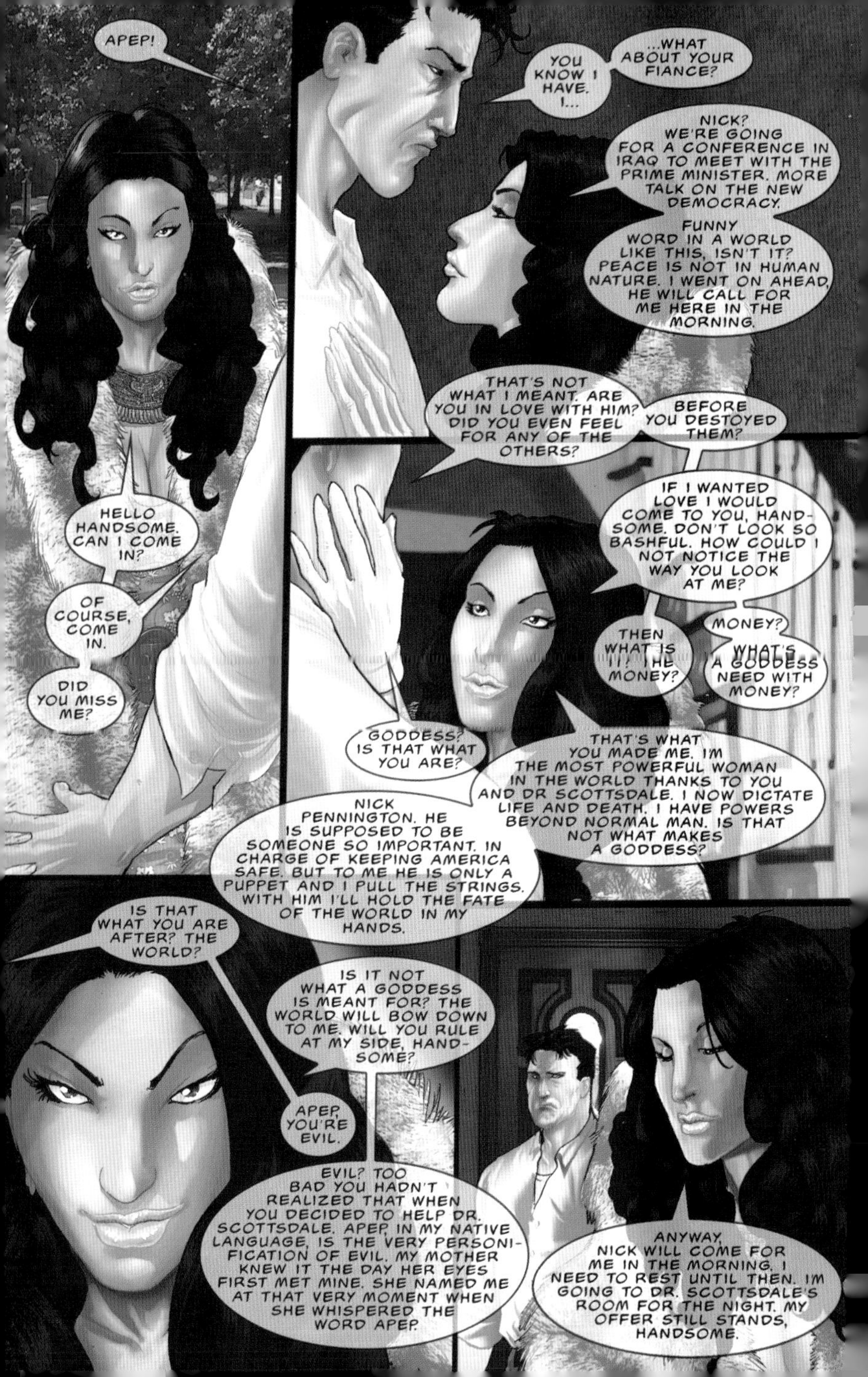
APEP!
HELLO HANDSOME. CAN I COME IN?
OF COURSE, COME IN.
DID YOU MISS ME?
YOU KNOW I HAVE. I...
...WHAT ABOUT YOUR FIANCE?
NICK? WE'RE GOING FOR A CONFERENCE IN IRAQ TO MEET WITH THE PRIME MINISTER. MORE TALK ON THE NEW DEMOCRACY.
FUNNY WORD IN A WORLD LIKE THIS, ISN'T IT? PEACE IS NOT IN HUMAN NATURE. I WENT ON AHEAD, HE WILL CALL FOR ME HERE IN THE MORNING.
THAT'S NOT WHAT I MEANT. ARE YOU IN LOVE WITH HIM? DID YOU EVEN FEEL FOR ANY OF THE OTHERS?
BEFORE YOU DESTOYED THEM?
IF I WANTED LOVE I WOULD COME TO YOU, HAND-SOME. DON'T LOOK SO BASHFUL. HOW COULD I NOT NOTICE THE WAY YOU LOOK AT ME?
THEN WHAT IS IT? THE MONEY?
MONEY?
WHAT'S A GODDESS NEED WITH MONEY?
GODDESS? IS THAT WHAT YOU ARE?
THAT'S WHAT YOU MADE ME. I'M THE MOST POWERFUL WOMAN IN THE WORLD THANKS TO YOU AND DR SCOTTSDALE. I NOW DICTATE LIFE AND DEATH. I HAVE POWERS BEYOND NORMAL MAN. IS THAT NOT WHAT MAKES A GODDESS?
NICK PENNINGTON. HE IS SUPPOSED TO BE SOMEONE SO IMPORTANT. IN CHARGE OF KEEPING AMERICA SAFE. BUT TO ME HE IS ONLY A PUPPET AND I PULL THE STRINGS. WITH HIM I'LL HOLD THE FATE OF THE WORLD IN MY HANDS.
IS THAT WHAT YOU ARE AFTER? THE WORLD?
IS IT NOT WHAT A GODDESS IS MEANT FOR? THE WORLD WILL BOW DOWN TO ME. WILL YOU RULE AT MY SIDE, HAND-SOME?
APEP, YOU'RE EVIL.
EVIL? TOO BAD YOU HADN'T REALIZED THAT WHEN YOU DECIDED TO HELP DR. SCOTTSDALE. APEP, IN MY NATIVE LANGUAGE, IS THE VERY PERSONI-FICATION OF EVIL. MY MOTHER KNEW IT THE DAY HER EYES FIRST MET MINE. SHE NAMED ME AT THAT VERY MOMENT WHEN SHE WHISPERED THE WORD APEP.
ANYWAY, NICK WILL COME FOR ME IN THE MORNING. I NEED TO REST UNTIL THEN. I'M GOING TO DR. SCOTTSDALE'S ROOM FOR THE NIGHT. MY OFFER STILL STANDS, HANDSOME.

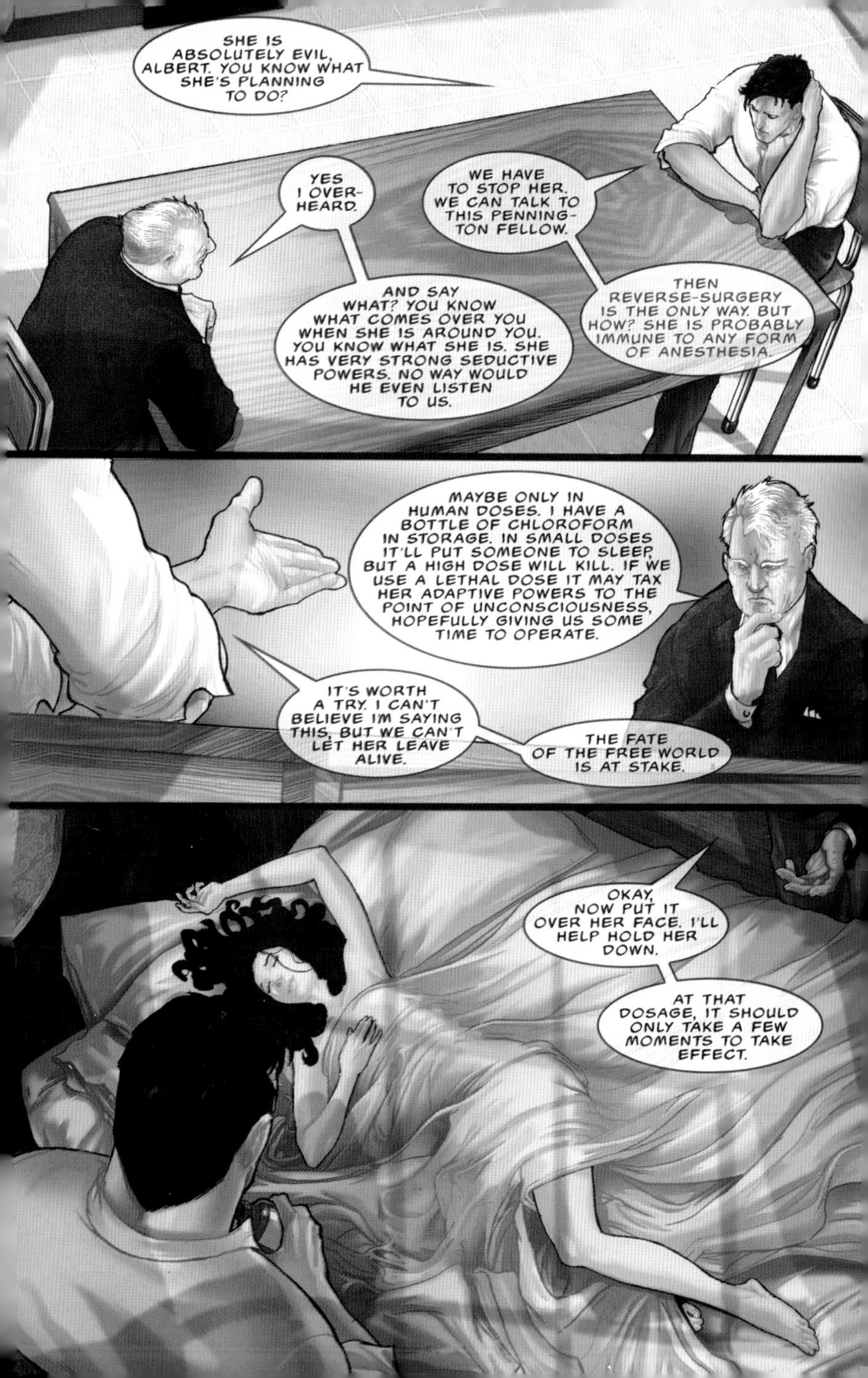
SHE IS ABSOLUTELY EVIL, ALBERT. YOU KNOW WHAT SHE'S PLANNING TO DO?
YES I OVER-HEARD.
WE HAVE TO STOP HER. WE CAN TALK TO THIS PENNING-TON FELLOW.
AND SAY WHAT? YOU KNOW WHAT COMES OVER YOU WHEN SHE IS AROUND YOU. YOU KNOW WHAT SHE IS. SHE HAS VERY STRONG SEDUCTIVE POWERS. NO WAY WOULD HE EVEN LISTEN TO US.
THEN REVERSE-SURGERY IS THE ONLY WAY. BUT HOW? SHE IS PROBABLY IMMUNE TO ANY FORM OF ANESTHESIA.
MAYBE ONLY IN HUMAN DOSES. I HAVE A BOTTLE OF CHLOROFORM IN STORAGE. IN SMALL DOSES IT'LL PUT SOMEONE TO SLEEP, BUT A HIGH DOSE WILL KILL. IF WE USE A LETHAL DOSE IT MAY TAX HER ADAPTIVE POWERS TO THE POINT OF UNCONSCIOUSNESS, HOPEFULLY GIVING US SOME TIME TO OPERATE.
IT'S WORTH A TRY. I CAN'T BELIEVE IM SAYING THIS, BUT WE CAN'T LET HER LEAVE ALIVE.
THE FATE OF THE FREE WORLD IS AT STAKE.
OKAY, NOW PUT IT OVER HER FACE. I'LL HELP HOLD HER DOWN.
AT THAT DOSAGE, IT SHOULD ONLY TAKE A FEW MOMENTS TO TAKE EFFECT.

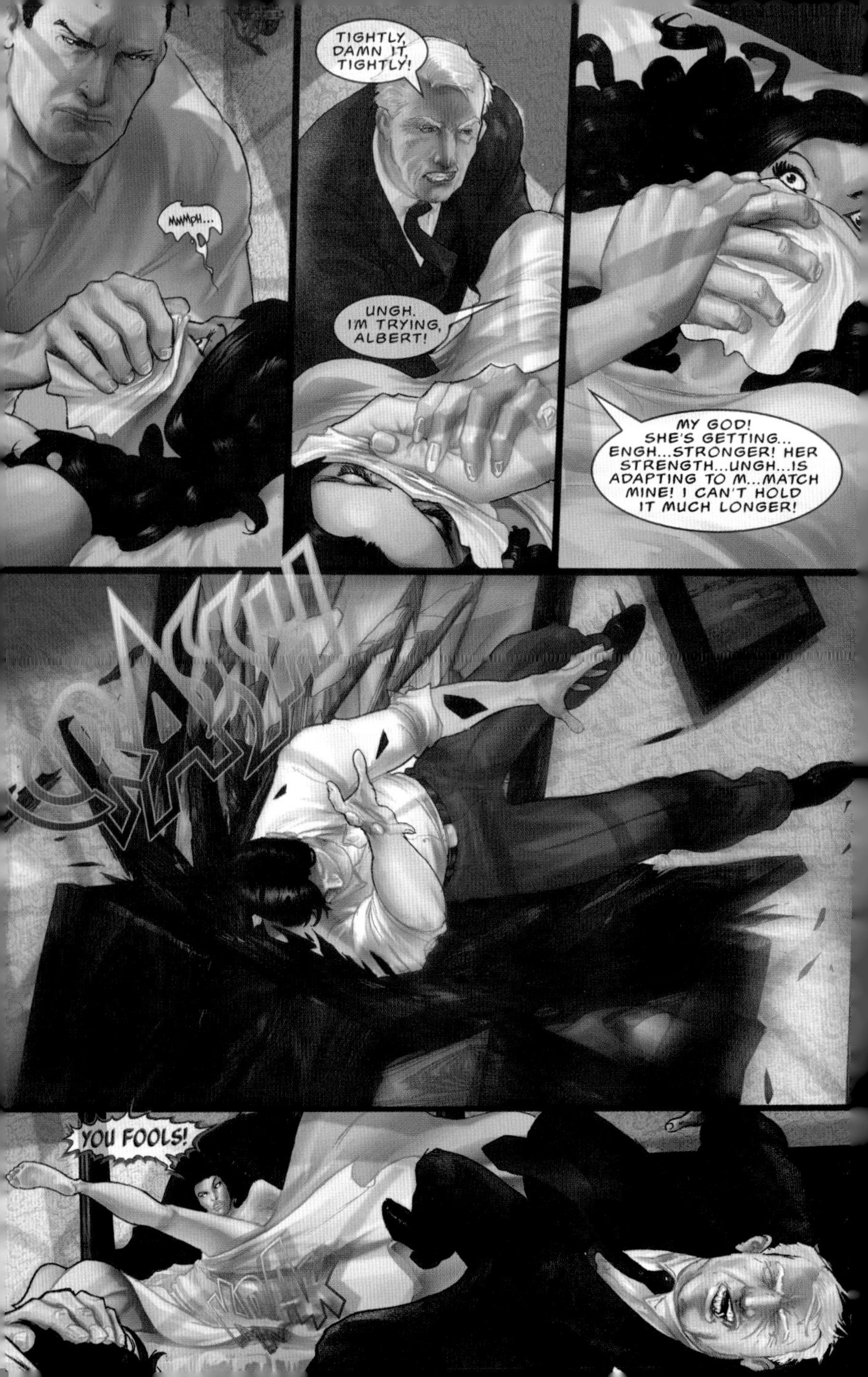
MMMPH...
TIGHTLY, DAMN IT, TIGHTLY!
UNGH. I'M TRYING, ALBERT!
MY GOD! SHE'S GETTING... ENGH...STRONGER! HER STRENGTH...UNGH...IS ADAPTING TO M...MATCH MINE! I CAN'T HOLD IT MUCH LONGER!
YOU FOOLS!

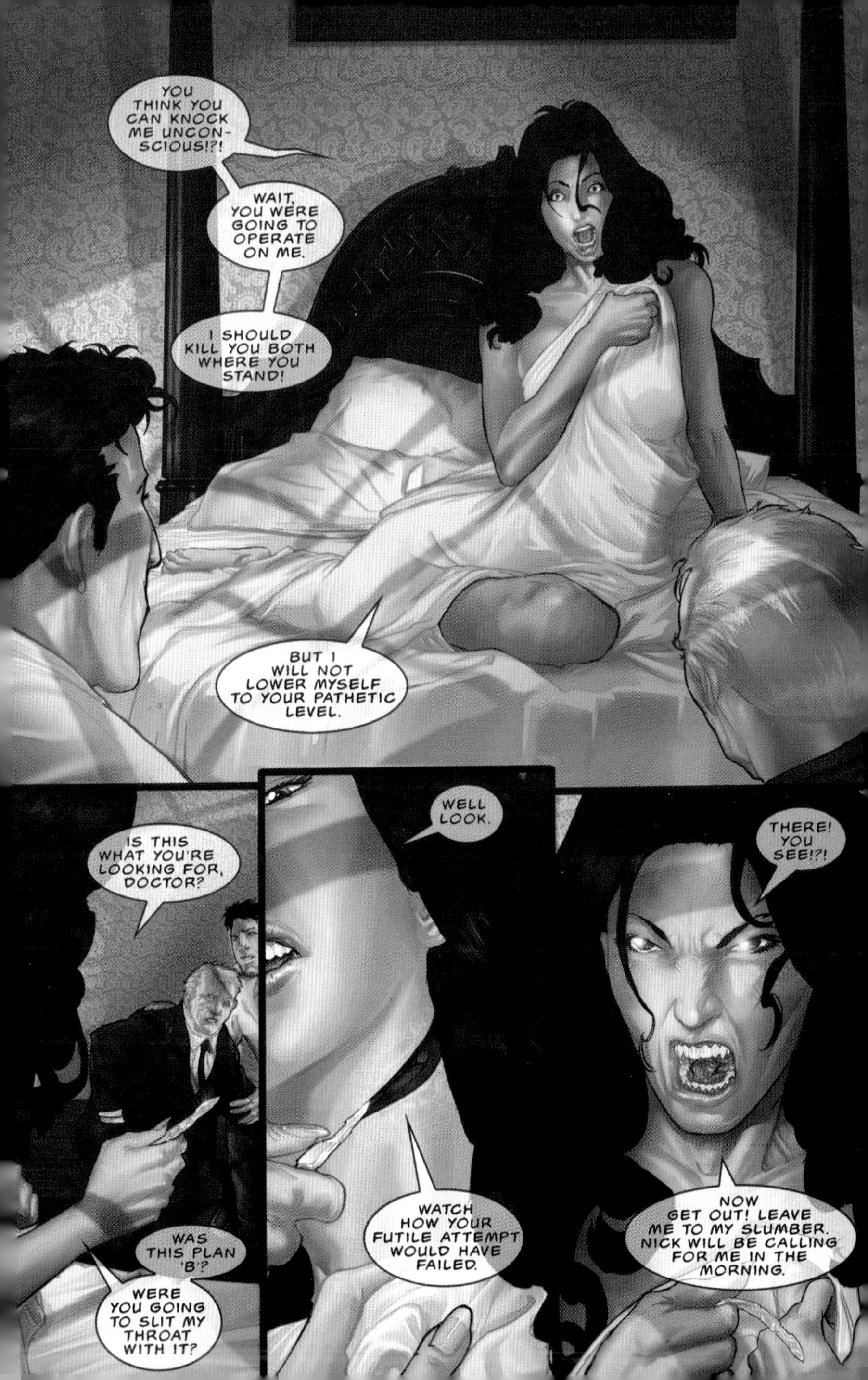
YOU THINK YOU CAN KNOCK ME UNCON- SCIOUS!?!
WAIT, YOU WERE GOING TO OPERATE ON ME.
I SHOULD KILL YOU BOTH WHERE YOU STAND!
BUT I WILL NOT LOWER MYSELF TO YOUR PATHETIC LEVEL.
IS THIS WHAT YOU'RE LOOKING FOR, DOCTOR?
WAS THIS PLAN 'B'?
WERE YOU GOING TO SLIT MY THROAT WITH IT?
WELL LOOK.
WATCH HOW YOUR FUTILE ATTEMPT WOULD HAVE FAILED.
THERE! YOU SEE!?!
NOW GET OUT! LEAVE ME TO MY SLUMBER. NICK WILL BE CALLING FOR ME IN THE MORNING.

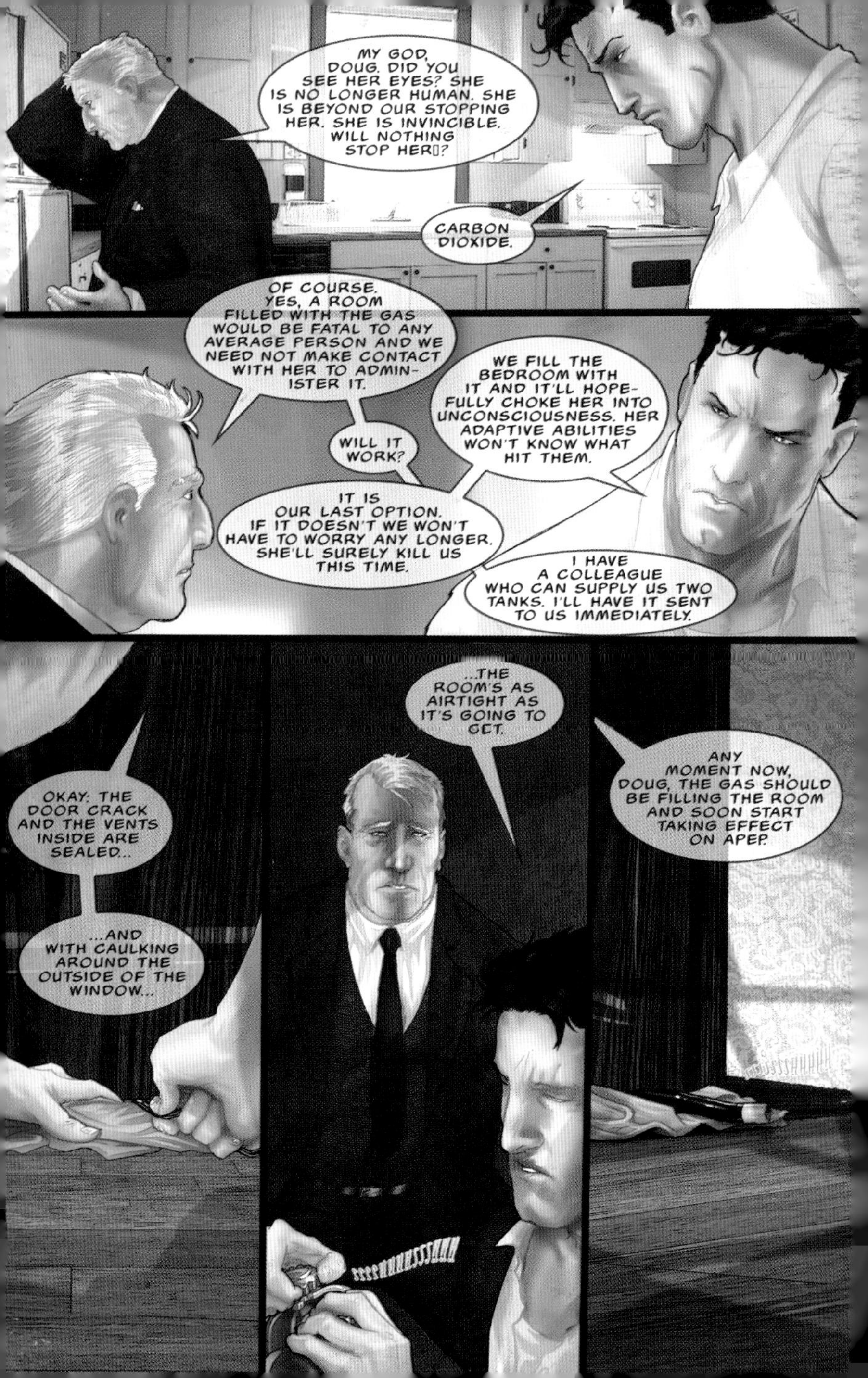
MY GOD, DOUG. DID YOU SEE HER EYES? SHE IS NO LONGER HUMAN. SHE IS BEYOND OUR STOPPING HER. SHE IS INVINCIBLE. WILL NOTHING STOP HER?
CARBON DIOXIDE.
OF COURSE. YES, A ROOM FILLED WITH THE GAS WOULD BE FATAL TO ANY AVERAGE PERSON AND WE NEED NOT MAKE CONTACT WITH HER TO ADMINISTER IT.
WILL IT WORK?
WE FILL THE BEDROOM WITH IT AND IT'LL HOPEFULLY CHOKE HER INTO UNCONSCIOUSNESS. HER ADAPTIVE ABILITIES WON'T KNOW WHAT HIT THEM.
IT IS OUR LAST OPTION. IF IT DOESN'T WE WON'T HAVE TO WORRY ANY LONGER. SHE'LL SURELY KILL US THIS TIME.
I HAVE A COLLEAGUE WHO CAN SUPPLY US TWO TANKS. I'LL HAVE IT SENT TO US IMMEDIATELY.
OKAY: THE DOOR CRACK AND THE VENTS INSIDE ARE SEALED...
...AND WITH CAULKING AROUND THE OUTSIDE OF THE WINDOW...
...THE ROOM'S AS AIRTIGHT AS IT'S GOING TO GET.
SSSSHHHHSSSHHH
ANY MOMENT NOW, DOUG, THE GAS SHOULD BE FILLING THE ROOM AND SOON START TAKING EFFECT ON APEP.

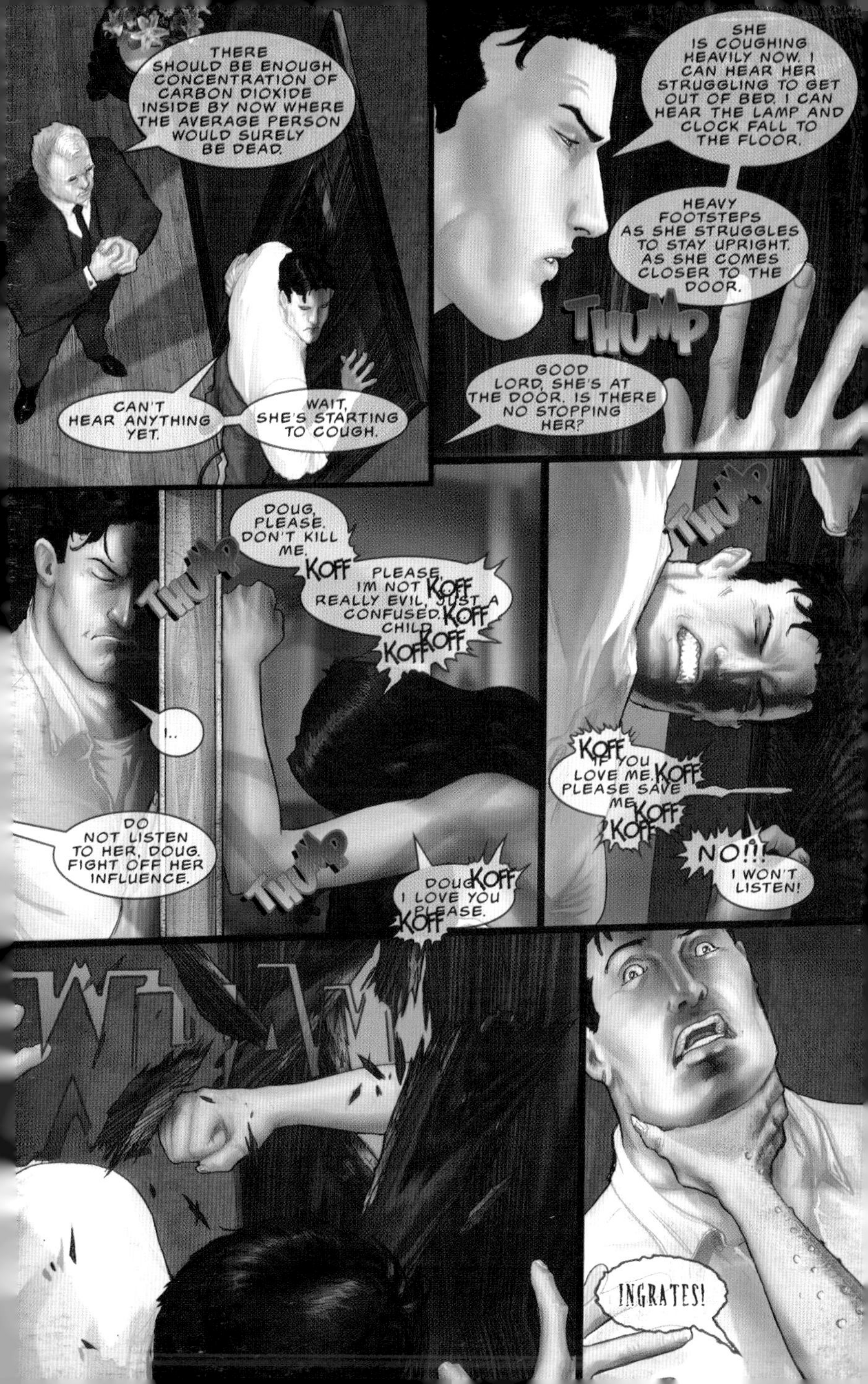
THERE SHOULD BE ENOUGH CONCENTRATION OF CARBON DIOXIDE INSIDE BY NOW WHERE THE AVERAGE PERSON WOULD SURELY BE DEAD.
CAN'T HEAR ANYTHING YET.
WAIT, SHE'S STARTING TO COUGH.
SHE IS COUGHING HEAVILY NOW. I CAN HEAR HER STRUGGLING TO GET OUT OF BED. I CAN HEAR THE LAMP AND CLOCK FALL TO THE FLOOR.
HEAVY FOOTSTEPS AS SHE STRUGGLES TO STAY UPRIGHT. AS SHE COMES CLOSER TO THE DOOR.
THUMP
GOOD LORD, SHE'S AT THE DOOR. IS THERE NO STOPPING HER?
THUMP
DOUG, PLEASE. DON'T KILL ME.
KOFF
PLEASE, I'M NOT KOFF REALLY EVIL, JUST A CONFUSED. KOFF CHILD KOFF KOFF
I..
DO NOT LISTEN TO HER, DOUG. FIGHT OFF HER INFLUENCE.
THUMP
DOUG KOFF I LOVE YOU PLEASE. KOFF
THUMP
KOFF IF YOU LOVE ME. KOFF PLEASE SAVE ME KOFF KOFF
NO!!! I WON'T LISTEN!
INGRATES!

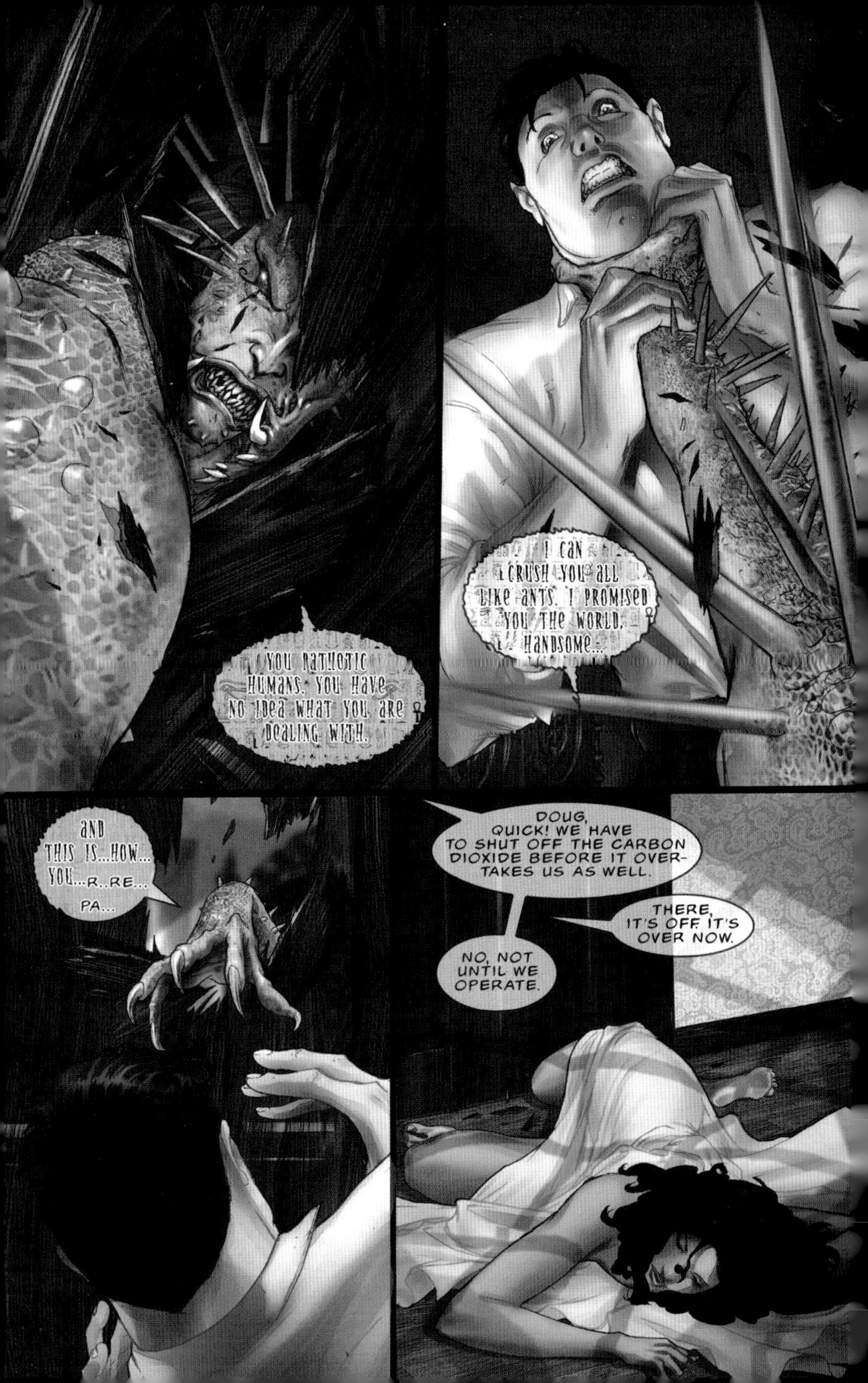
YOU PATHETIC HUMANS. YOU HAVE NO IDEA WHAT YOU ARE DEALING WITH.
I CAN CRUSH YOU ALL LIKE ANTS. I PROMISED YOU THE WORLD, HANDSOME...
AND THIS IS...HOW... YOU...R..RE... PA...
DOUG, QUICK! WE HAVE TO SHUT OFF THE CARBON DIOXIDE BEFORE IT OVER-TAKES US AS WELL.
THERE, IT'S OFF. IT'S OVER NOW.
NO, NOT UNTIL WE OPERATE.

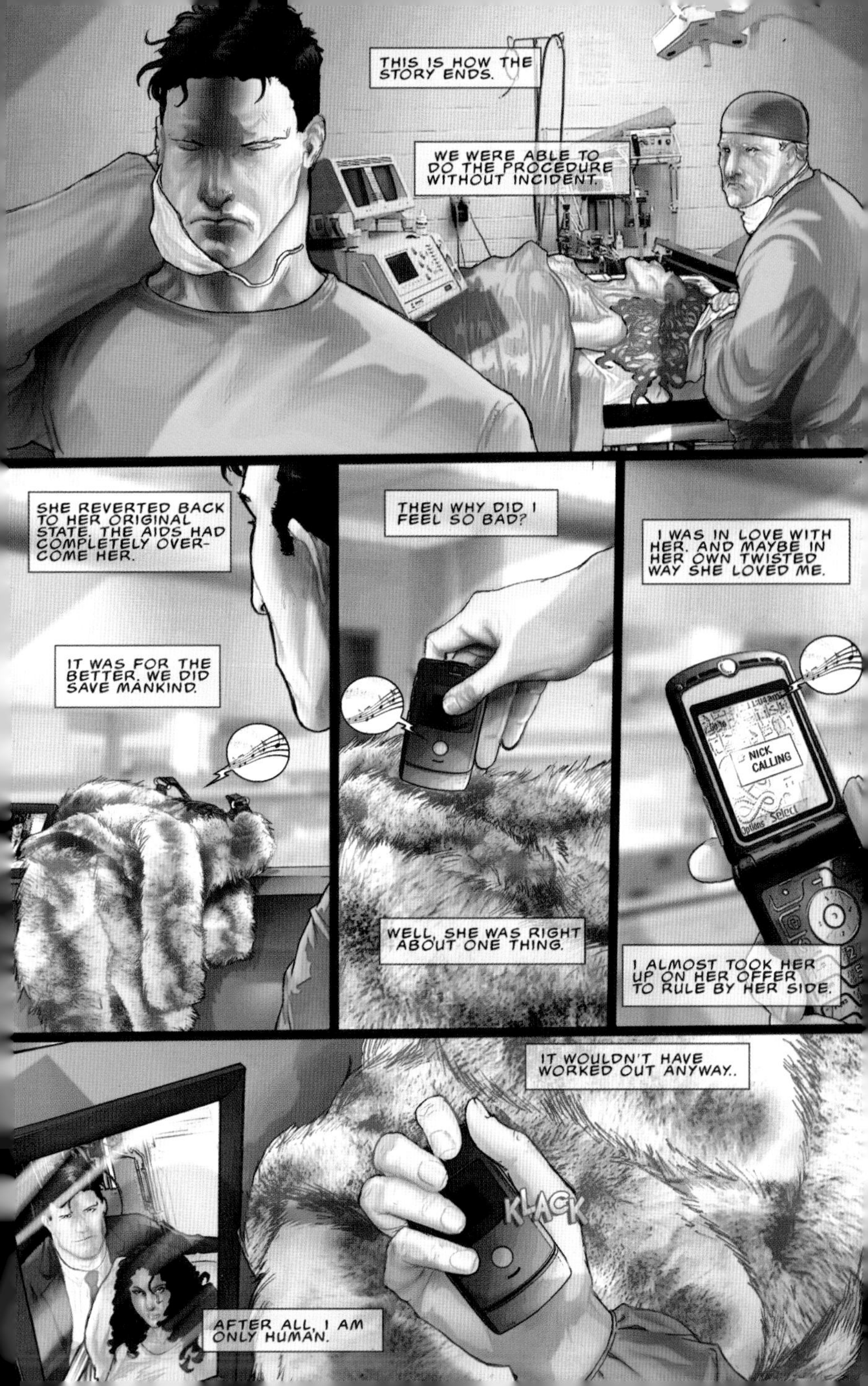
THIS IS HOW THE STORY ENDS.
WE WERE ABLE TO DO THE PROCEDURE WITHOUT INCIDENT.
SHE REVERTED BACK TO HER ORIGINAL STATE. THE AIDS HAD COMPLETELY OVER-COME HER.
IT WAS FOR THE BETTER. WE DID SAVE MANKIND.
THEN WHY DID I FEEL SO BAD?
WELL, SHE WAS RIGHT ABOUT ONE THING.
I WAS IN LOVE WITH HER. AND MAYBE IN HER OWN TWISTED WAY SHE LOVED ME.
NICK CALLING
Options Select
I ALMOST TOOK HER UP ON HER OFFER TO RULE BY HER SIDE.
IT WOULDN'T HAVE WORKED OUT ANYWAY..
KLACK
AFTER ALL, I AM ONLY HUMAN.

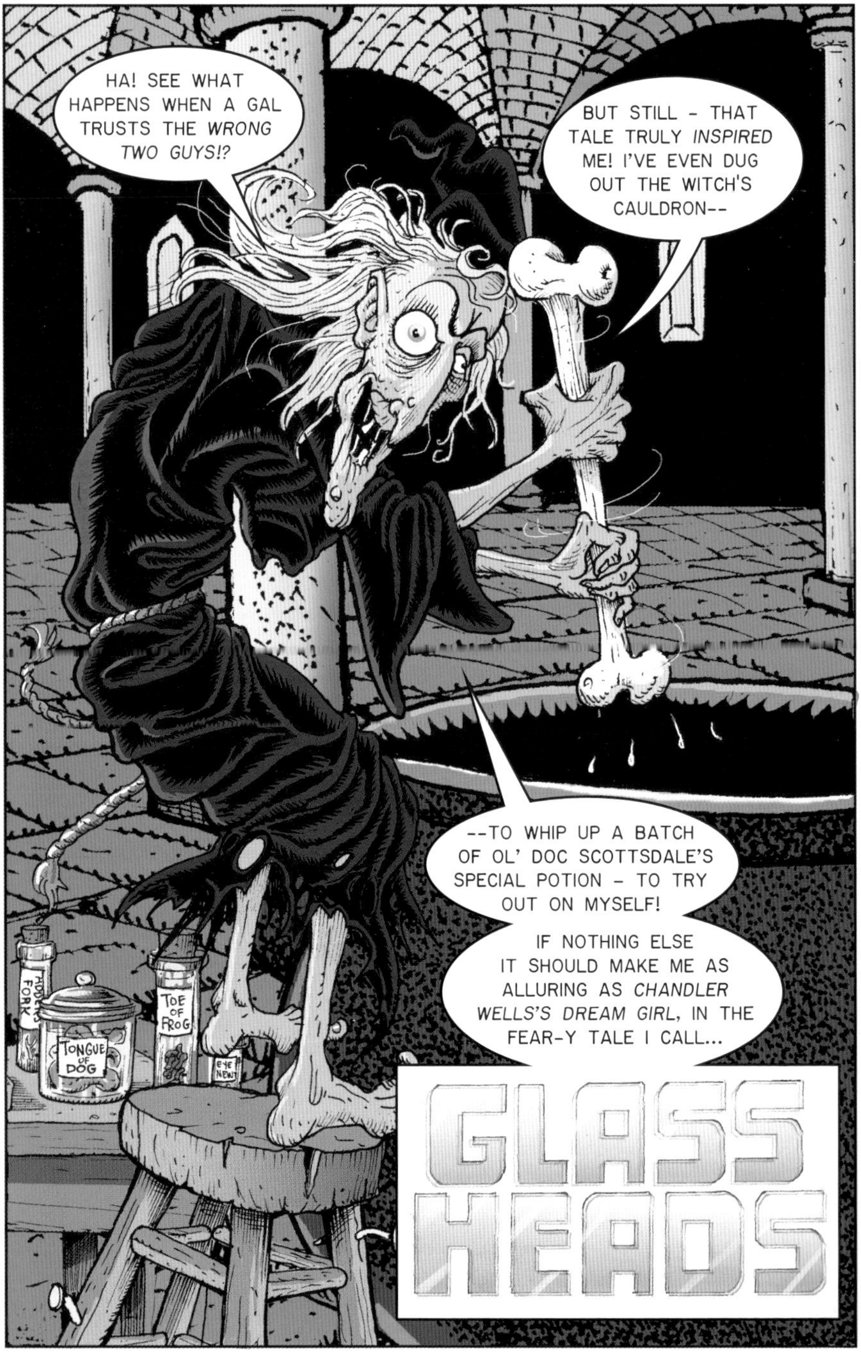
HA! SEE WHAT HAPPENS WHEN A GAL TRUSTS THE *WRONG TWO GUYS!?*
BUT STILL - THAT TALE TRULY *INSPIRED* ME! I'VE EVEN DUG OUT THE WITCH'S CAULDRON--
--TO WHIP UP A BATCH OF OL' DOC SCOTTSDALE'S SPECIAL POTION - TO TRY OUT ON MYSELF!
IF NOTHING ELSE IT SHOULD MAKE ME AS ALLURING AS *CHANDLER WELLS'S DREAM GIRL*, IN THE FEAR-Y TALE I CALL...
GLASS HEADS
ADDER'S FORK
TONGUE OF DOG
TOE OF FROG
EYE NEWT

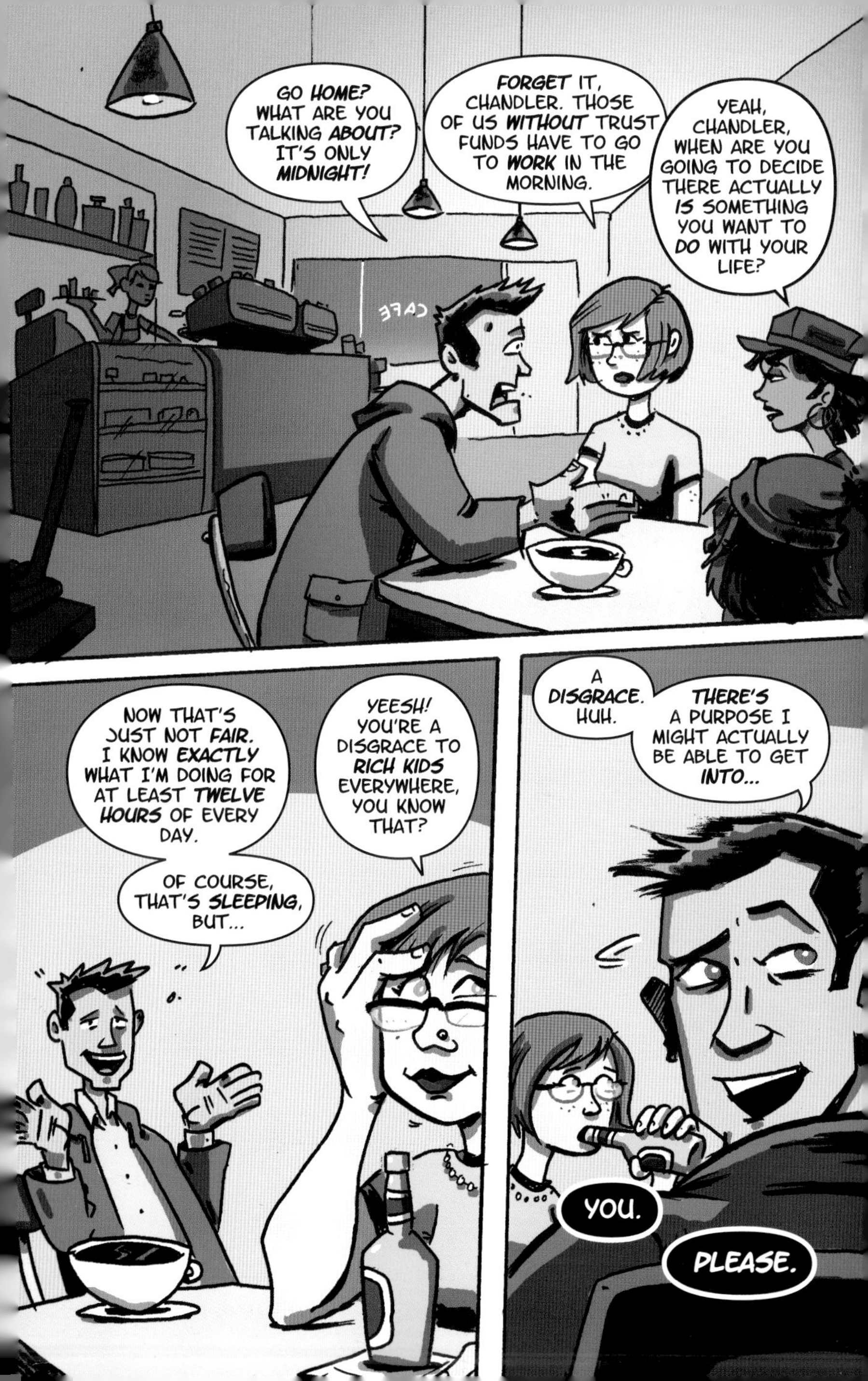
GO HOME? WHAT ARE YOU TALKING ABOUT? IT'S ONLY MIDNIGHT!
FORGET IT, CHANDLER. THOSE OF US WITHOUT TRUST FUNDS HAVE TO GO TO WORK IN THE MORNING.
YEAH, CHANDLER, WHEN ARE YOU GOING TO DECIDE THERE ACTUALLY IS SOMETHING YOU WANT TO DO WITH YOUR LIFE?
CAFE
NOW THAT'S JUST NOT FAIR. I KNOW EXACTLY WHAT I'M DOING FOR AT LEAST TWELVE HOURS OF EVERY DAY.
OF COURSE, THAT'S SLEEPING, BUT...
YEESH! YOU'RE A DISGRACE TO RICH KIDS EVERYWHERE, YOU KNOW THAT?
A DISGRACE. HUH.
THERE'S A PURPOSE I MIGHT ACTUALLY BE ABLE TO GET INTO...
YOU.
PLEASE.

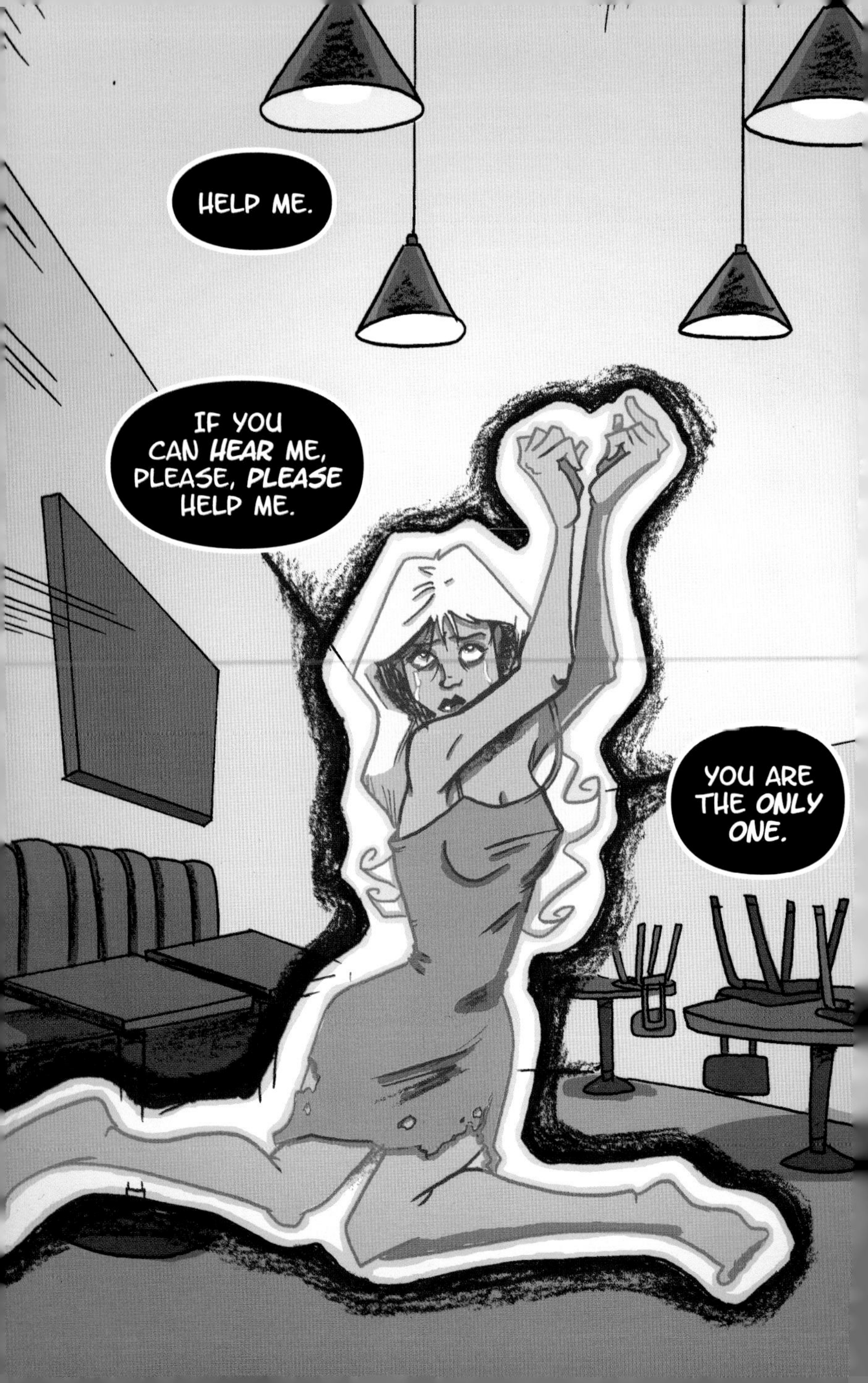
HELP ME.
IF YOU CAN HEAR ME, PLEASE, PLEASE HELP ME.
YOU ARE THE ONLY ONE.

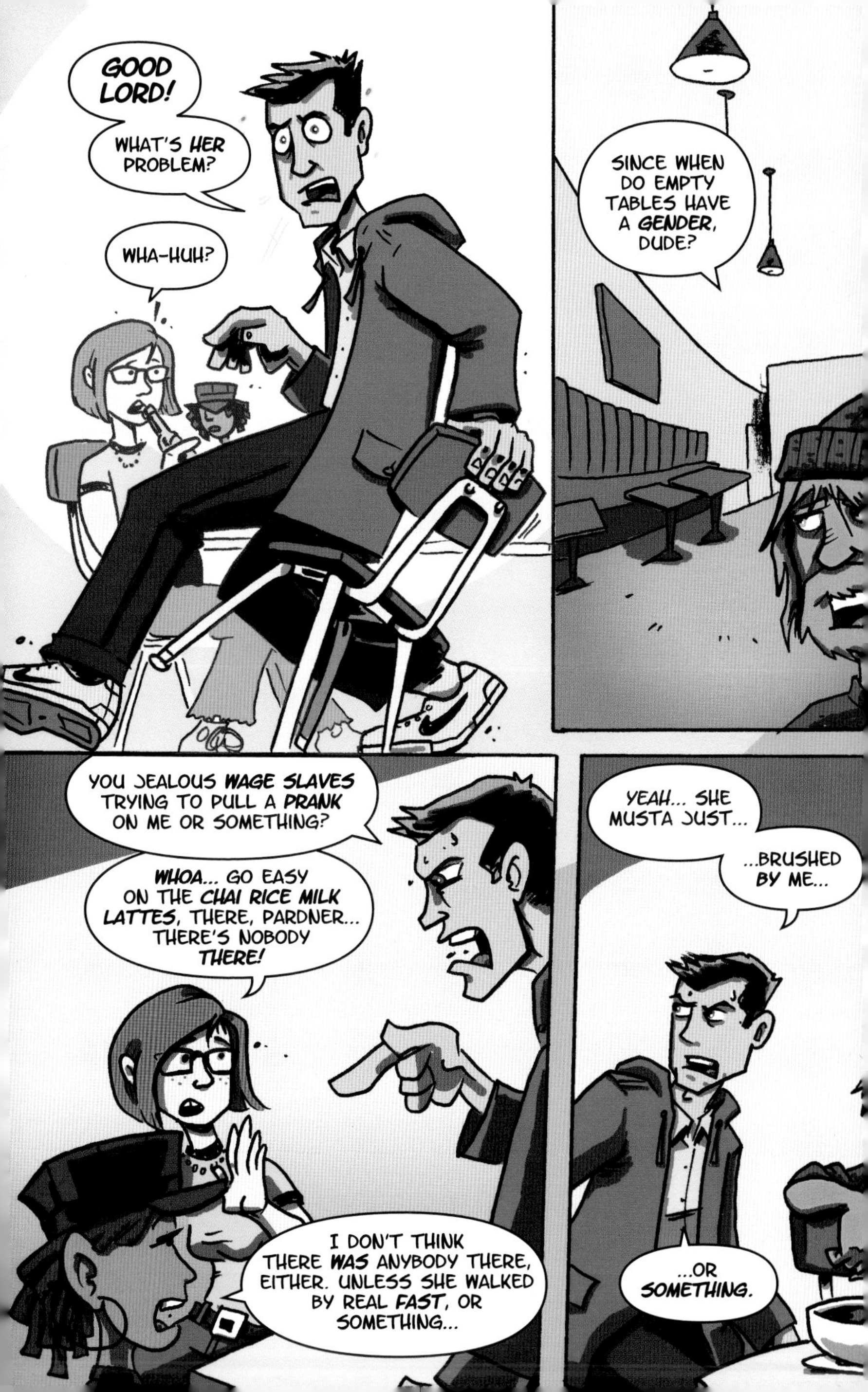
GOOD LORD!
WHAT'S HER PROBLEM?
WHA-HUH?
SINCE WHEN DO EMPTY TABLES HAVE A GENDER, DUDE?
YOU JEALOUS WAGE SLAVES TRYING TO PULL A PRANK ON ME OR SOMETHING?
WHOA... GO EASY ON THE CHAI RICE MILK LATTES, THERE, PARDNER... THERE'S NOBODY THERE!
I DON'T THINK THERE WAS ANYBODY THERE, EITHER. UNLESS SHE WALKED BY REAL FAST, OR SOMETHING...
YEAH... SHE MUSTA JUST...
...BRUSHED BY ME...
...OR SOMETHING.

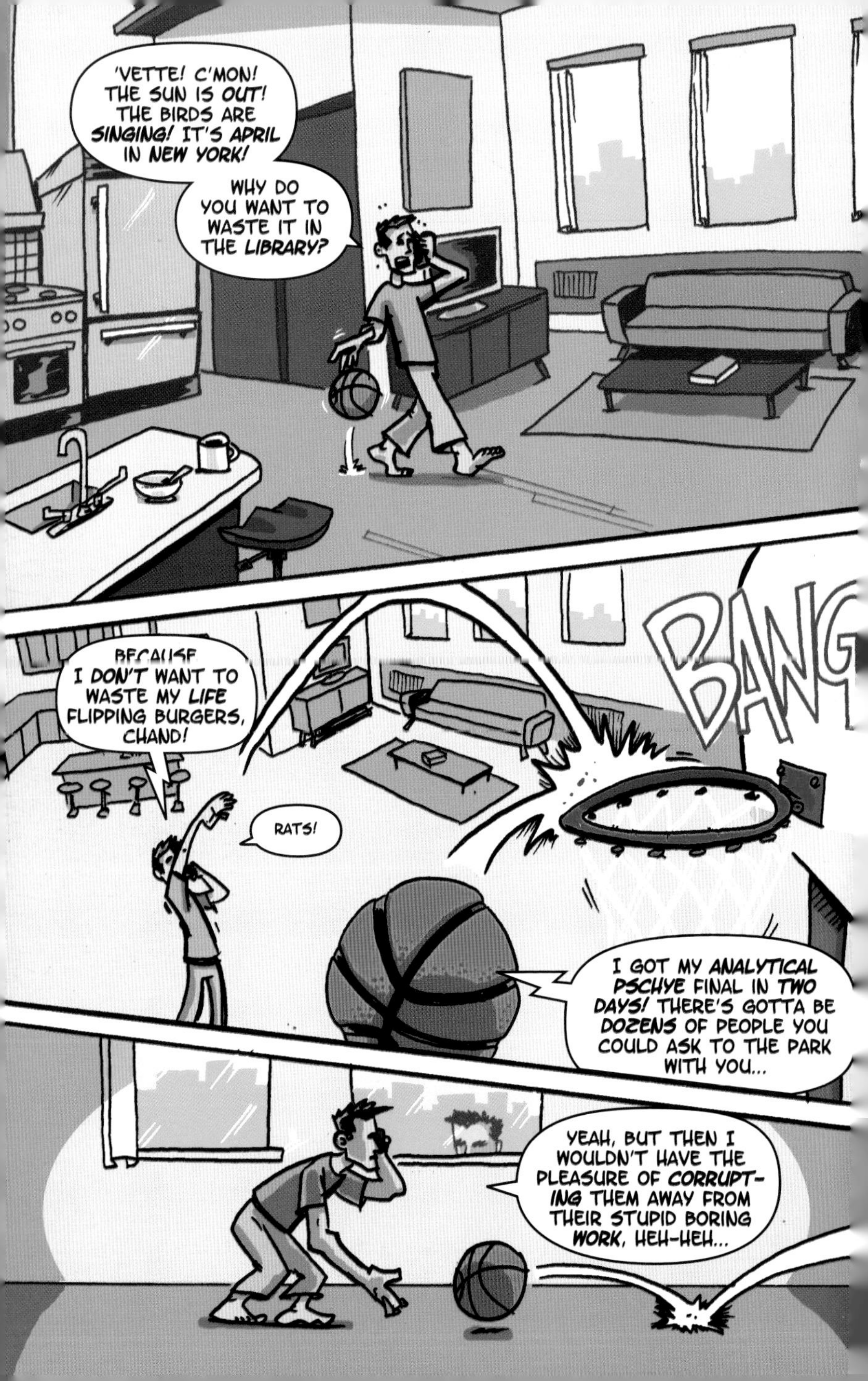
'VETTE! C'MON! THE SUN IS OUT! THE BIRDS ARE SINGING! IT'S APRIL IN NEW YORK!
WHY DO YOU WANT TO WASTE IT IN THE LIBRARY?
BECAUSE I DON'T WANT TO WASTE MY LIFE FLIPPING BURGERS, CHAND!
BANG
RATS!
I GOT MY ANALYTICAL PSCHYE FINAL IN TWO DAYS! THERE'S GOTTA BE DOZENS OF PEOPLE YOU COULD ASK TO THE PARK WITH YOU...
YEAH, BUT THEN I WOULDN'T HAVE THE PLEASURE OF CORRUPT-ING THEM AWAY FROM THEIR STUPID BORING WORK, HEH-HEH...

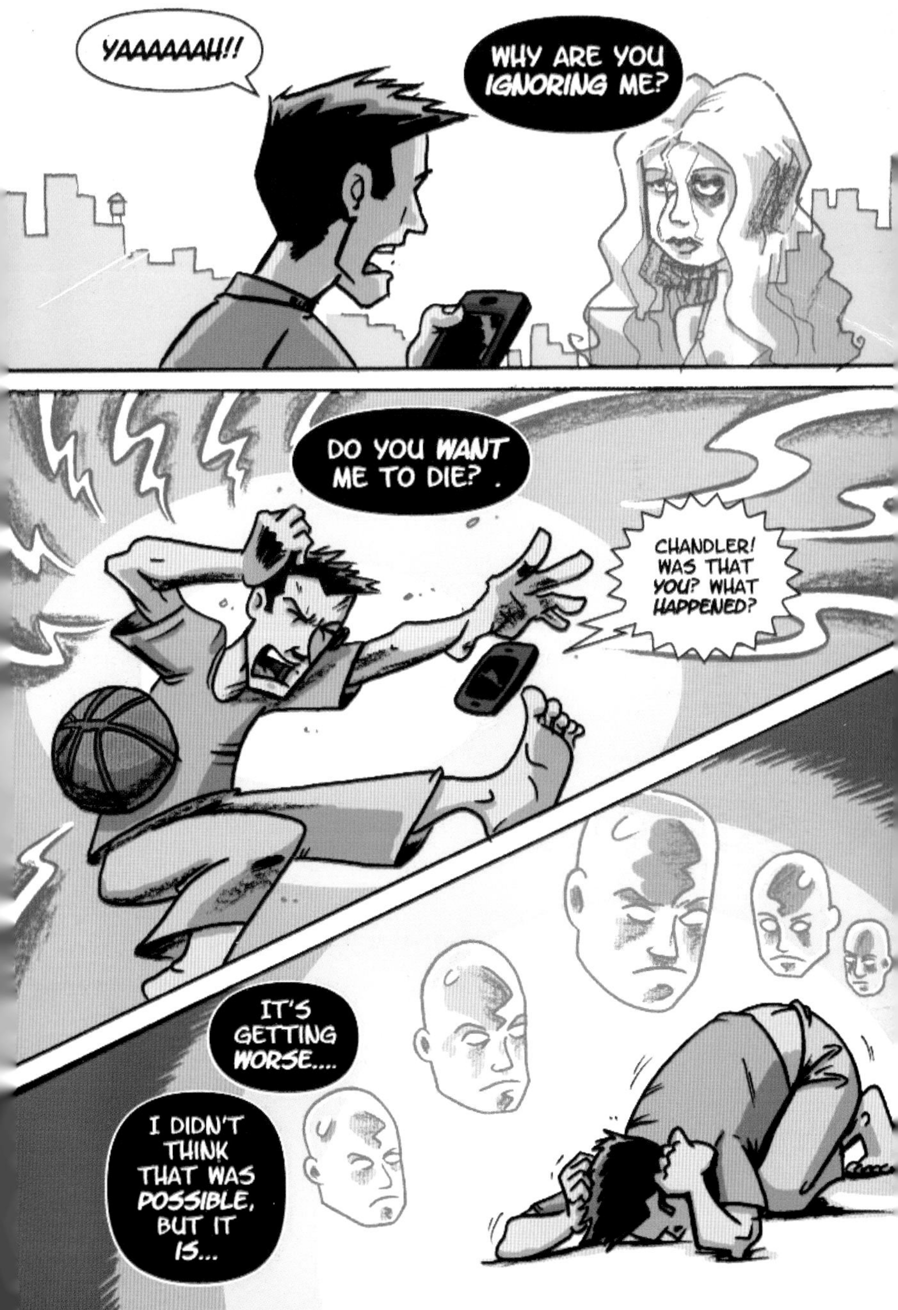
YAAAAAAH!!
WHY ARE YOU IGNORING ME?
DO YOU WANT ME TO DIE?
CHANDLER! WAS THAT YOU? WHAT HAPPENED?
IT'S GETTING WORSE....
I DIDN'T THINK THAT WAS POSSIBLE, BUT IT IS...

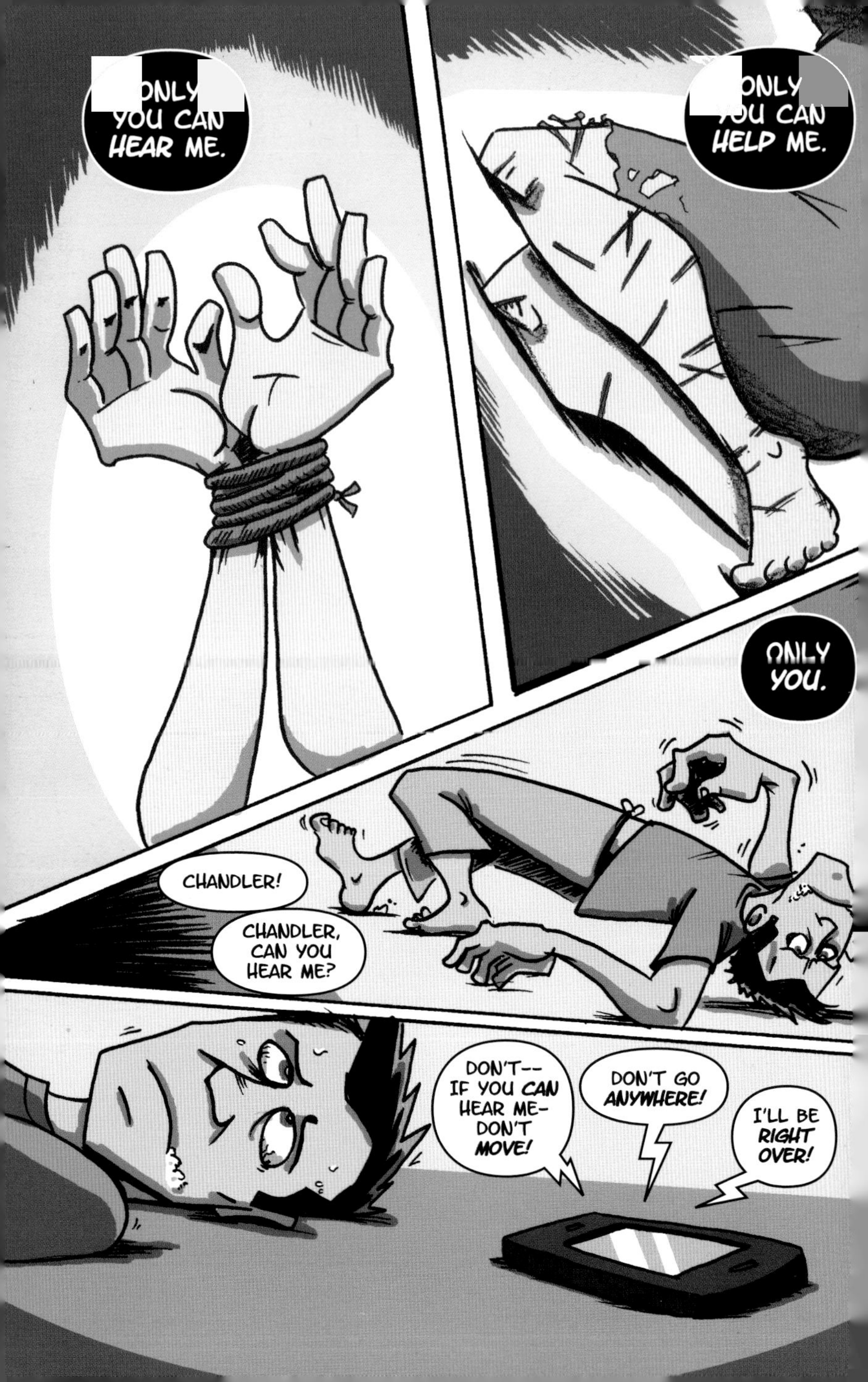
ONLY YOU CAN HEAR ME.
ONLY YOU CAN HELP ME.
ONLY YOU.
CHANDLER!
CHANDLER, CAN YOU HEAR ME?
DON'T-- IF YOU CAN HEAR ME- DON'T MOVE!
DON'T GO ANYWHERE!
I'LL BE RIGHT OVER!

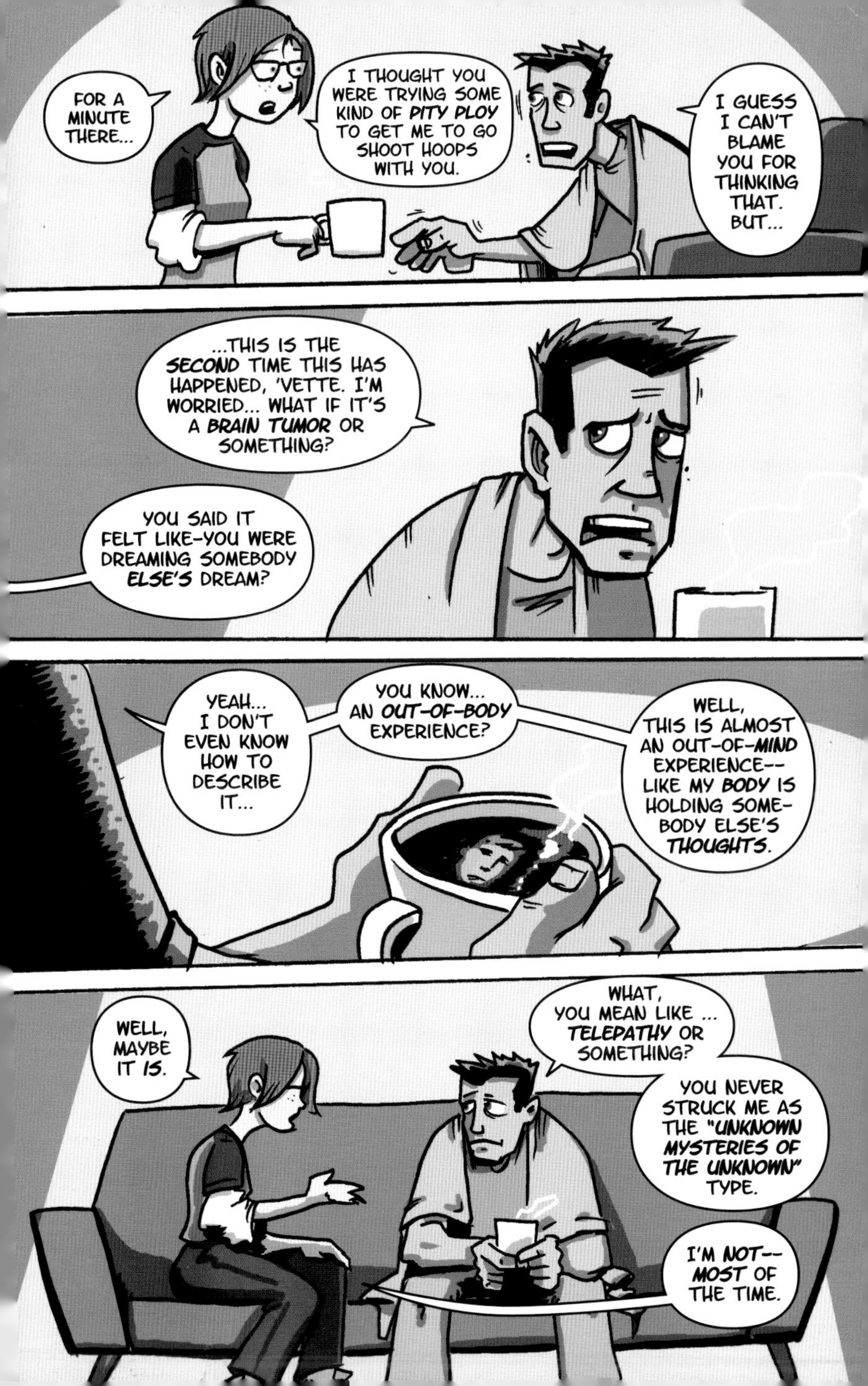
FOR A MINUTE THERE...
I THOUGHT YOU WERE TRYING SOME KIND OF PITY PLOY TO GET ME TO GO SHOOT HOOPS WITH YOU.
I GUESS I CAN'T BLAME YOU FOR THINKING THAT. BUT...
...THIS IS THE SECOND TIME THIS HAS HAPPENED, 'VETTE. I'M WORRIED... WHAT IF IT'S A BRAIN TUMOR OR SOMETHING?
YOU SAID IT FELT LIKE--YOU WERE DREAMING SOMEBODY ELSE'S DREAM?
YEAH... I DON'T EVEN KNOW HOW TO DESCRIBE IT...
YOU KNOW... AN OUT-OF-BODY EXPERIENCE?
WELL, THIS IS ALMOST AN OUT-OF-MIND EXPERIENCE-- LIKE MY BODY IS HOLDING SOMEBODY ELSE'S THOUGHTS.
WELL, MAYBE IT IS.
WHAT, YOU MEAN LIKE ... TELEPATHY OR SOMETHING?
YOU NEVER STRUCK ME AS THE "UNKNOWN MYSTERIES OF THE UNKNOWN" TYPE.
I'M NOT-- MOST OF THE TIME.

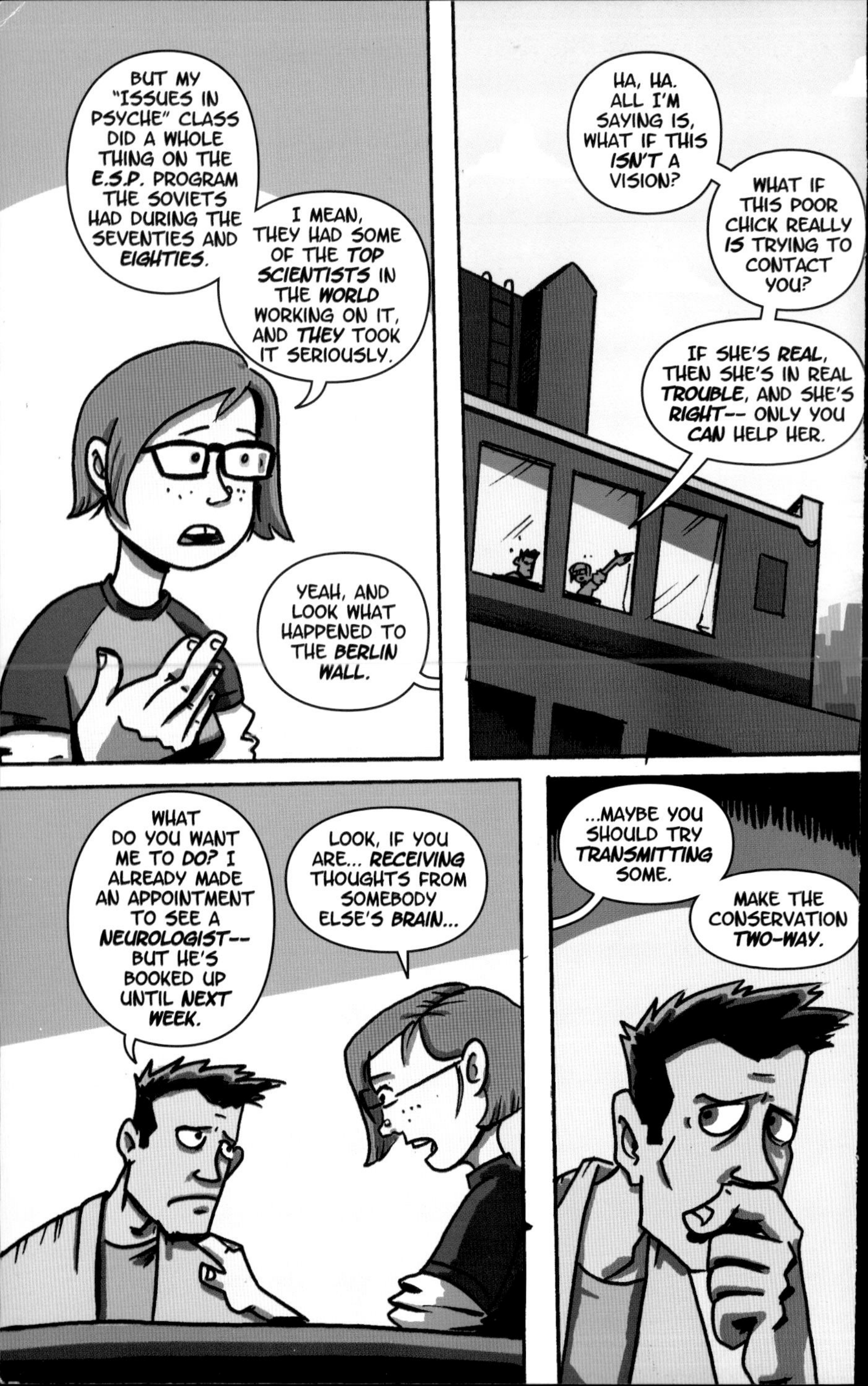
BUT MY "ISSUES IN PSYCHE" CLASS DID A WHOLE THING ON THE E.S.P. PROGRAM THE SOVIETS HAD DURING THE SEVENTIES AND EIGHTIES.
I MEAN, THEY HAD SOME OF THE TOP SCIENTISTS IN THE WORLD WORKING ON IT, AND THEY TOOK IT SERIOUSLY.
YEAH, AND LOOK WHAT HAPPENED TO THE BERLIN WALL.
HA, HA. ALL I'M SAYING IS, WHAT IF THIS ISN'T A VISION?
WHAT IF THIS POOR CHICK REALLY IS TRYING TO CONTACT YOU?
IF SHE'S REAL, THEN SHE'S IN REAL TROUBLE, AND SHE'S RIGHT-- ONLY YOU CAN HELP HER.
WHAT DO YOU WANT ME TO DO? I ALREADY MADE AN APPOINTMENT TO SEE A NEUROLOGIST-- BUT HE'S BOOKED UP UNTIL NEXT WEEK.
LOOK, IF YOU ARE... RECEIVING THOUGHTS FROM SOMEBODY ELSE'S BRAIN...
...MAYBE YOU SHOULD TRY TRANSMITTING SOME.
MAKE THE CONSERVATION TWO-WAY.

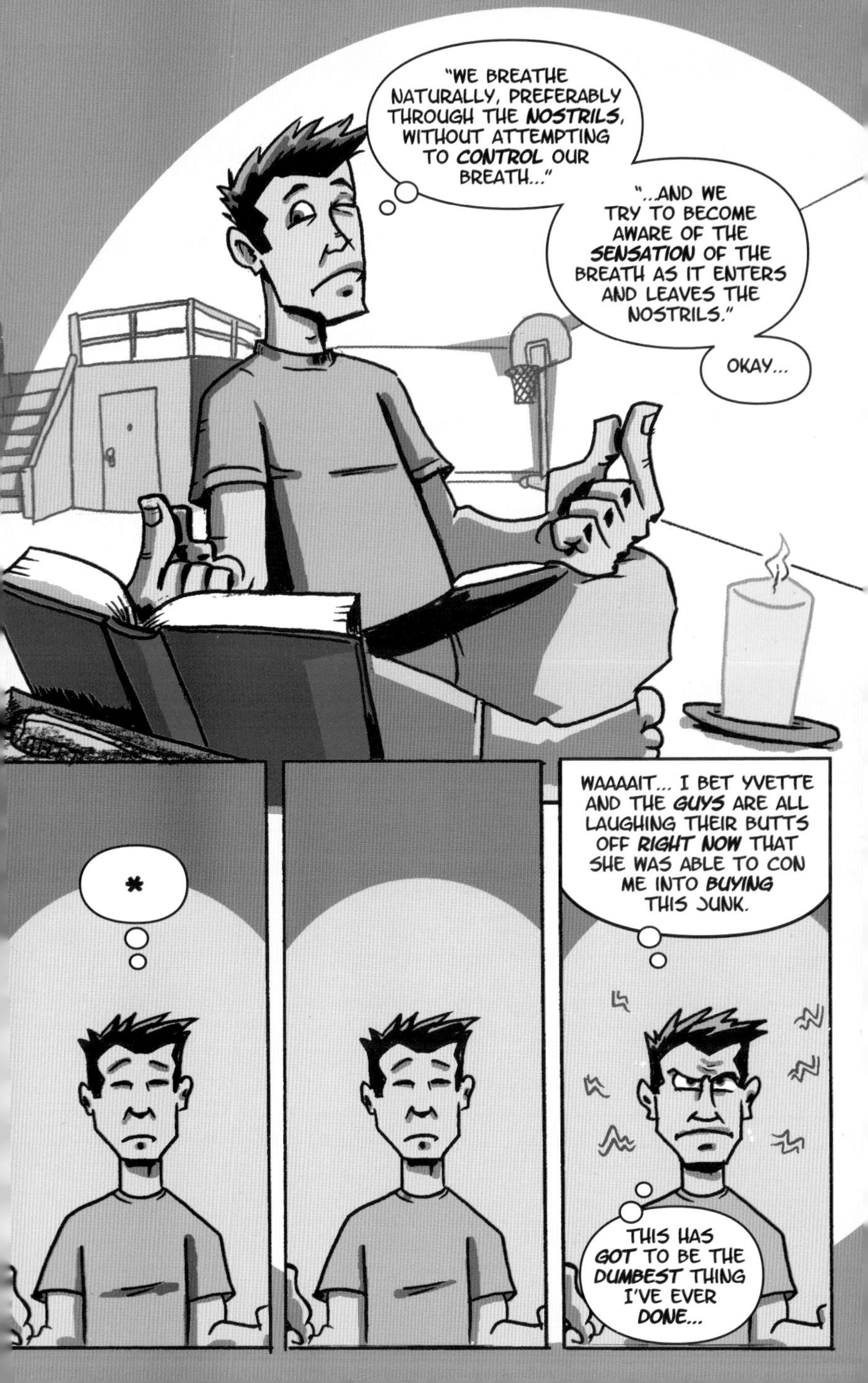

"WE BREATHE NATURALLY, PREFERABLY THROUGH THE NOSTRILS, WITHOUT ATTEMPTING TO CONTROL OUR BREATH..."
"...AND WE TRY TO BECOME AWARE OF THE SENSATION OF THE BREATH AS IT ENTERS AND LEAVES THE NOSTRILS."
OKAY...
*
WAAAAIT... I BET YVETTE AND THE GUYS ARE ALL LAUGHING THEIR BUTTS OFF RIGHT NOW THAT SHE WAS ABLE TO CON ME INTO BUYING THIS JUNK.
THIS HAS GOT TO BE THE DUMBEST THING I'VE EVER DONE...

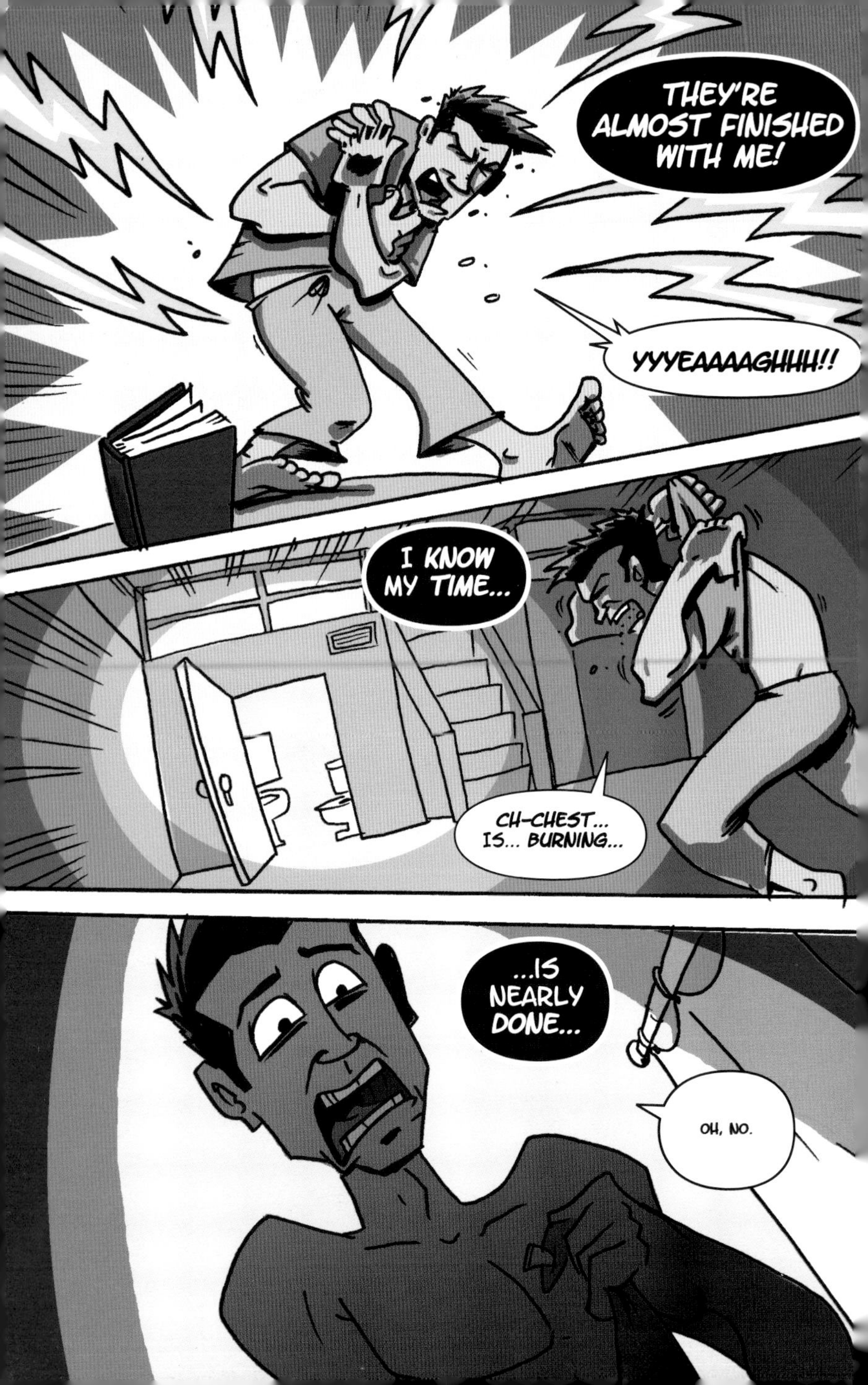
THEY'RE ALMOST FINISHED WITH ME!
YYYEAAAAGHHH!!
I KNOW MY TIME...
CH-CHEST... IS... BURNING...
...IS NEARLY DONE...
OH, NO.

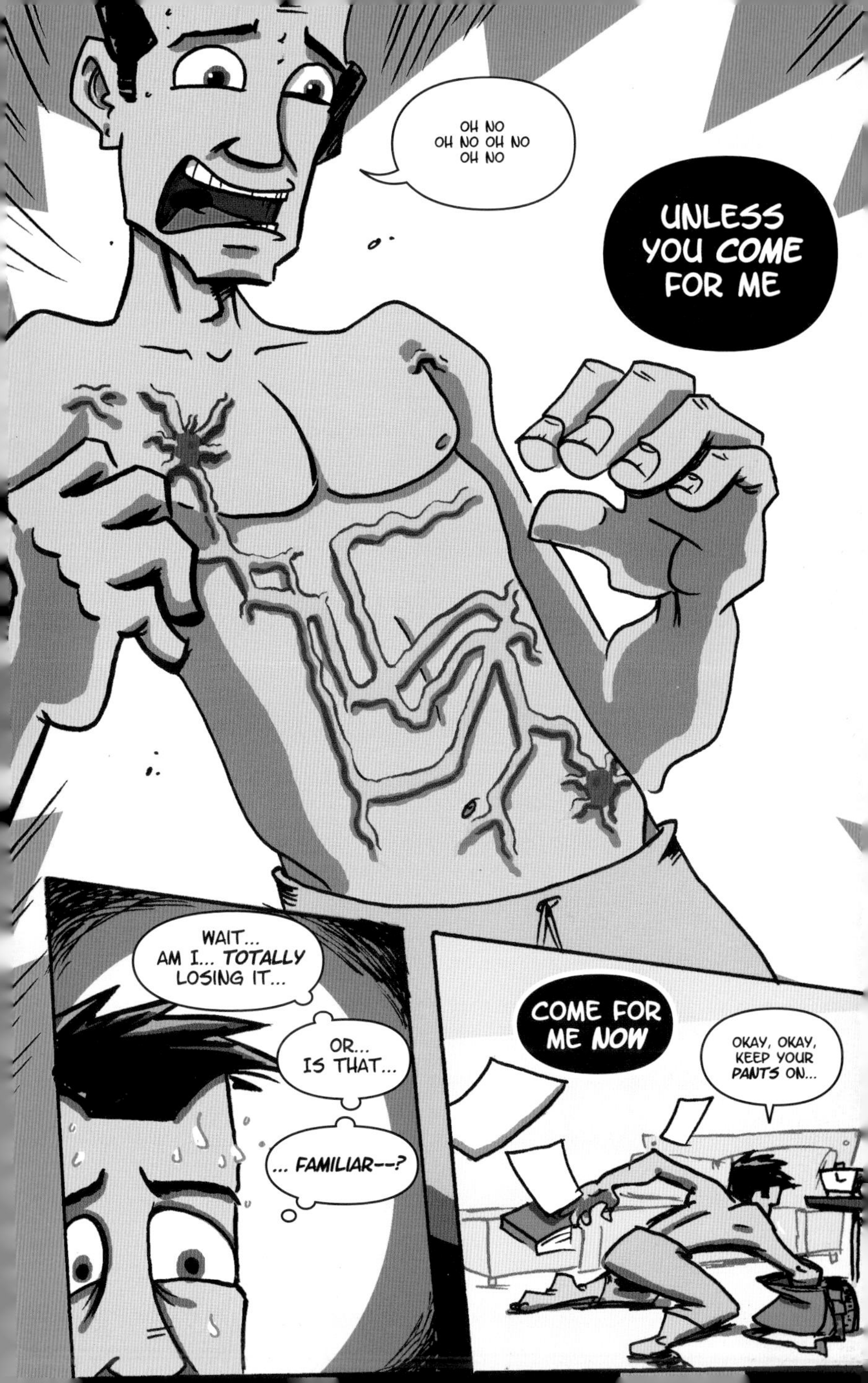
OH NO
OH NO OH NO
OH NO
UNLESS YOU COME FOR ME
WAIT... AM I... TOTALLY LOSING IT...
OR... IS THAT...
... FAMILIAR--?
COME FOR ME NOW
OKAY, OKAY, KEEP YOUR PANTS ON...

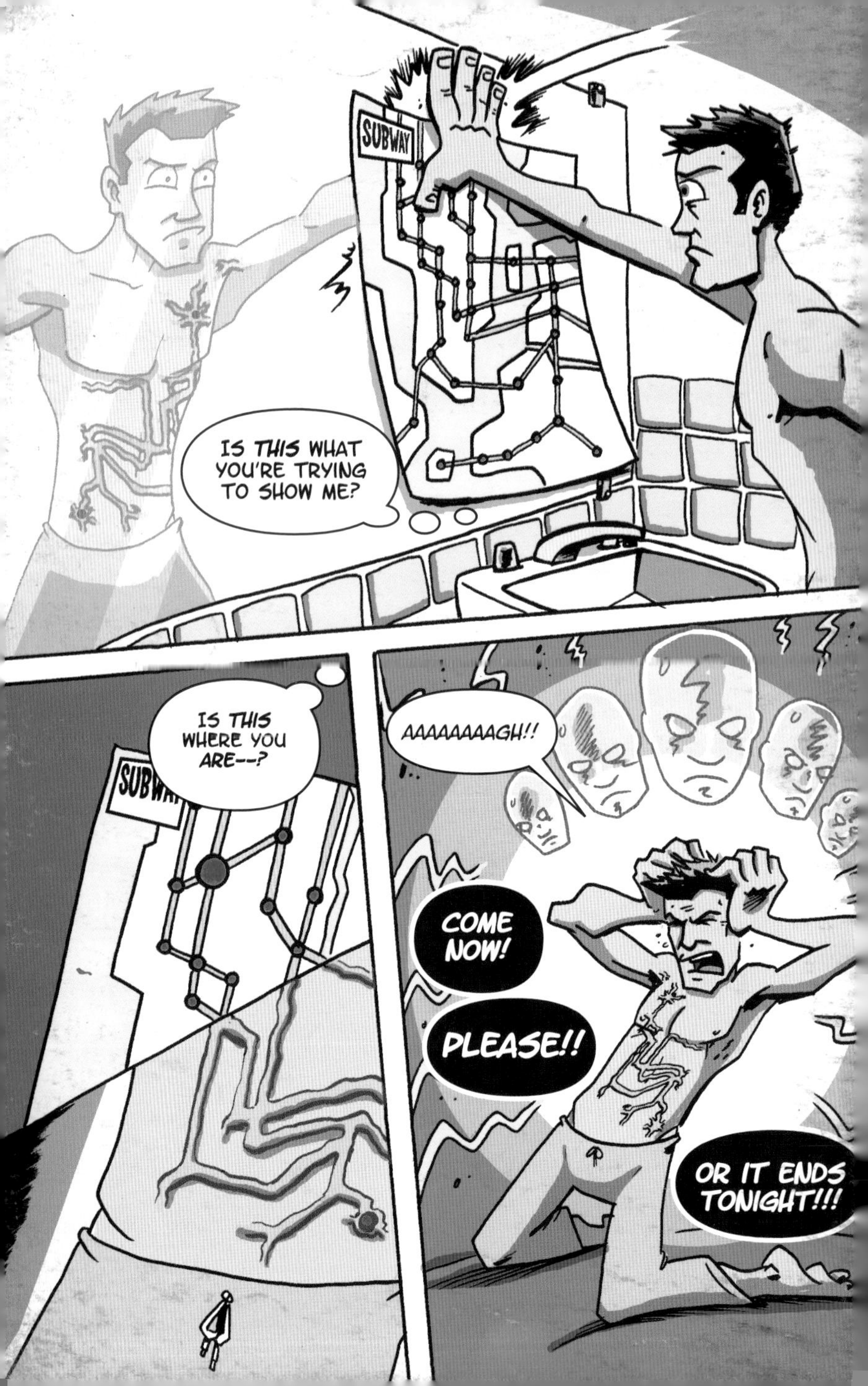
SUBWAY
IS THIS WHAT YOU'RE TRYING TO SHOW ME?
IS THIS WHERE YOU ARE--?
SUBWAY
AAAAAAAAGH!!
COME NOW!
PLEASE!!
OR IT ENDS TONIGHT!!!

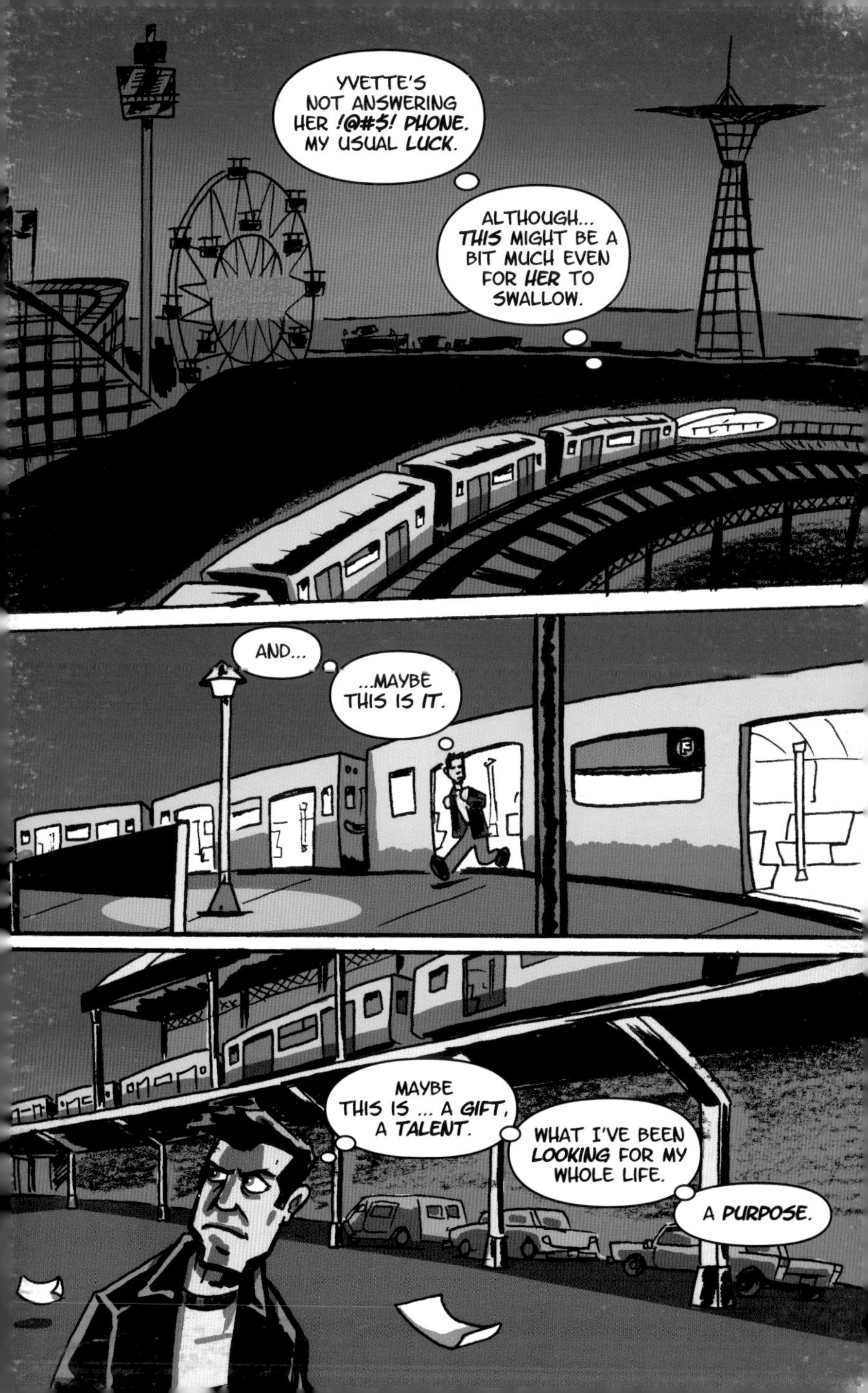
YVETTE'S NOT ANSWERING HER !@#$! PHONE. MY USUAL LUCK.
ALTHOUGH... THIS MIGHT BE A BIT MUCH EVEN FOR HER TO SWALLOW.
AND...
...MAYBE THIS IS IT.
MAYBE THIS IS ... A GIFT, A TALENT.
WHAT I'VE BEEN LOOKING FOR MY WHOLE LIFE.
A PURPOSE.

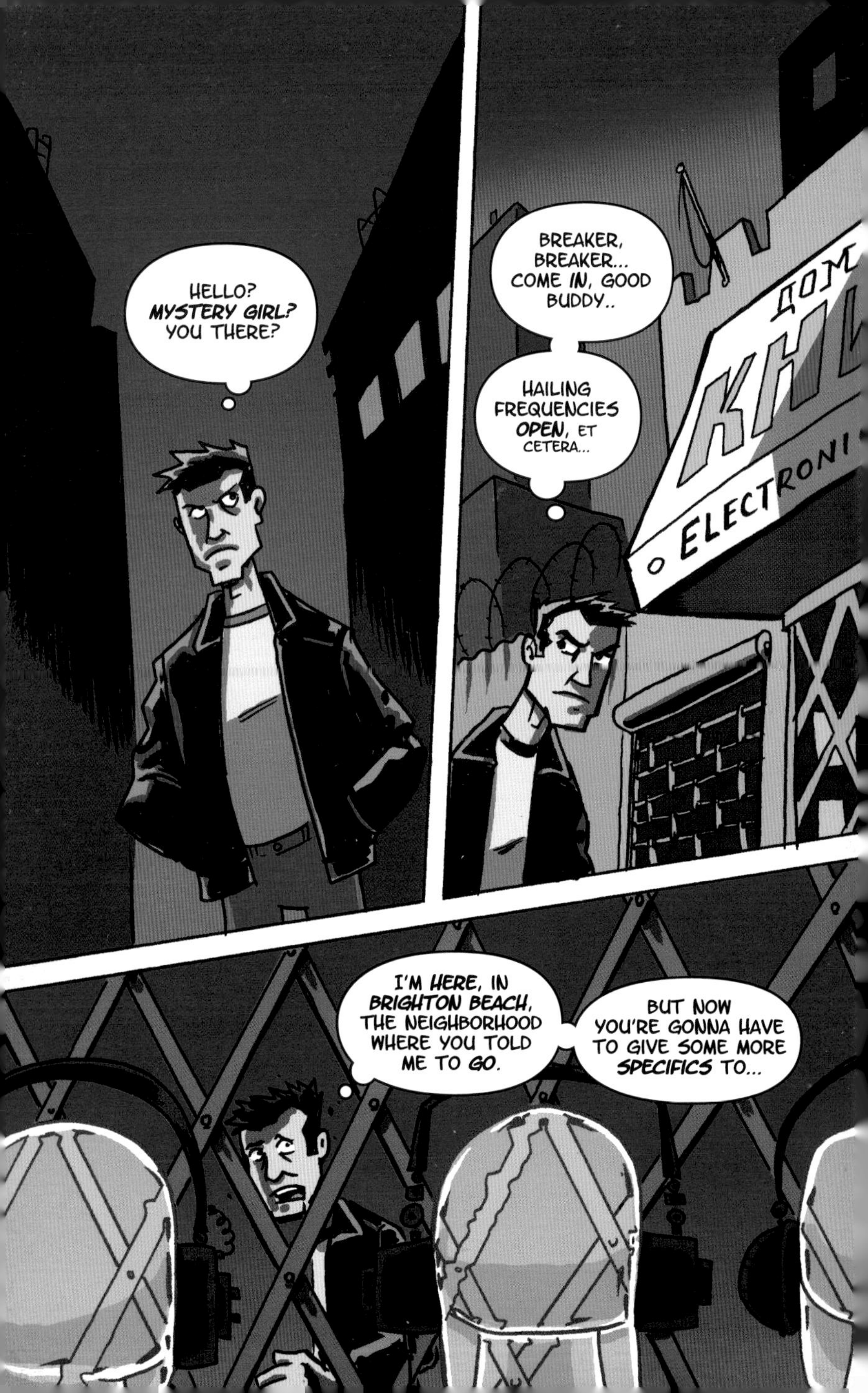
HELLO? *MYSTERY GIRL?* YOU THERE?
BREAKER, BREAKER... COME *IN*, GOOD BUDDY..
HAILING FREQUENCIES *OPEN*, ET CETERA...
ДОМ
ELECTRONI
I'M *HERE*, IN *BRIGHTON BEACH*, THE NEIGHBORHOOD WHERE YOU TOLD ME TO *GO*.
BUT NOW YOU'RE GONNA HAVE TO GIVE SOME MORE *SPECIFICS* TO...

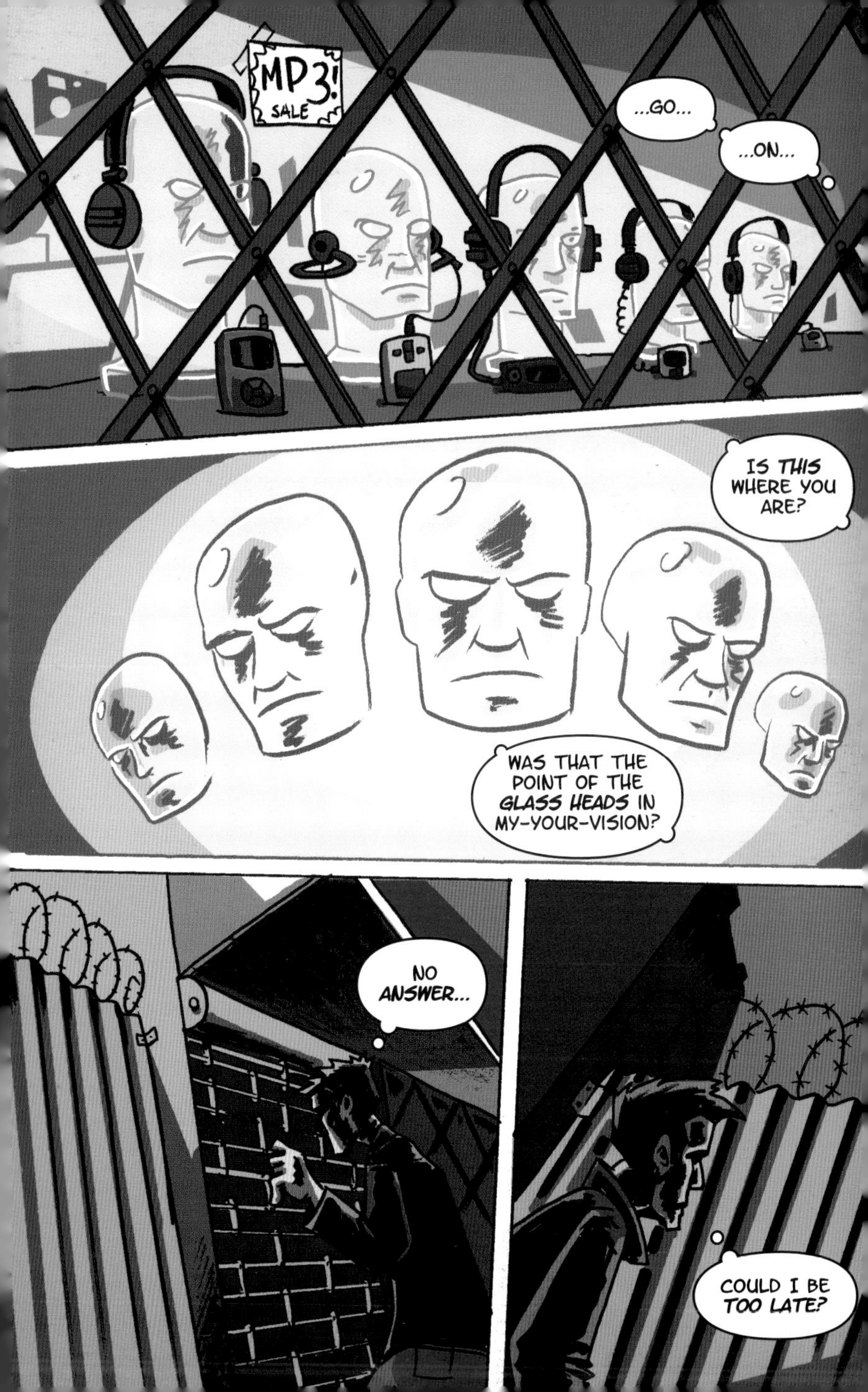
MP3! SALE
...GO...
...ON...
IS THIS WHERE YOU ARE?
WAS THAT THE POINT OF THE GLASS HEADS IN MY-YOUR-VISION?
NO ANSWER...
COULD I BE TOO LATE?

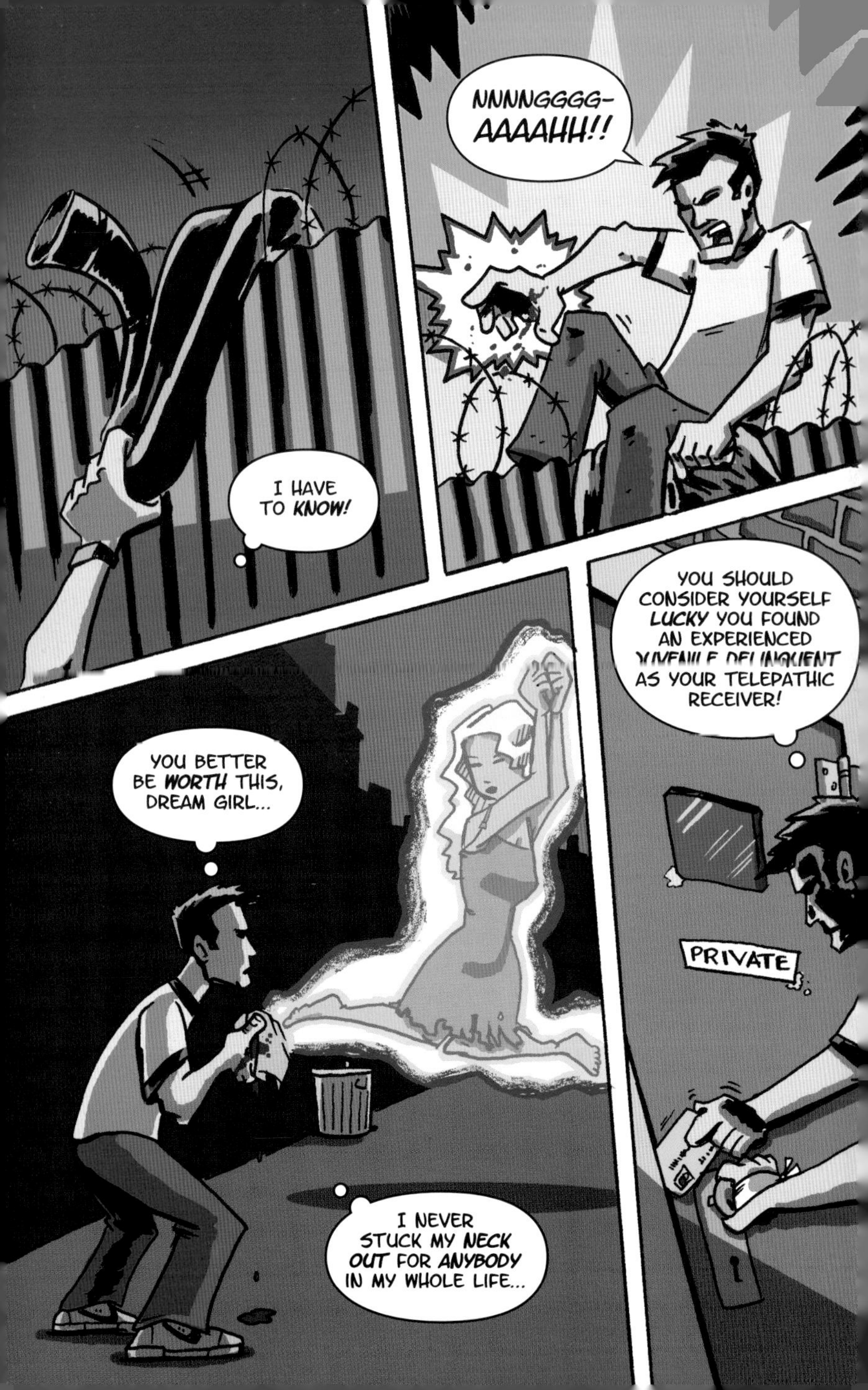
I HAVE TO KNOW!
NNNNGGGG-AAAAHH!!
YOU BETTER BE WORTH THIS, DREAM GIRL...
I NEVER STUCK MY NECK OUT FOR ANYBODY IN MY WHOLE LIFE...
YOU SHOULD CONSIDER YOURSELF LUCKY YOU FOUND AN EXPERIENCED JUVENILE DELINQUENT AS YOUR TELEPATHIC RECEIVER!
PRIVATE

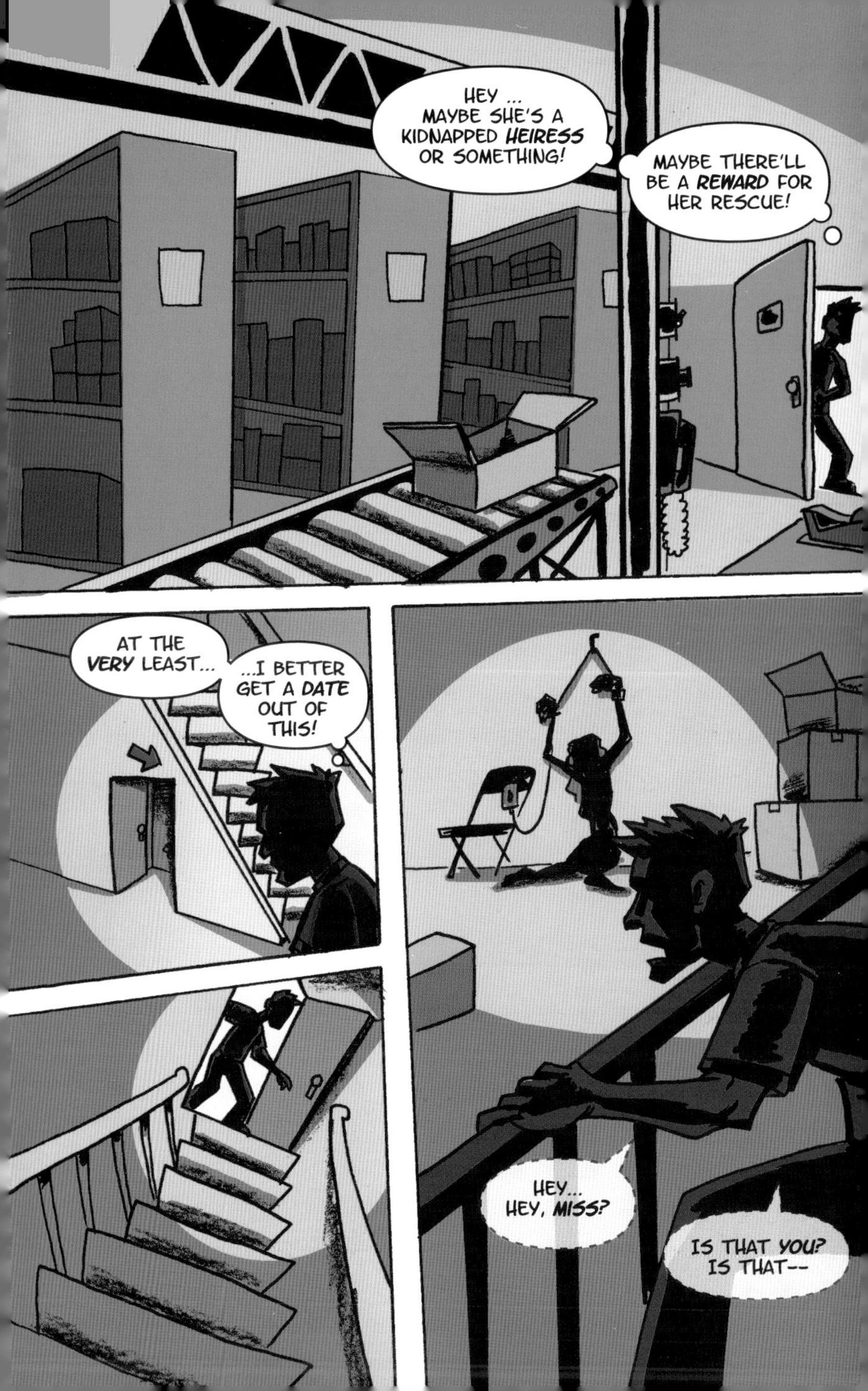
HEY ... MAYBE SHE'S A KIDNAPPED HEIRESS OR SOMETHING!
MAYBE THERE'LL BE A REWARD FOR HER RESCUE!
AT THE VERY LEAST...
...I BETTER GET A DATE OUT OF THIS!
HEY... HEY, MISS?
IS THAT YOU? IS THAT--

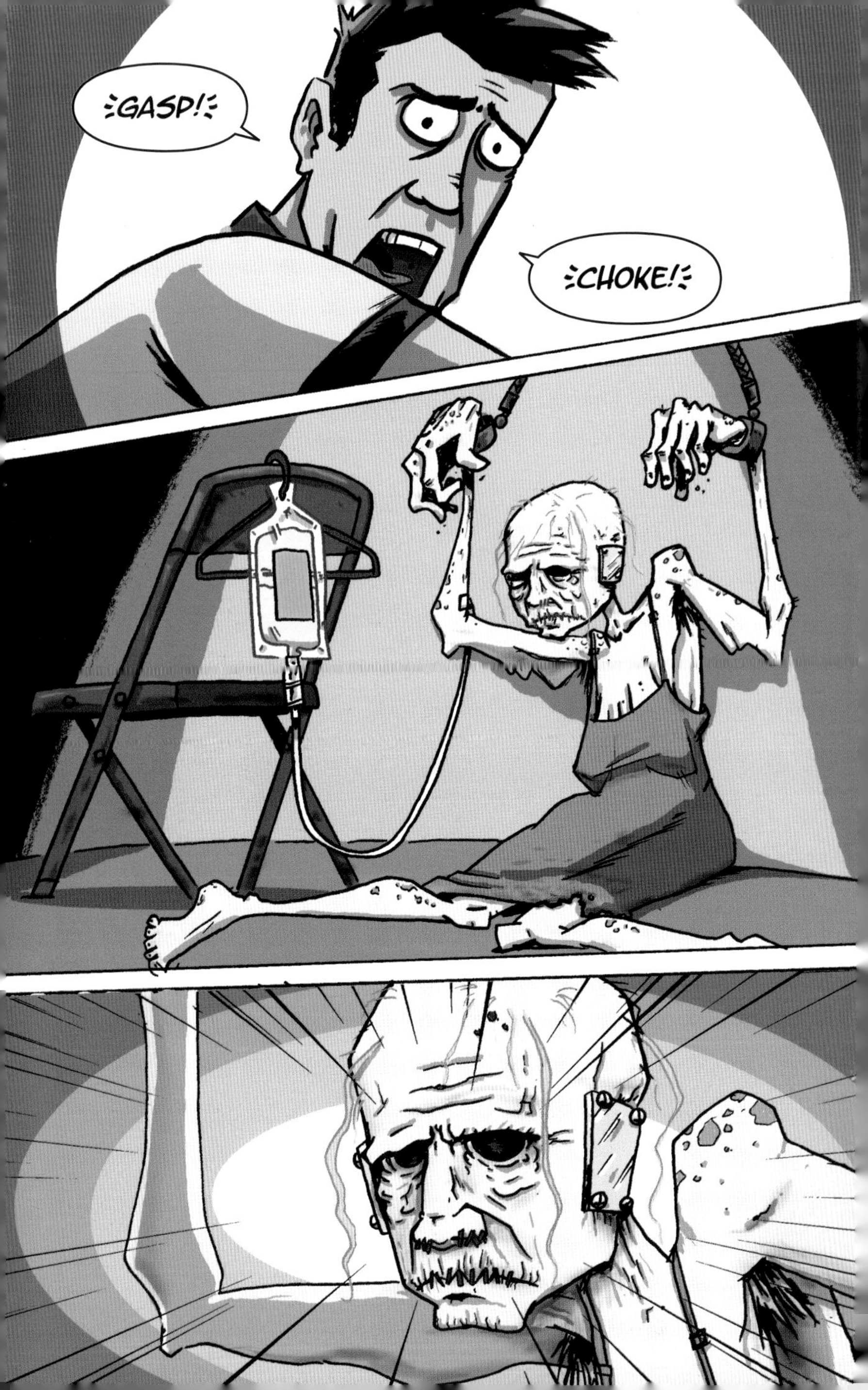
GASP!
CHOKE!

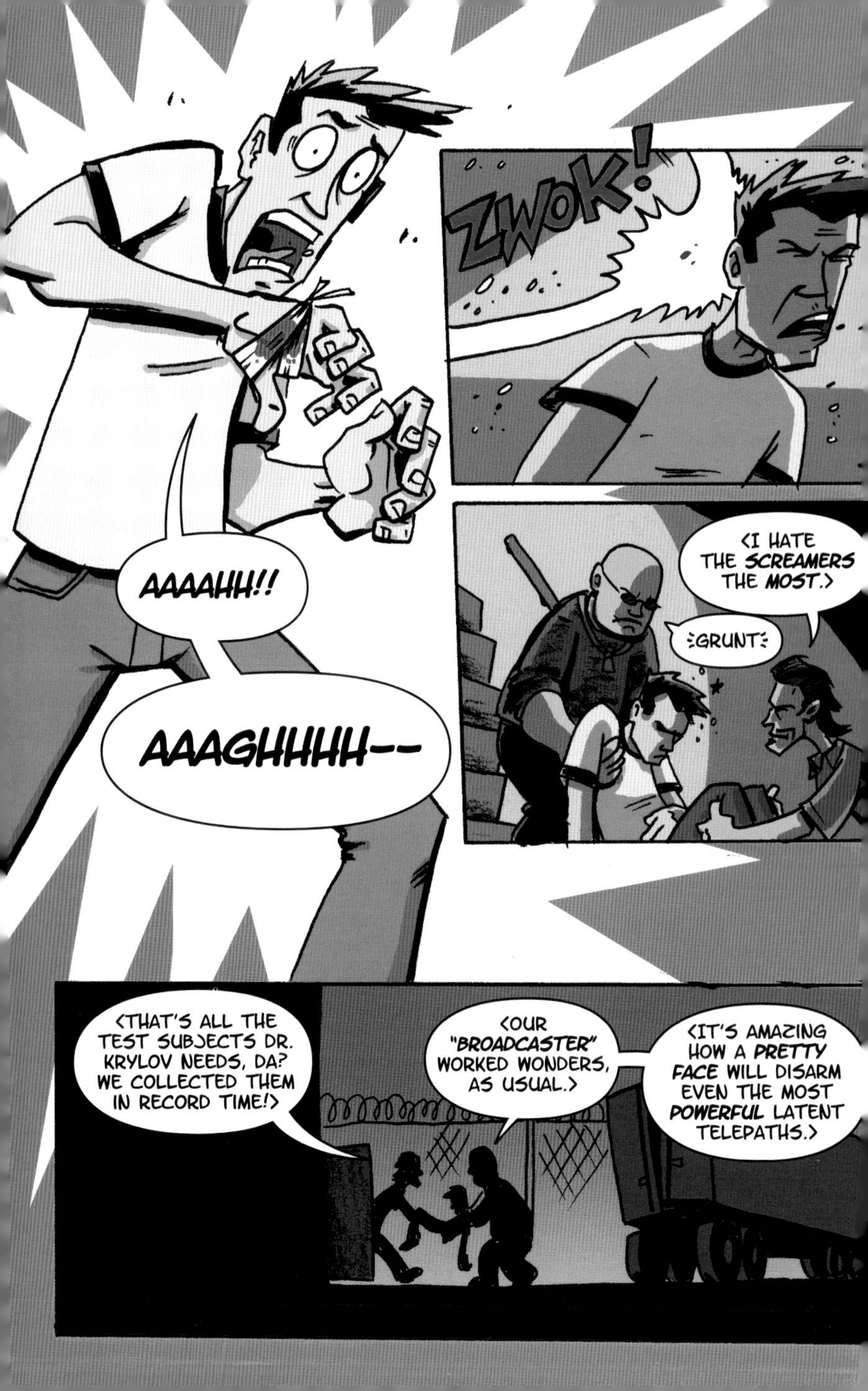
ZWOK!
AAAAHH!!
AAAGHHHH--
<I HATE THE SCREAMERS THE MOST.>
GRUNT
<THAT'S ALL THE TEST SUBJECTS DR. KRYLOV NEEDS, DA? WE COLLECTED THEM IN RECORD TIME!>
<OUR "BROADCASTER" WORKED WONDERS, AS USUAL.>
<IT'S AMAZING HOW A PRETTY FACE WILL DISARM EVEN THE MOST POWERFUL LATENT TELEPATHS.>

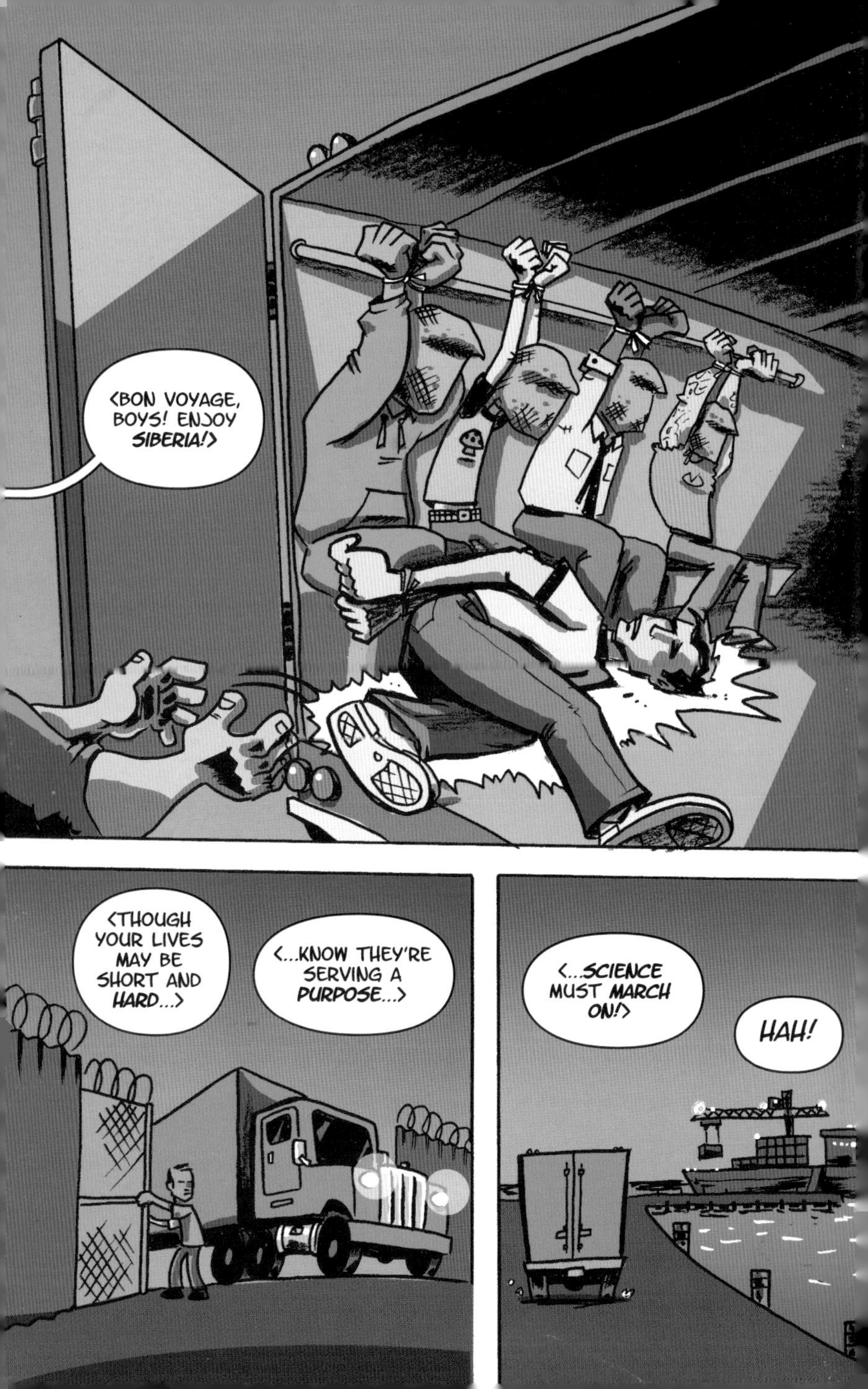
<BON VOYAGE, BOYS! ENJOY SIBERIA!>
<THOUGH YOUR LIVES MAY BE SHORT AND HARD...>
<...KNOW THEY'RE SERVING A PURPOSE...>
<...SCIENCE MUST MARCH ON!>
HAH!

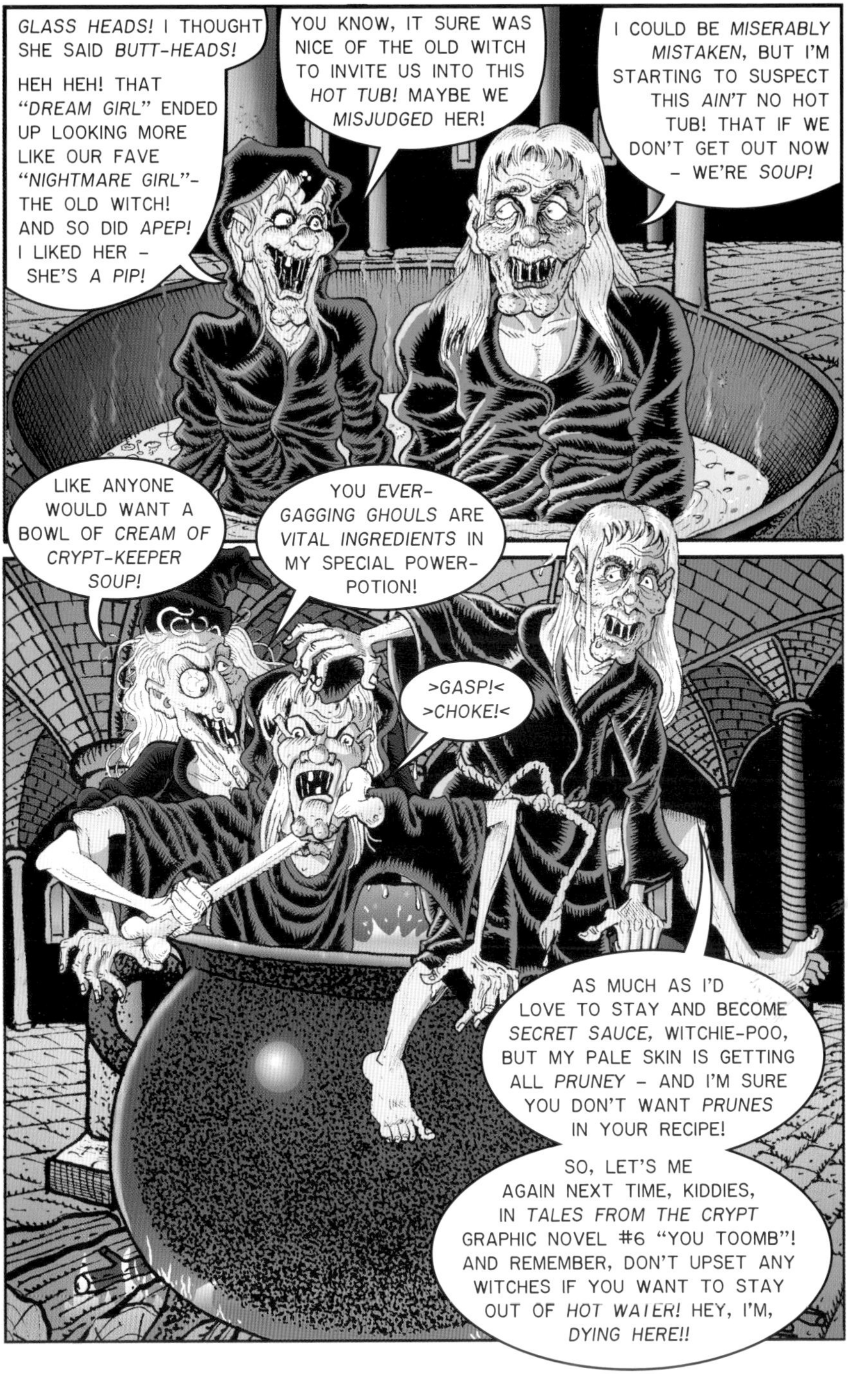
GLASS HEADS! I THOUGHT SHE SAID BUTT-HEADS!
HEH HEH! THAT "DREAM GIRL" ENDED UP LOOKING MORE LIKE OUR FAVE "NIGHTMARE GIRL"- THE OLD WITCH! AND SO DID APEP! I LIKED HER - SHE'S A PIP!
YOU KNOW, IT SURE WAS NICE OF THE OLD WITCH TO INVITE US INTO THIS HOT TUB! MAYBE WE MISJUDGED HER!
I COULD BE MISERABLY MISTAKEN, BUT I'M STARTING TO SUSPECT THIS AIN'T NO HOT TUB! THAT IF WE DON'T GET OUT NOW - WE'RE SOUP!
LIKE ANYONE WOULD WANT A BOWL OF CREAM OF CRYPT-KEEPER SOUP!
YOU EVER-GAGGING GHOULS ARE VITAL INGREDIENTS IN MY SPECIAL POWER-POTION!
>GASP!< >CHOKE!<
AS MUCH AS I'D LOVE TO STAY AND BECOME SECRET SAUCE, WITCHIE-POO, BUT MY PALE SKIN IS GETTING ALL PRUNEY - AND I'M SURE YOU DON'T WANT PRUNES IN YOUR RECIPE!
SO, LET'S ME AGAIN NEXT TIME, KIDDIES, IN TALES FROM THE CRYPT GRAPHIC NOVEL #6 "YOU TOOMB"! AND REMEMBER, DON'T UPSET ANY WITCHES IF YOU WANT TO STAY OUT OF HOT WATER! HEY, I'M, DYING HERE!!

THE HARDY BOYS

A NEW GRAPHIC NOVEL EVERY 3 MONTHS!

#10 "A Hardy Day's Night"
ISBN - 978-1-59707-070-6
#11 "Abracadeath"
ISBN - 978-1-59707-080-5
#12 "Dude Ranch O' Death"
ISBN - 978-1-59707-088-1
#13 "The Deadliest Stunt"
ISBN - 978-1-59707-102-4
NEW! #14 "Haley Danielle's Top Eight!"
ISBN – 978-159707-113-0
Also available – Hardy Boys #1-9
All: Pocket sized, 96-112 pp., full-color, $7.95
Also available in hardcover! $12.95

NEW!

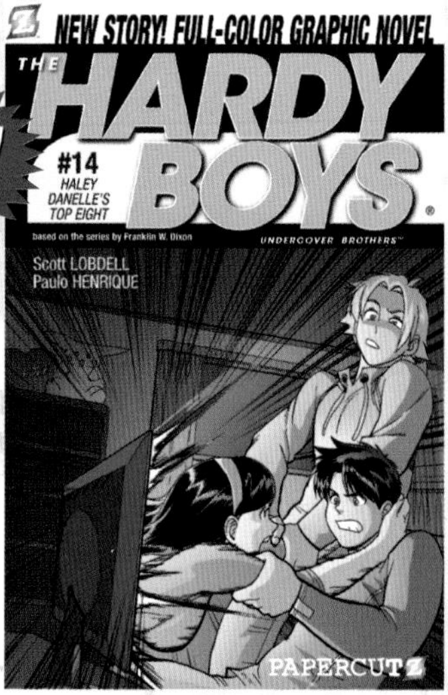
NEW STORY! FULL-COLOR GRAPHIC NOVEL
THE HARDY BOYS
#14
HALEY DANELLE'S TOP EIGHT
based on the series by Franklin W. Dixon
UNDERCOVER BROTHERS
Scott LOBDELL
Paulo HENRIQUE
PAPERCUTZ

THE HARDY BOYS
Graphic Novels #1-4 Box Set
ISBN – 978-1-59707-040-9
THE HARDY BOYS
Graphic Novels #5-8 Box Set
ISBN – 978-1-59707-075-1
THE HARDY BOYS
Graphic Novels #9-12 Box Set
ISBN-978-1-59707-125-3
All: Full-color, $29.95

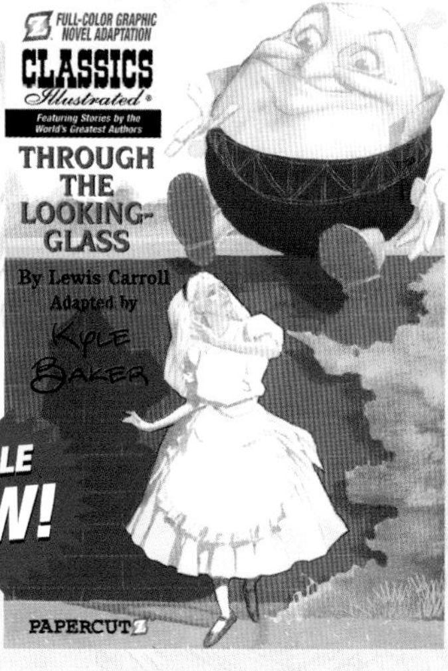
FULL-COLOR GRAPHIC NOVEL ADAPTATION
CLASSICS Illustrated
Featuring Stories by the World's Greatest Authors
THROUGH THE LOOKING-GLASS
By Lewis Carroll
Adapted by
KYLE BAKER
PAPERCUTZ

CLASSICS *Illustrated*

#1 "Great Expectations"
ISBN 978-159707-097-3
#2 "The Invisible Man"
ISBN 978-159707-106-2
NEW! #3 "Through the Looking Glass"
ISBN 978-159707-115-4
All: 6 1/2 x 9, 56 pp., full-color, $9.95

ON SALE NOW!

Please add $4.00 postage and handling. Add $1.00 for each additional title.
Make check payable to NBM publishing.
Send To:
Papercutz, 40 Exchange Place, Suite 1308,
New York, New York 10005, 1-800-886-1223
www.papercutz.com

WATCH OUT FOR PAPERCUTZ

Welcome to a scary edition of the Papercutz Backpages, the place to find out all the latest news about the graphic novel publishers of THE HARDY BOYS, NANCY DREW, TALES FROM THE CRYPT, BIONICLE, and CLASSICS ILLUSTRATED. I'm Jim Salicrup, your Editor-in-Chief, and prime Papercutz promoter! We've got lots to talk about, so let's get right to it...

Things have taken a scary turn here at Papercutz! Don't panic -- we're not talking about any of our graphic novels suddenly vanishing from bookstore shelves! We're not talking that kind of scary! Thanks to your continued support, our sales are stronger than ever, and if any of our titles have vanished off the shelves, it's only because they are temporarily sold out! No, we're talking TALES FROM THE CRYPT scary -- and how it's suddenly seeming to take over the pages of CLASSICS ILLUSTRATED and CLASSICS ILLUSTRATED DELUXE!

CLASSICS ILLUSTRATED #4 features world-famous cartoonist Gahan Wilson's creepy cartoons illustrated Edgar Allan Poe's "The Raven and Other Poems." And if that wasn't scary enough, CLASSICS ILLUSTRATED DELUXE #3 features an all-new adaptation by Marion Mousse of Mary Shelly's monster-masterwork "Frankenstein"!

Why have our CLASSICS ILLUSTRATED titles turned into a virtual vault of horror? The answer is obvious! After all, what is a "classic" if not a story so powerfully compelling that it leads to countless retellings? But we suspect that you've never experienced Poe's poems as seen through macabre cartoonist Gahan Wilson's bloodshot eyes, or the tale of Victor Frankenstein and his monster as dramatically brought to life, so to speak, by the dark visions of Marion Mousse.

Despite how many times the Frankenstein story has been told, it's as thought-provoking and as frightening now as the day it was when originally published in 1818. If you've never read the original novel you may be surprised that it's not the over-the-top crazy story so many adaptations may imply, but rather it's a serious tale tackling many major issues. Mousse takes great pains to restore many of Victor Frankenstein's motivations that lead to his "mad quest" to solve the ultimate mystery of life and death (as opposed to simply creating a monster).

In the pages that follow you'll see for yourself, the skill and artistry that Mousse brings to faithfully adapting this terrifying classic. Keep in mind, that the pages of CLASSICS ILLUSTRATED DELUXE are much larger than these pages, so to truly savor these pages, and to avoid eyestrain, be sure to pick up CLASSICS ILLUSTRATED DELUXE #3!

Thanks,

Jim

Caricature drawn
by Rick Parker

THE OLD EDITOR

FOR MORE THAN A YEAR, I STUDIED ALL THE FORMS AND CONSEQUENCES OF DEATH: THE FLESH DECOMPOSING, SLOWLY ROTTING...

...THE MATTER OF WHICH WE'RE ALL MADE, DEGRADING AND WASTING AWAY BEFORE VANISHING AS THOUGH THROUGH MAGIC.

FRANKENSTEIN...

...OUR LOCAL CELEBRITY HARD AT WORK.

...

DOCTOR KREMPE...

YOUR WHIMSICAL THEORIES ARE THE MOCKERY OF ALL INGOLSTADT, FRANKENSTEIN!

WHY THEN? IF YOU PREFER DIGGING THROUGH FLESH TO DELIGHTING IN THAT CREDULOUS AUDIENCE.

STILL CHASING AFTER YOUR MAD HEROES?! CORNELIUS AGRIPPA, PARACELSUS...

DON'T TELL ME THAT YOU'RE STILL A DISCIPLE OF THOSE COOKED-UP ABSURDITIES?!

PHILLIPUS AUREOLUS VON HOHENHEIM, KNOWN AS PARACELSUS, EMINENT ALCHEMIST, WHO CLAIMED TO HAVE EXPERIMENTED ON THE FAMOUS ELIXIR OF ETERNAL YOUTH AND CREATED...

...THE HOMUNCULUS, A SMALL LIVING BEING IN THE FORM OF A HUMAN!

I KNOW ALL THAT, FRANKENSTEIN!

SO YOU CONTINUE AND CONTINUE TO PERSIST! YOU PERSIST IN RIDICULING YOUR PROFESSORS, IN DISCREDITING OUR HONORABLE INSTITUTION?!!

WELL THEN! SO, I HEREAFTER FORBID YOU TO USE COURSE MATERIAL SUCH AS HUMAN REMAINS OUTSIDE OF YOUR COURSES!

UNTIL NOW, I'D MADE NO ASSUMPTIONS ABOUT YOUR CHARACTER, YOUNG MAN.

YES, I WAS HESITATING...I WAS HESITATING BETWEEN A YAHOO AND AN ENLIGHTENED SCIENTIST. NOW I KNOW.

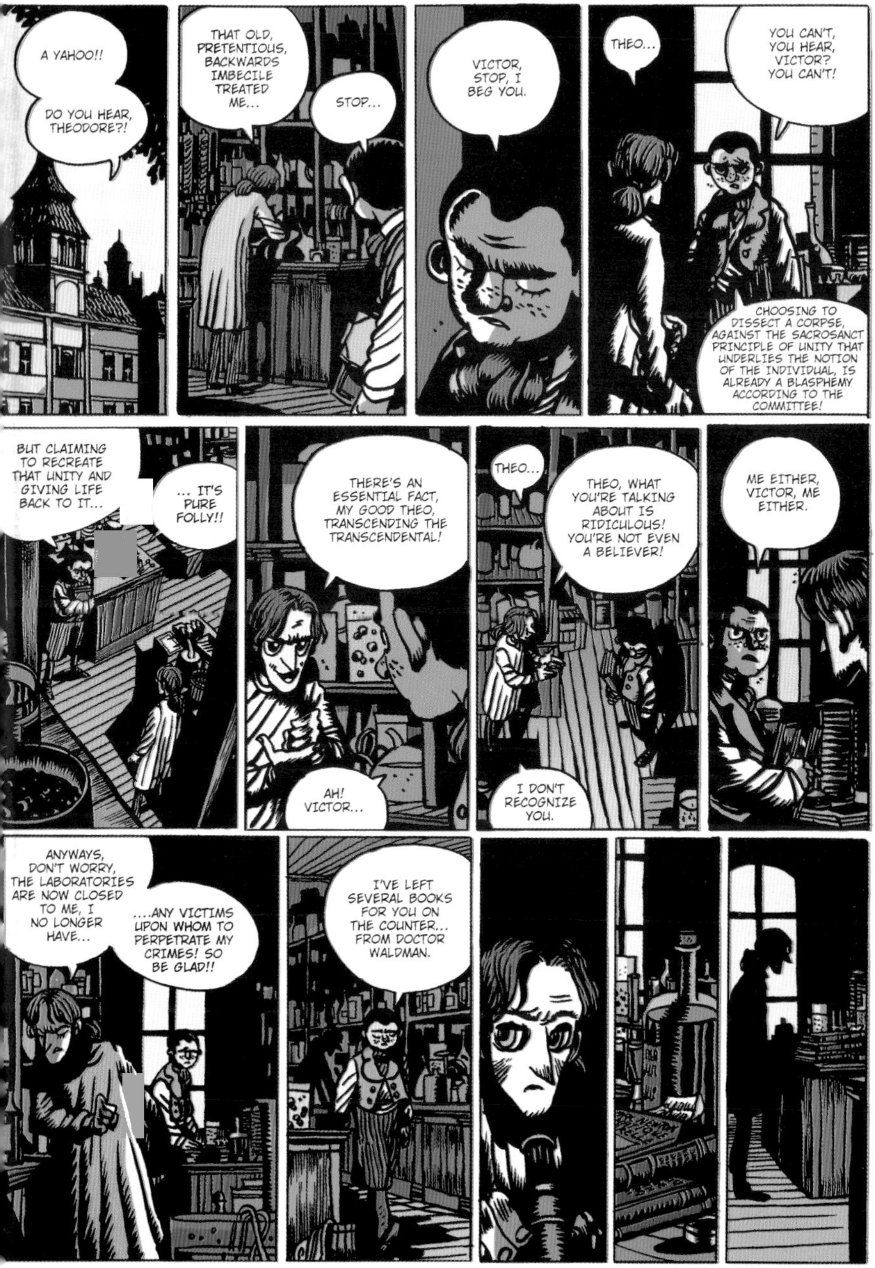
A YAHOO!!
DO YOU HEAR, THEODORE?!
THAT OLD, PRETENTIOUS, BACKWARDS IMBECILE TREATED ME...
STOP...
VICTOR, STOP, I BEG YOU.
THEO...
YOU CAN'T, YOU HEAR, VICTOR? YOU CAN'T!
CHOOSING TO DISSECT A CORPSE, AGAINST THE SACROSANCT PRINCIPLE OF UNITY THAT UNDERLIES THE NOTION OF THE INDIVIDUAL, IS ALREADY A BLASPHEMY ACCORDING TO THE COMMITTEE!
BUT CLAIMING TO RECREATE THAT UNITY AND GIVING LIFE BACK TO IT...
... IT'S PURE FOLLY!!
THERE'S AN ESSENTIAL FACT, MY GOOD THEO, TRANSCENDING THE TRANSCENDENTAL!
AH! VICTOR...
THEO...
THEO, WHAT YOU'RE TALKING ABOUT IS RIDICULOUS! YOU'RE NOT EVEN A BELIEVER!
I DON'T RECOGNIZE YOU.
ME EITHER, VICTOR, ME EITHER.
ANYWAYS, DON'T WORRY, THE LABORATORIES ARE NOW CLOSED TO ME, I NO LONGER HAVE...
....ANY VICTIMS UPON WHOM TO PERPETRATE MY CRIMES! SO BE GLAD!!
I'VE LEFT SEVERAL BOOKS FOR YOU ON THE COUNTER... FROM DOCTOR WALDMAN.

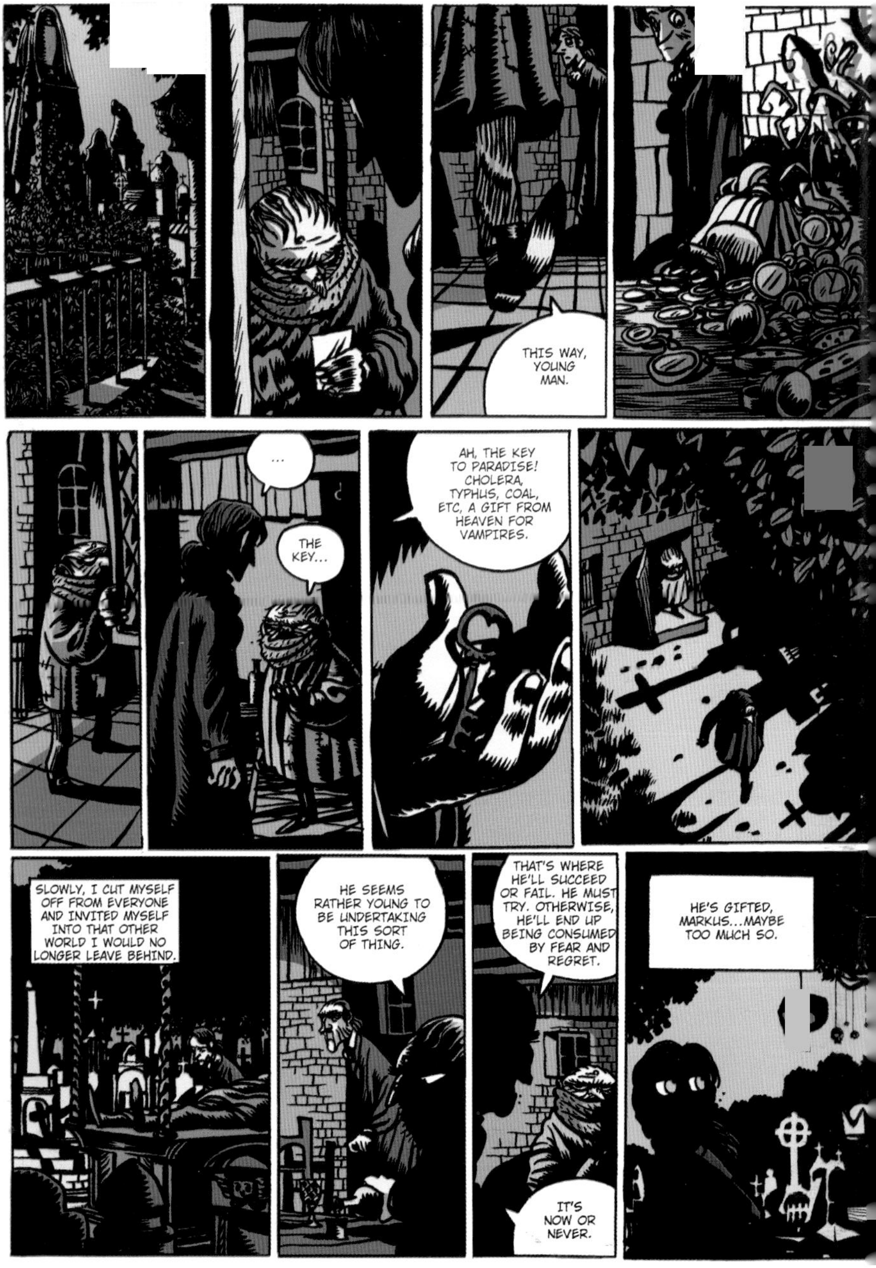
THIS WAY, YOUNG MAN.
...
THE KEY...
AH, THE KEY TO PARADISE! CHOLERA, TYPHUS, COAL, ETC, A GIFT FROM HEAVEN FOR VAMPIRES.
SLOWLY, I CUT MYSELF OFF FROM EVERYONE AND INVITED MYSELF INTO THAT OTHER WORLD I WOULD NO LONGER LEAVE BEHIND.
HE SEEMS RATHER YOUNG TO BE UNDERTAKING THIS SORT OF THING.
THAT'S WHERE HE'LL SUCCEED OR FAIL. HE MUST TRY. OTHERWISE, HE'LL END UP BEING CONSUMED BY FEAR AND REGRET.
IT'S NOW OR NEVER.
HE'S GIFTED, MARKUS...MAYBE TOO MUCH SO.

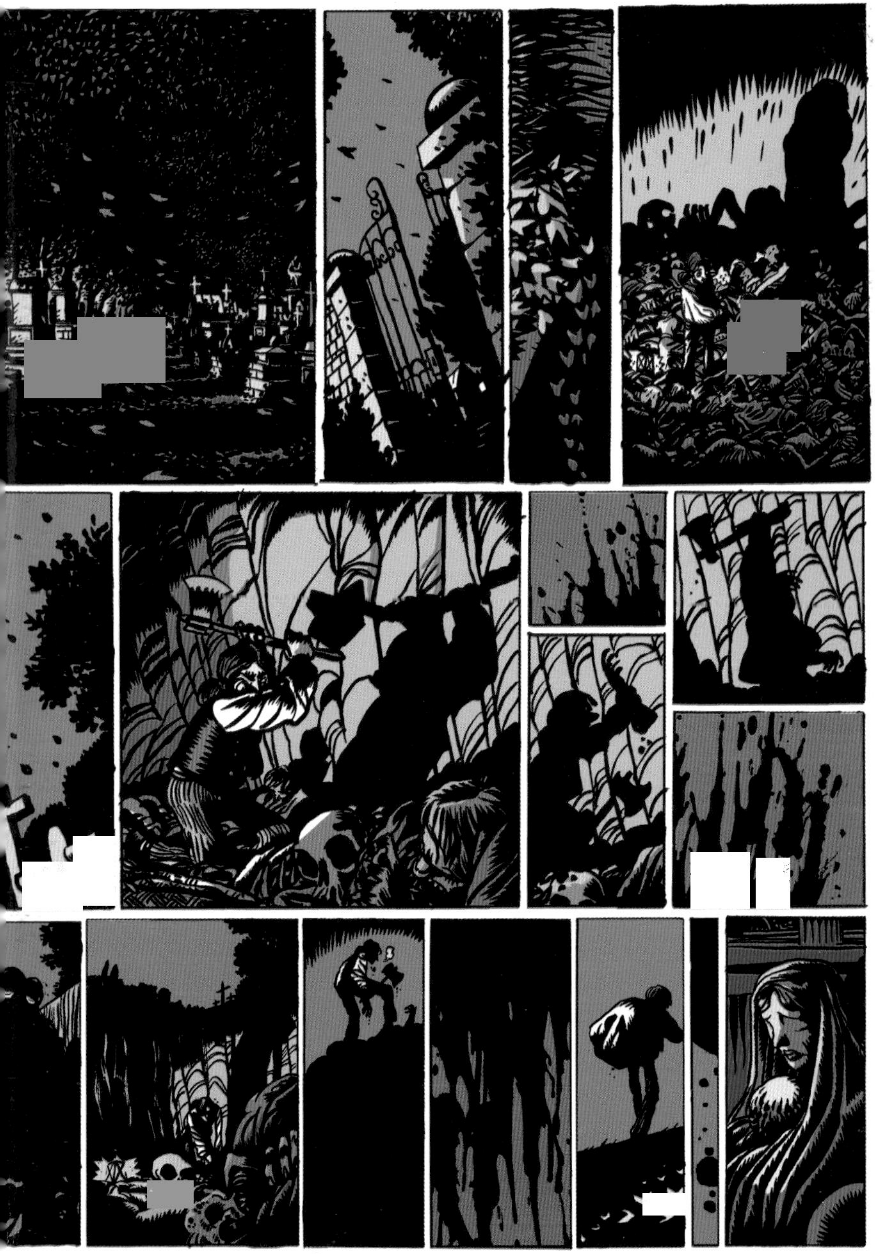

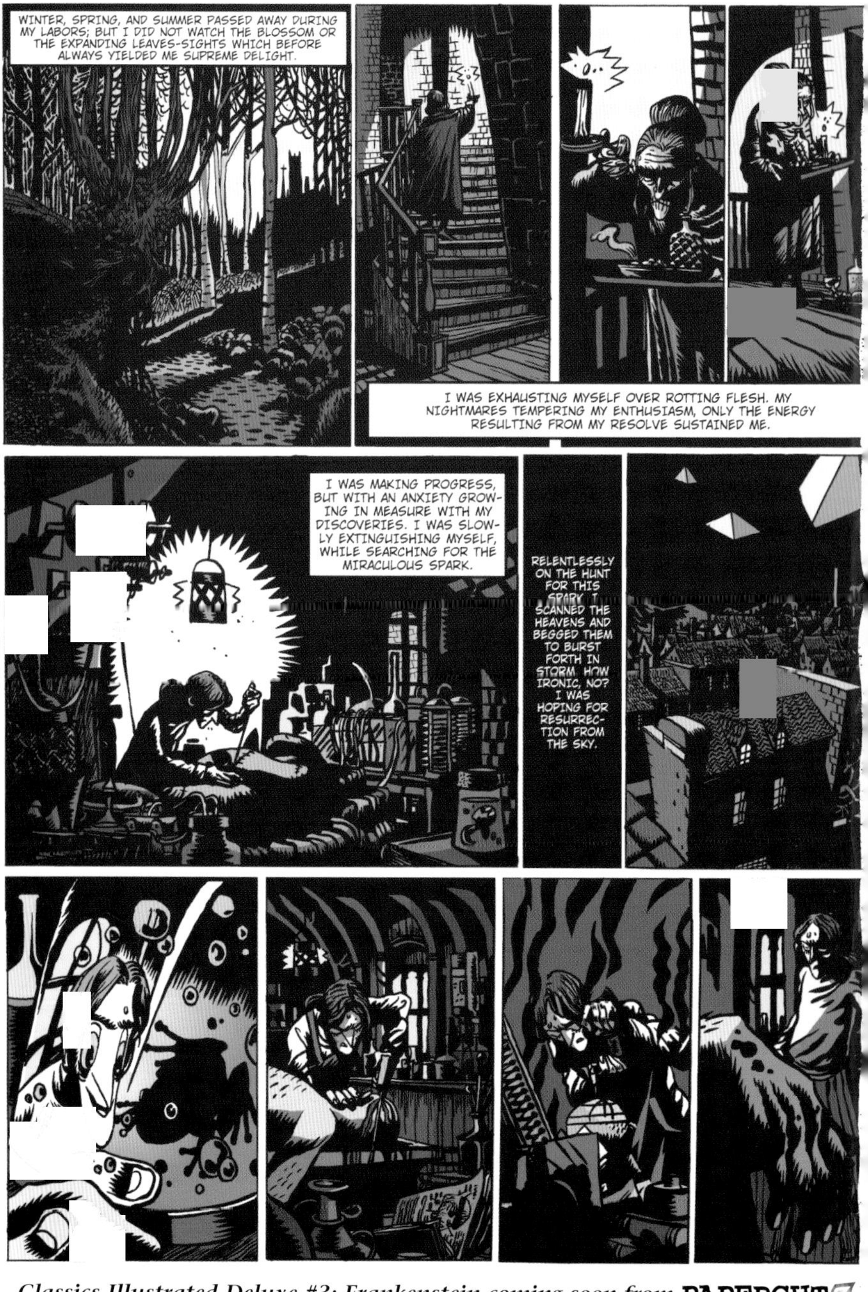
WINTER, SPRING, AND SUMMER PASSED AWAY DURING MY LABORS; BUT I DID NOT WATCH THE BLOSSOM OR THE EXPANDING LEAVES-SIGHTS WHICH BEFORE ALWAYS YIELDED ME SUPREME DELIGHT.
I WAS EXHAUSTING MYSELF OVER ROTTING FLESH. MY NIGHTMARES TEMPERING MY ENTHUSIASM, ONLY THE ENERGY RESULTING FROM MY RESOLVE SUSTAINED ME.
I WAS MAKING PROGRESS, BUT WITH AN ANXIETY GROWING IN MEASURE WITH MY DISCOVERIES. I WAS SLOWLY EXTINGUISHING MYSELF, WHILE SEARCHING FOR THE MIRACULOUS SPARK.
RELENTLESSLY ON THE HUNT FOR THIS SPARK, I SCANNED THE HEAVENS AND BEGGED THEM TO BURST FORTH IN STORM. HOW IRONIC, NO? I WAS HOPING FOR RESURRECTION FROM THE SKY.